EDGE OF THE WOODS

Emily Slate Mystery Thriller
Book 12

ALEX SIGMORE

Dark Woods Press

EDGE OF THE WOODS: EMILY SLATE MYSTERY THRILLER
BOOK 12

1st Edition

ebook ISBN 978-1-957536-38-5

Print ISBN 978-1-957536-39-2

Prologue

IF MARNIE TOOK ANOTHER STEP, she was going to throw up.

She pitched forward, her lungs on fire, and waited for the inevitable. Her legs burned and sweat poured down her back. The fact that she had two layers of wool on wasn't helping things, either. What had she been thinking? Why had she agreed to do this?

"Hey. You okay?"

Marnie glared up at Josh from under hooded eyes, projecting as much spite and death his way as possible. *Okay?* Like hiking three miles out into the woods up a slope that would make an Olympic skier blush was anything close to okay.

"Don't lean over like that, stand up and take deep—"

Bile rose in her throat and she felt the familiar sensation of her stomach emptying out the wrong end. A sensation usually reserved after one too many margaritas, or anytime she ate sushi. Marnie didn't even bother trying to hide as she spewed her guts all over the dry sticks and branches. Life out here in the woods had retreated for the winter and wouldn't be back for at least another month. She took a few minutes to make sure no other sudden movements might cause another catastrophe before she straightened back up, feeling surprisingly better.

"Here," Josh said, handing her a bottle of water. "I told you to stay hydrated."

She snatched the bottle out of his hand. The cool water wasn't as welcome as she'd hoped, seeing as the temperature had dropped as soon as the sun had dipped behind the mountains. But at least it got the taste of half-digested turkey sandwich out of her mouth. She swished the water around for a moment before spitting it back out and taking a fresh drink. The water felt good against her raw throat, but nothing would soothe the fact she was out in the middle of freaking nowhere, miles from the nearest fireplace or heater and night was quickly approaching.

She handed the bottle back to Josh who took it, a sheepish look on his face. "I tried to—"

Marnie held up a hand. "Let's just get there."

"Right," he said, turning and continuing along the trail.

Marnie took a deep breath, attempted to center herself, and continued after him. This whole hike had been Josh's idea of a romantic get-together. Something the both of them could do to reconnect. They both worked long hours, barely saw each other during the day and what little free time they did have always seemed to end with the two of them asleep on the couch. A change had been necessary, but this hadn't been what Marnie had in mind. She had been thinking somewhere a little more tropical, with one of those spas where they put the hot rocks on your back while you listened to the nearby ocean. Like they ever could have afforded that. The thought almost made her laugh out loud.

Nope, *this* was what they could afford. A weekend hike out into the middle of nowhere. It wasn't all bad, she supposed. There had been fresh snow a few days ago, coating most of the terrain in a soft blanket of white. While the trail itself had already melted away, the white contrast with the bare branches of the trees made everything stand out, making the woods look like they stretched out forever.

"Evening," Josh said, causing Marnie to look back up as she trudged after him. A couple of hikers coming in the opposite direction down the slope smiled as they passed, offering their greetings as well. She had to admit, the hiking community was a friendly bunch.

Once they were out of earshot, Marnie took the opportunity to voice her concerns. "It's going to be dark soon. Shouldn't we stop?"

"Well, we would have been there already if we'd gotten on the trail earlier," Josh said without a hint of accusation in his voice, but she knew it was there anyway. *She* was the reason they hadn't left on time. He never came right out and said it, but it was always there, lurking in the background of their lives. Her perpetual inability to do anything "on time".

Marnie sighed. She missed her couch and her warm blanket. Maybe they were just destined to live out their lives apart from each other most of the time. She didn't see a hike in the woods changing that, or anything else. She'd been naïve, and just like that echoes of her mother's voice reverberated through her head.

"Just tell me how much farther," she finally replied after absorbing the silence between them for a minute.

"We're close, only about ten more minutes. I went on this trail hundreds of times as a kid. I know it by heart."

Right. His time in the scouts. Josh had always been connected to nature in a way she hadn't. She was thrilled he enjoyed it so much, but at the same time, it was just another barrier between them. Something *else* they didn't have in common. Not for the first time thoughts passed through her brain wondering if they'd be better off apart. Wouldn't Josh be happier with someone who shared an interest in the things he liked to do? Would *she* be any better off? At least she wouldn't be fighting a sore throat from throwing up her lunch and her legs wouldn't be killing her. That would at least be a start.

"Evening," she heard Josh say. She looked up again, having found that if you didn't watch where you were walking at all times while hiking you were likely to trip. A man approached them from the other direction. He looked like the total package, dressed in camo gear and trucker hat pulled down so Marnie couldn't see his eyes. What she did notice was the leather sling on his back that was molded in the shape of a rifle. She stopped to let the man pass, though he didn't offer thanks or even a word to either of them.

"C'mon," Josh said, already back on the trail. "We're not too far now."

But Marnie couldn't help but watch the hunter walk away, back down the trail. Was it even hunting season? Why would he be out here? Weren't there other, designated areas where people hunted?

She picked up the pace to catch up with Josh, finding her legs didn't hurt nearly as much as before. "Hey," she said, keeping her voice low. "Did you see that?"

"What?" he asked in that maddeningly oblivious way he often did.

"That guy. He had a gun."

Josh chuckled. "Yeah, lots of people carry them out here. Even though it's winter, sometimes you don't know what you'll find."

"You think he was hunting?" she asked.

"If so, I'd say he had a bad day of it." He didn't even slow down, just kept up that steady pace of his. But Marnie's heart was in her chest. For some reason knowing someone was out here with a loaded weapon only made her more anxious. Why had she agreed to this?

About five minutes after passing the hunter the hike leveled off, and another ten minutes later she finally saw the small wooden shack in the distance, right off the main trail.

"Thank God," she muttered, having calmed down now that they had some distance from the man with the gun.

"See, told you. Right where I said it would be," Josh said as they approached. He pulled off his pack and set it in the opening of the structure. It was about eight feet tall, with a sloped roof and had been built about a foot off the ground. Three sides were completely enclosed, except for openings around the roof and the fourth side was only halfway exposed, the other half covered by old wood. Marnie imagined eight or ten adults could fit inside if they had to. She poked her head inside to survey their home for the night, but had to pull out a flashlight. Light was draining from the sky quick.

"Whoa, no way," she said, jumping back as her light caught movement at the far end of the structure.

"What?" Josh asked. He'd already begun unpacking his sleeping bag and the propane stove kit.

"I saw a rat. Right there, in the corner." Marnie pointed with the light, but there was nothing except dust particles catching the beam.

"Yeah, probably. But they won't bother us while we're in there," Josh replied nonchalantly.

"*No,*" she said. "This is where I draw the line. I'm not sleeping with rats."

"Don't worry, the fire will keep them away," he replied, setting up the stove in the old burned-out firepit a few feet from the structure. It was surrounded by rocks and looked like it had been there a while.

Marnie closed her eyes, took a deep breath, and let it back out. What was she going to do, hike back down to the car? It had taken them an hour-and-a-half to get out here. It would be dark in fifteen minutes at best and she'd never find her way back on her own. Like it or not, she was stuck here for the night. "Fine. Then you're sleeping in that corner."

Josh chuckled, pulling her close and kissing the top of her head. "Whatever you say." She had to admit the embrace was a nice change of pace. He'd been more relaxed ever since they'd begun hiking, enough that it was noticeable. Maybe coming out here hadn't been a bad idea after all.

But she would see herself in *hell* before she even thought about getting naked with rats running around. Josh would just have to wait until they got back home.

As the food warmed on the small propane heater, Josh built them a fire which was burning bright just as the last bit of purple light left the sky. Because the canopy was bare, Marnie could see hundreds—no, thousands of stars every time she looked up. She didn't look up enough back at home.

The ready meals Josh had packed turned out to be surprisingly good and as the night wore on, Marnie felt herself relaxing more and more. She even stopped caring about the rat so much. By the time they were halfway through their White Claws and had taken half a gummy each, she'd fully relaxed into the scene. The woods were so peaceful, so quiet. No wonder people always talked about getting back to nature. And she'd almost missed this because…why? She'd wanted more of the same? Because there was a reality show on that she just *had* to see? Because if she did anything other than her normal routine she'd have to face the fact that life was not turning out how she'd wanted and that every time she looked into a mirror all she saw was boring ol' Marnie, already set in her ways at the ripe old age of twenty-seven?

She leaned back in the collapsible chair Josh had insisted she add to her pack, staring up at the stars. This couldn't be her life. She couldn't let things play out like this. She needed to take some risks, enjoy life a little bit more. Do some things outside her comfort zone. Otherwise, what was the point of it all?

Marnie smiled. She was going to start suggesting they take more of these hikes together. Just get away from everything for a while, focus on each other. She turned, looking at Josh's face lit by the fire. He was staring at her, smiling. He reached his hand over and she took it, giving it a squeeze. She might have to rethink her rule about the sleeping bags.

As she was about to suggest they figure it out, a sound like the crack of a whip reverberated through the woods. Something wet splashed on her face and for a second she thought it had somehow started raining on a cloudless night. But when she looked back at Josh, she realized it hadn't been rain, but blood.

She shut her eyes quickly, praying that it was the combination of alcohol and drugs that was making her hallucinate. She hadn't seen that. It couldn't be real.

But when she opened her eyes again, his dead eyes stared right back at her.

Marnie screamed as loud as she could, the sound ringing through the forest.

Chapter One

TAKING the end of the bandage, I slowly pull it back to reveal the raw, red skin underneath. There's a straight line drawing right across my neck, as if someone has taken a red pen and marked me up. Like I've been some little kid's art project. It's a harsh reminder of how close I keep coming to losing everything. The other reminder is lying in the room down the hall. A man I have come to love and trust as much as anyone in my life, and he almost lost his, doing my dirty work. I scowl at the raw skin. Even the small punctures where the stitches held me together are still visible. I can't go back in there looking like this. He was freaked out enough about the bandage. Liam needs to heal, and he doesn't need to be worrying about me as he does it.

I toss the bandage in the trash before rooting around in my travel bag for my concealer. It only takes a few dabs, but the skin is still raw and it hurts. Still, I manage to cover it up so that my brush with death is little more than a shadow on my otherwise unremarkable neck. A nice little souvenir from the town of Bellefluer where I just finished up a case with my best friend and fellow agent, Zara Foley. All courtesy of a makeshift cult under the guise of being a Wiccan society and who didn't like the FBI poking their noses in the town's business.

Unfortunately, I had to make a quick exit after finding Liam had been hospitalized after almost being in a house fire. They've kept him mostly sedated over the past forty-eight hours to help his lungs heal, and Dr. Riley tells me he's doing remarkably well. He's already off the oxygen mask and only needs a few more days of observation before he can go home.

I haven't left his side since.

Taking one more look in the mirror, I do my best to fluff my stringy hair. A shower sounds really good now but I'm not leaving this hospital without Liam. He's been at Hickory County Hospital for a total of three full days though according to Dr. Riley, should be ready to leave in the next day or so, assuming this last round of tests comes back with good news. Thankfully, he didn't inhale the smoke for too long and his lungs were only slightly singed. With the oxygen therapy from Dr. Riley's team, Hickory Medical has done a pretty good job of patching him up. When I'd first arrived I'd wanted to transport him to a larger, more capable hospital, but after considering all the options, Dr. Riley and Liam both decided staying would help him heal faster.

Whatever helps him get out of here and back home quicker. I have a lot of making up to do. Because he's been out of it for most of the time, we haven't really had a chance to talk. Not to mention the fact he's not supposed to be saying anything while he's healing. It's been ludicrous; the few short conversations we've had he's had to write his responses out on a notepad. It's frustrating and slow and I just want to tell him how sorry I am and how much I love him for just being him, but I can't do that here. Not in the middle of a hospital.

We just need to get home where I can take care of him like he's taken care of me so many times before.

Satisfied I'm not going to do any better in the mirror, I pull my small bag together and leave the public restroom, headed back for Liam's room. His door is cracked, but I can tell the lights are on. I put on my best smile and enter slowly after knocking.

"Good Morning?"

He's sitting up in the bed, the TV across from him on a random news channel, though he's looking out the window at the woods surrounding the hospital. It's just outside Mill-bridge, the town where Liam was investigating the house that caught on fire. The house that my mother presumably grew up in.

"Morning," he croaks out when he sees me.

"Hey," I say gently. "Aren't you still supposed to be on silent mode?"

"Doc came in this morning, wanted me to start speaking again, just to make sure everything is looking okay."

I nod. *Of course* the doctor comes along during the thirty minutes I'm not in here. "Sorry, I just needed to freshen up." The reality is I needed a minute to pull myself together. All I've been able to think about the past few days is how close Liam came to dying. About how it should have been me looking through that house, not him. I should have just waited until the issue in Bellefleur was over before heading up here, instead of being impatient about it.

He holds his hand out for mine and I take it before sitting down beside him. "Doesn't look like you need any freshening to me," he says softly.

"You are a bad liar," I tell him. Despite washing my face and spritzing some deodorant on, I know I have an odor about me. One that only a hot shower will fix. "Did the doctor say anything else?"

"He's just waiting on the results of the last test," Liam says. He's still wearing the oxygen tubes that are connected to his nose.

"For almost getting burned alive you sound pretty good," I try teasing, but it comes out flat. As much as I try to keep reminding myself that I can't change what happened and that I had no way of knowing he was in any danger at all, it still pulls at me, like a loose thread. My primary concern when he arrived in Millbridge had been someone recognizing him as FBI, but I never thought anyone would go to these kinds of lengths. Then again, that's exactly what Saffi and Cora had tried to do down in Bellefleur. And I'm going to have the scar to prove it.

He gives my hand a small squeeze. "You okay? You look lost."

I almost scoff but stop myself. "You're not supposed to be worrying about me. You just focus on getting better. While you've got that thing on, try some deep breaths in through the nose and out through the mouth. See if you feel any constriction or pain." He arches a skeptical eyebrow at me. "It's what they had me do after that mess down in Charleston," I tell him. The funny thing is, I know exactly how he feels right now. I've been there myself. Though my case wasn't as severe as his.

He gives me one of those resigned smiles of his that just make my heart melt and draws in a deep breath before letting it go. It's almost imperceptible, but I know Liam, and I see the wince of pain. "Okay, cowboy, that's enough," I tell him after he does it a second time with the same result. "Give yourself some time. We're going to hold off on the marathon training for a while."

"But no, I love running marathons," he jokes. He takes the small plastic cup beside his bed and draws a long sip through the straw before turning back to me. "So can we talk about it now?"

I let go of his other hand and shift uncomfortably in my seat. "You really should rest. It's just—"

"Em," he says, his voice more serious. "I've been trying to have this conversation with you for three days. Don't you want to know what happened?"

Why am I being so evasive? This is Liam. And I promised I would always be honest with him. I look him dead in the eye. "No. I don't. It's tainted. Because learning whatever you know about…the *situation* means that I have to accept responsibility for putting you there. If you don't tell me, then maybe somehow it balances out. Maybe me not knowing is my punishment for doing that to you."

"Listen to me," he says. "You didn't do anything to me. I went there of my own free will. Do you think it's easy watching you under the constant pressure from these letters that keep appearing? If anything, me going was selfish."

Now I can't help but laugh. "No. I've been putting way too much on you, expecting way too much. And this time it almost got you killed. Remember when I told you I wasn't sure if I could handle a relationship like this because of the risk? Because it was possible one day you might not be there anymore? I never thought *I* would be the one to put you in that situation." Before he can argue I hold up a hand. "You wouldn't have been there if not for me. You wouldn't be *here* if not for me."

"Emily, stop it," he says. I'm struck by the sharpness of his voice. It's almost as if he's angry, but not at almost dying. Instead, I think he's angry at me for trying to take the blame.

Remember what Dr. Frost says, "Your guilt is a shield. It's what keeps other people out and you locked up. You need to open those doors. Stop holding everything by yourself."

"I don't want to hear one more word about you being responsible for this, understand?" Liam says, his voice as serious as I've ever heard it.

I look deep into his eyes and nod, though part of me knows the promise is only on the outside. It is going to take some serious work to get me to stop blaming myself internally for this. But this is a first step. As soon as I accept that possibility, that maybe I don't have to beat myself up over this, I might start to feel lighter than I have in the past few days.

"Thank you," I say, reaching out and taking his hand again. "Thank you for just…being you."

His face softens and he smiles back. He reaches over on the table that holds his water and anything else they need to bring him and retrieves the picture he'd taken from my mother's house. He hands it back to me.

I've spent most of the last three days avoiding looking at this picture because of what it has represented. I really only got one good look at it when I first arrived. But now I'm out of excuses. It's an old black and white, but the quality is pretty good. I take a close look, really examining the faces of each of the family members. This is the first time I've ever seen a picture of my grandparents, or even my mom as a child. But it's undoubtedly her. She carried those dimples all the way into adulthood. The smile on her face is unmistakable.

But what's more concerning is the baby bump my grandmother is cradling in the picture. She looks happy and about five or six months along. There's no date on the picture, but my mother seems to be around six or so. Which means I may still have a living aunt or uncle out there who would be in their fifties by now.

"I need to tell you about what I saw there," Liam says. "In the house."

I have to admit I've been curious, though I've held off from contacting the locals about the fire for fear of tipping someone off that I'm here. Whoever is doing this obviously wanted me to come to Millbridge. And that's part of why I feel so responsible for Liam. Maybe if I had come, the house wouldn't have burned down. Because I'm not willing to accept that it was just an accident that *happened* to take place in the few minutes Liam was in the house. I also don't believe he'd ever do anything that could have caused the fire. Which means someone was there, someone was watching him. And they didn't like what they saw.

And according to him, at least, what he said when I first

arrived, that person was my mother. But at the time, and even now, I'm still willing to chalk that up to Liam being under the influence of the drugs or whatever it was Riley had him on, and also having just been through a traumatic experience. There is no way he saw my mother at that house. My mother died almost two decades ago. I remember it vividly.

But that doesn't mean someone else wasn't there. As soon as Liam is healed up, I plan on taking care of this once and for all.

"I'm going to find out who did this to you," I say, staring at the picture. "I can at least do that much."

"Not without backup," he says. "Just give me a few days. Then I'll be good as new."

"Oh, my God!" We both look over at the strange voice to find two people standing in the doorway. The woman is in her sixties, thin but fresh-faced. She wears her age well. The man is broad-chested and a little rounder around the belly, and sports a blonde moustache and beard, both of which are graying. I've only ever seen these two people on Liam's phone, never in person before. I stand up, on alert. Liam also sits up straighter, his eyes wide. He clears his throat before he speaks.

"Hi, Mom. Hi, Dad."

Chapter Two

ONE MINUTE LIAM'S hospital room is calm, serene, like a relaxing spa. But as soon as his parents arrive, it's like the entire place has been turned into a whirlwind. They both blow into the room, assaulting us both with questions before either of us can even get a word out.

"What's the diagnosis? Is he going to make it? How much smoke got in his lungs? How long does he have to be in the hospital?"

And it's not like the questions come from one of them. It's from both, and the father, Sean, has a thick Irish accent which makes it difficult for me to understand what he's saying at certain times. Frankly, I'm overwhelmed and sneak a glance at Liam. He's wearing a pinched smile and I'm starting to realize why I haven't met these people yet. Because already they're *a lot.*

"Where were you when he was hurt?" the mother, Brianna asks me directly even before either of us can answer their questions.

"Um…" I say, clasping my hands behind my back like that will do any good. All it does is make me look like I'm being dressed down in front of a superior officer. And in some ways that's how it feels. "First off, it's nice to meet you Mrs. Coll. Liam has told me a lot—"

"Never mind that." She cuts me off. "Why weren't you there to back him up? Isn't that what you're supposed to do in the FBI?"

"Mom," Liam says.

"Shh, you don't talk. You have lung damage. You let your mother handle this."

I have to bite my lip to keep from laughing at the woman's obvious mischaracterization of the scenario. I know Liam has told them about me, but I've never actually had a conversation with them in my life. I shoot a glance at the father who is standing off to the side, watching the whole conversation. But then I realize he's actually watching *me*, and I recall that he's a retired police officer. He's doing exactly what Zara and I do to suspects when we have them in an interrogation room. One of us will ask the questions, try to catch the suspect off guard, while the other looks for any clues or tells that the suspect might not be giving us the whole truth. Fortunately, I'm skilled in keeping my emotions in check when I need to.

"I was in Louisiana, on a case," I tell her.

"So you just let him come up here by himself, to a strange town and—"

Liam reaches a hand out and takes his mother's arm. "Mom, please. Emily's not my babysitter. No one expected this to happen."

"I should say not," she replied. "I already spent an hour on the phone chewing out that Fletcher Wallace. How he could have approved of—"

"Wait, you called my boss?" Liam asks.

"No, he called us," Brianna replies. "How do you think we found out about you being here? You certainly didn't call us up to let us know."

"Fine thing about that, yeah?" Sean says, crossing his arms. "Your mother's been worried sick."

Thankfully, at least for now, they seem to have turned their attention back on their son. At least I don't feel like I'm in the spotlight anymore. "I don't ask for much, Liam, I really don't," his mother continues. "But would it kill you to at least tell me where you are?"

"That's kind of hard to do," he replies, frustration leaking into his voice, though he's doing a good job not showing it. "A lot of what I do is classified."

"Was this?"

He squirms in his bed. "Well, no. This was technically on my own time."

"You mean you weren't even gettin' paid for this little excursion?" Sean asks.

Liam shoots a guilty look at me like he knows he's just opened up a brand-new can of worms. "No, I was just... looking into something on my own."

"Why an the hell would you do that?" Sean asks. "You jus' got that job. An you're already takin' personal time off?"

Liam opens his mouth when I catch his mother's gaze on me. *Shit.* I forgot to watch for her, she's been eyeing me this whole time. I can see it in the gleam of her eye. It's like she knows Liam was up here in Millbridge for me, not for himself. The look she's giving me is downright *loathing*. So much for hoping the first time I met Liam's parents would go well. But she doesn't say anything else about it, just turns her attention back to her son. Though she does position herself in a way so that she's between the two of us. Her hand is on his shoulder while Liam tries to explain—somewhat unsuccessfully—what he was doing in Millbridge without implicating me.

I sigh. "It's my fault," I finally say. "He was up here looking for something for me. I've been receiving—"

"So you got my son doin' your dirty work fer ya, huh?"

Mr. Coll's accent seems to get stronger the more upset he becomes.

"I mean, I—"

"Dad, it wasn't like that," Liam says. "Emily didn't ask me to come up here. And she already feels guilty enough about it, so just cut her some slack." He trips on the last word, which induces a coughing fit.

"Back up, give him some air," Mrs. Coll says, stepping back and running into me, forcibly pushing me away. I want to point out that Liam hadn't had so much as one cough until they arrived.

Liam coughs for a few more moments before getting it under control, but it sounds deep and ragged. And it's loud enough that I catch a nurse poking her head in the door. "Is he—let me grab the doctor."

"Liam, honey, are you all right?" Mrs. Coll asks, leaning over him and patting his back like he's a five-year-old. I roll my eyes. Liam and I had the "meeting the family" talk and decided it was something that was best held off for a while, both because of everything we'd both been through and my own particular demons with both blood and non-blood relatives. Now I see that it was probably a delay tactic on his part as much as it was for my own benefit. They've only been here five minutes and already I can see this isn't going to be easy.

A minute later Dr. Riley comes rushing into the room with a stethoscope in hand. He ignores both Mr. and Mrs. Coll and goes straight for Liam. "Breathe deep for me. Three times." Liam does as he's told as the doctor holds the stethoscope on his chest, moving it slightly with each breath. I catch that wince of pain on Liam's face again as he does it.

Dr. Riley pulls the stethoscope away and wraps it back around his neck. "Did you feel any fluid when you were coughing? Like there was something in your lungs?"

Liam shakes his head.

Riley regards him for a second. "Based on your most

recent X-rays I don't think it's anything to be concerned about." He then turns to the three of us. "But I want to reiterate he needs *rest*. Another few days in the hospital won't hurt, but they won't do him any good either. He needs to get home, take it easy. I've already spoken to your boss and recommended you take the next two weeks off."

"Two weeks!" Mr. Coll booms. "For a little smoke in his lungs?"

Riley turns to him. "Yes, two weeks. To give everything proper time to heal. His is a high-activity job, one that requires a lot of lung capacity. I would prefer to see them entirely healed before he goes back on duty."

"Can't he jus' work the desk or somethin'?"

"Dad," Liam croaks out. "It's fine. I'll talk to Wallace."

I want to interject and throw in my two cents, but I feel like I'm out of my depth here. I'll just be happy when we can get Liam back to his apartment and away from his parents. They're definitely not doing him any favors by being here. I half consider asking the desk nurse for a Xanax.

"Well, you have my recommendation," Riley says, then shoots me a quick look as if he expects me to take care of this. "Meanwhile, I'm going to get started on the paperwork to have you discharged. It shouldn't be more than three or four hours and we'll have you out of here."

Inwardly I sigh a breath of relief.

"I'll go start gettin' the car ready," Mr. Coll says and my heart is back in my throat.

"Wait, what's happening?" I ask.

Mrs. Coll turns to me. "You heard the doctor. He needs rest. We're taking him back to Stillwater where he can recuperate."

"Back to…Stillwater?" I ask as if my mind can't wrap itself around what she's saying.

She nods. "Yes, dear. I'm sure you take good care of your dog, but this is *a person*. He needs special care. Around-the-clock supervision. You won't be able to do that while you're working. Liam has told us all about how busy you are."

I sneak a quick glance and Liam is giving me the most emphatic shaking of his head *no* as he can, which amounts to a slight movement back and forth, but his eyes are practically bulging.

"Don't worry, I know how to take care of my son," she says. "You can see each other in a few weeks once he's back on the job. Unless, of course, he decides he'd be better off back at his old position." She turns leans down to Liam. "Your father has already spoken to Chief Salazar. He said he would be happy to have you back at your old post if you no longer wanted to work for the FBI."

"Whoa, wait a second," I say, unable to help myself. "Who said anything about him quitting his job?"

"Well you do have to admit, it's a dangerous position. And it doesn't leave a lot of time for anything else," Mrs. Coll says. I feel like I'm being hit by a cyclone and there's no relief from it. Why would Liam ever quit his job? I mean, sure, he's had a few close calls. And he's been held against his will on one occasion. But he's never indicated to me anything other than a willingness to do the job. I thought he was a lot happier working at the FBI than he was being a small-town detective. Not that there was anything wrong with that, it was just that he'd confessed to me that it didn't feel like he could make a difference in Stillwater.

"Em," Liam croaks out again, reaching for me. "I'm not quitting. That's just Mom being wishful."

His mother takes his outstretched hand before I can. "Let's just see how you feel in a few weeks." She turns back to me. "Thank you, for all you've done for our son. But we'll take it from here."

I feel like I'm being summarily dismissed, not only as a person, but from this relationship.

"Mom, stop doing this," Liam says. "Emily has always been there for me. I'm not going anywhere without her."

"Don't be silly," she replies. "You can see your girlfriend when you get back to D.C. You heard the doctor; you need to go home and rest."

Dr. Riley clears his throat. "Yes, and presumably that would be with as little activity as possible." He sneaks me another look of concern.

"What are you saying?" Mrs. Coll asks, spinning on him. I'm not sure if she caught the look between us or not, but I really need to watch her. She is more perceptive than she lets on.

"Just that if Liam is going to heal, he needs to be in a calm, quiet environment."

"Don't worry, he's always felt safe at home. We still even have his bedroom just as he left it."

"Mom, this really isn't—" Liam begins before Brianna shushes him.

"He couldn't get better care anywhere else."

I can practically see the horror on Liam's face of having to move back in with his parents for a few weeks. Dr. Riley sighs. "I'll prepare a list of instructions."

"Mom," Liam says. "I'm a grown man. I don't need to go back—"

"You have been through something terrible," she replies before he can finish. "And I never get to see you anymore. You'll come back home, rest up, and spend some quality time with your family. And that's the end of it."

"Then Emily is coming too," he says.

She turns to me and offers a wan smile. "I'm sure Emily needs to get back to work."

"Oh, no I have plenty of paid time off saved up. In fact my last boss had to force me to take vacations. It's no problem." I think I see the ghost of a scowl on Mrs. Coll's face, but it's gone in an instant. "That's wonderful. But I'm afraid we don't have any extra room."

"Not a problem," I say, putting on the biggest smile I can muster. "I'm sure I can find a nearby motel."

She hesitates a moment, then turns back to her son, without saying another word. I'm not sure if I should consider that a win or not. But I'll take it.

Only, what have I just gotten myself into?

Chapter Three

"It's like she's practically challenging me to a duel," I say, my voice hushed even though I'm outside the hospital. I'm afraid I might see Brianna Coll leaning out one of the windows above me, listening in on my private conversation with Zara.

"She sounds like a real ball buster."

"Honestly it's surprising to see how normal Liam turned out after meeting both of them," I reply. "You should have seen it, they practically charged into the room like they were on a mission to fuck everything up."

She laughs. "Sounds like you're facing the gauntlet. Are you really going to stay the entire time?"

"How can I avoid it now? If I don't come, she'll think I'm spineless. And if I do, it'll be like going in for battle every day." I sigh. "Not to mention I need to ask Wallace for more time off now. And after that trip you and I took I'm not sure he's going to grant it."

"Don't you have like...four years' worth of time saved up?" she asks.

"Yeah, but two requests back to back like this. I'm not sure that's going to work with his little budget he likes to keep."

"What if you only came by every few days?"

"And leave him to fend for himself?" I ask, incredulous. "He may not blame me for almost getting him killed, but I get the feeling if I left him alone with his parents for more than ten minutes he'd never forgive me." I run my hand down my face. My grimy, unshowered face. I can't think of worse circumstances in which to meet my boyfriend's parents. "Did you get back okay?"

"Yep, buttoned everything up down in Bellefleur. That has to be one of the weirdest cases I've ever worked on."

"I'm just glad you were there," I say. "And so you told Wallace—"

"Yes, *nosy*. I told him I wanted back on field duty. God, sometimes you are worse than my mother."

I snort. "At least I'm not worse than Liam's mother. If I do end up staying, I don't know how I'm going to keep my cool around her. She's one of those people who takes any chance they can to insult you and pretend like it's a compliment."

"Then I guess you'll just have to fight back," she says. "In the best way you know how."

I take a deep breath, gathering my strength. At least it will be nice to get back to Stillwater. And maybe relax for a bit, or at least try to. "You going to be good with Timber until I get back?"

"Do you think I'd ever let an opportunity to puppy sit pass?" she coos. "Before I left for Bellefleur I figured out how to get him to climb in the bed and get under the covers by himself. You should see it; he puts his head on the pillow and everything. He's just like people!"

I shake my head, laughing. "God, you need a boyfriend. And fast."

"I already have one, thankyouverymuch."

"Oh you mean the secret-agent-slash-not-secret-agent who sends you cute little love letters every now and again but never signs them?"

"Hey! He's off doing spy stuff. Can I blame him if he can't get back to the States but every so often?"

"Have you even seen him since New York?"

"Not in person, no. But I'm pretty confident I'll see him again soon."

"What makes you say that?" I ask, picking at the brick of the building.

"Because when I got home there was a large bouquet waiting for me and a little note with an 'A' on it. *That's* how."

I smile. Zara has had so many boyfriends come and go over the past year I know she has to be feeling some whiplash. But she's not the kind of person that needs a guy around all of the time either. She works perfectly well enough on her own. Still, I haven't seen her this excited about a guy in…well, ever since I met her. I just hope this one works out. "When you get back from him jetting you off to Rome or whatever let me know, k? I want to hear all about it."

"Yeah, as soon as I find all this extra time in my schedule I'll be sure to do that. What are you going to do about everything else?"

"Everything else?"

"The whole reason you needed to go to Ohio in the first place, remember? Wasn't there supposed to be something important you were going to do?" I know why she's not coming right out and saying it, and I'm grateful. I haven't given her any details about what Liam found, but Zara knows me well enough to know that my focus has been on anything but my own problems since I found out Liam was in the hospital.

"I know," I say. It's been brewing in the back of my mind, I'm just not sure I can commit to it right now. How would it look if Liam went back to Stillwater and I stayed here? If it weren't for his overbearing parents, he'd probably encourage me to go down that route, but I feel like I have a duty to him first. "I'm supposed to be meeting with one of the detectives that's up here investigating the fire later. But I can't stay and deal with this now. I shouldn't have gone to Bellefleur. I should have just come up here and handled it."

"Then it might be you in that hospital bed instead of him."

"Nothing I haven't handled before," I say, my voice nonchalant.

"Em, you need to be careful," she chides, her words turning serious. "In the past few months you've been hospitalized twice already. Both times seriously. You can't keep going full steam like this."

She's right. I've been pretending like this all hasn't taken a toll on me, but it has. My body barely has a chance to heal from one disaster before another one strikes. I can feel myself slowing down, not healing as quickly as I used to, despite the fact I'm not even thirty yet. This job can beat you down and spit you out, and I've been taking a beating lately. "Maybe two weeks away from work and everything else is just what I need."

"Just try not to annoy the crap out of Liam while you're there. You get antsy when you don't have anything to do. Make this time as much about you as it is about him."

"What, like go for massages?"

She chuckles. "Something like that. Or maybe a nice hike. You know, once he's feeling up to it. Something to keep you occupied."

"I'll keep that in mind." As I'm talking I spot a patrol car pull up in the hospital parking lot. "I gotta run. Tell Timber hi for me and I'll be home soon. In fact, I may need to stop by anyway and pick up some of Liam's stuff before heading to Stillwater."

"Will do. Drive safe."

We hang up and I make a bee-line for the detective stepping out of the Hickory County cruiser that parked close to the front entrance.

"Detective Michaels?" I ask as I approach, holding my hand out. "I'm Special Agent Slate. We spoke on the phone."

"Mm-hm." He's stoic, watching me under hooded eyes and I'm thrown for a moment before he speaks again. "There hasn't been any change in the investigation since our call."

"Is there anything I can do to help?" I ask. "After all, a federal agent was—"

"No," he replies sharply. "We expect an arson specialist in town later today. He's going to perform an investigation and give us an official report."

I'm surprised by his attitude. Then again, he probably thinks I'm going to try and take the investigation away from him. Why is it local LEOs always think that? "Did you find anyone else in the house?"

"No one other than Agent Coll, and technically he was beside the home, not inside it at the time."

"He said he saw another figure on the property. And someone had to pour that kerosine down those stairs. You haven't found any evidence to support any of that?"

"Like I said, we're still in the early stages," he says, standing a little straighter like I've ruffled his feathers. "We'll know more in the coming days and weeks."

"As soon as a suspect is found, the federal government will be filing charges. They tried to kill him."

"I'm aware," he replies, and I can tell his patience with me is just about up, but I'm not about to let him go yet.

"I also need to know what, if any, evidence you recover from the scene. I don't care how big or small. If you find it in the cinders, I want to know about it." I hand him my card, which he takes after half a second's hesitation.

He examines the card a moment before stuffing it in his pocket. "We'll be in touch," he says, pulling a wide-brim hat out of his car and setting it on his head.

"Thank you," I say, following him back in. "If you need

anything else from Agent Coll, you better get it now. He's being discharged this afternoon."

He doesn't say anything else, though he does pick up the pace. I leave him to it. He'll probably get a few follow-ups with Liam before heading back. I desperately want to head out to that scene, shifting through the rubble of my family's past, but I have other responsibilities. Other duties. I'll just have to deal with the letters later, once Liam is feeling better. Maybe then I can finally put this whole thing to rest.

Given my luck, I'm not so sure.

Chapter Four

It's past eight by the time I get to Stillwater. They managed to discharge Liam early, which meant we were able to get on the hour-and-a-half flight out of Millridge back to Dulles, but because of traffic I figured it was best I head for his place to pick up some of his essentials first before making the two-hour drive back into Stillwater. And apparently Mrs. Coll thought that was an excellent idea. The only one who didn't seem thrilled was Liam who gave me a "you better not leave me alone with them" look before I headed out.

I have to admit that face has been the source of all my amusement while I packed him a bag. When we get some alone time we're going to have a *lot* to talk about regarding his family. I smile, knowing this will be an inside joke of ours for years to come.

And of course I stopped by Zara's to give Timber some love before heading back out again. I don't like the thought of being away from him for two more weeks after my extended stay in Bellefleur, so I may venture back into the city a few times just so he doesn't feel so lonely all the time. I know I haven't been fair to him, leaving him alone or with the sitter, or even with Zara while I'm gone and I need to rectify that. Part of me thinks I should have just brought him with me, but I don't think bringing my eighty-pound dog into the mix would do me any favors with his mother. The entire drive back to Stillwater I can't help but formulate plans about how I—no, how *we* can make things better for him. I can't help but grin as a plan solidifies in my brain, one that I'll need to speak to Liam about at length. But not until all of this has calmed down. Our personal lives are *not* something I want to be discussing in front of his mother.

The other angle of all this is Wallace. I called him from the hospital, giving him a full update and report on Liam's condition, only to find the doctor had already spoken with him at length. Surprisingly he didn't balk at my request for more time off. I thought I would at least get a little pushback, but Wallace has been uncharacteristically chill lately and I don't know if he's only that way with me, or if it's been a permanent change in him somewhere.

There's no question he's still feeling the effects from the whole Simon Magus situation, where he had to be reined in by my old boss, Janice, and where the joint FBI/ATF operation was almost destroyed from within due to *his* decisions. In Fletcher Wallace's short time as my SAC, he hasn't exactly proved himself worthy of the job. Perhaps he's still feeling the heat from Janice and doesn't want me there making the situation any worse. Or maybe he just doesn't like me showing him up, and figures the best way to do that is to keep me out of the office as much as possible. It certainly would explain his odd behavior lately.

If I were more paranoid than I already am, I would suspect something else is going on. Especially after the whole debacle with The Organization and Deputy Director Cochran. But given the new administration, the complete restructuring of the FBI, and the fact there are safeguards upon safeguards regarding who is working in the division, there is no way he could be anything other than the genuine article.

It's also very possible I'm overthinking this. I have a bad history of people betraying me, so I always get a little nervous when someone isn't acting the way I think they should. I also have to remember I don't know Fletcher Wallace very well; this could be his natural state, and his earlier attitude toward me might have been nothing more than him getting used to the job. Plus, Zara, Nadia, and Elliott are there to keep an eye on him. One of them will let me know if anything seems suspicious.

By the time I crest the mountain and drive down the winding road into Stillwater, the sun has long since left the sky and the glittering lights of the town are visible below. For some reason my heart is beating a little faster coming back to this small town. This was the site of the case that could have been my last with the FBI. If I hadn't found Victoria Wright's killer, I might have ended up being benched with desk duty or worse. Janice took a big risk assigning me to that case, and I can't express how grateful I am that she did. It turned everything around for me and was probably the first real step forward I'd taken since Matt died.

Of course, this was also where I first saw Camille, though I didn't quite know it at the time. But as I drive back into town looking at all the familiar landmarks I can't help but feel a little nostalgia, even though it's only been a little over a year.

Liam gave me his address before we parted at the airport, but I find myself taking a short detour through downtown to drive past the town's police station. Even though I know Chief Burke is no longer inside, my face darkens as I drive past. I don't know, some part of me expected to see some remnant of him somewhere, but nothing stands out. Zara would say I just enjoy torturing myself, and she probably wouldn't be wrong.

I continue to Liam's parents' house in an area of town I didn't explore when I was here last time. It's in an established neighborhood which looks like it was built in the sixties or seventies. Most of the homes have some kind of wood paneling or siding, and thick trees fill the neighborhood, making some of the homes difficult to see from the street. When I get to number four-forty-two, I turn down the drive-way. It dips down before coming back up and around a wooded corner before the home comes into view. It's a modest one-story, though it looks like it may have a basement as the yard slopes away in the back. There are two cars in the drive-way, both facing the garage which is on the end of the home. There's only a single light on the side of the house providing the only illumination, so I'm careful to park where no one will hit me. At least I was able to grab my own car. I feel like I've been driving someone else's vehicle for a solid month.

I get out quickly and grab Liam's suitcase from the back, leaving my own. I have no intention of staying here not to mention Mrs. Coll has preemptively shot down the idea. As soon as I'm done I plan on grabbing a room at a local hotel. I'd stay at the motel I stayed at before, but after my experience in Bellfleur, no more motels for me.

Hobbling up the walkway to the front door with the suit-case in tow, I finally get it up and over the porch. The walkway is nothing but gravel so I can't drag the suitcase without completely destroying the landscaping. I have to stop and take a breath and remind myself that I'm doing this for Liam. Lights are on inside the house, but because the curtains are drawn I can't see anyone inside. Before ringing the bell I look out to the woods to try and see the street but can't spot it from the house, the woods are too thick.

I'm stalling. I know I'm stalling. *Just push the damn button.*

The bell inside rings and I step back, the suitcase at my side. I hear the deadbolt unlatch and the door opens to reveal Mrs. Coll, a scowl on her face which is only visible for a moment before dissolving into what I would call resting bitch face. From what little I've already learned about this woman I know that she doesn't do anything by accident. I was *meant* to see that scowl.

"Evening, Mrs. Coll," I say. "I have Liam's bag from his place."

She reaches out to take the bag and I can already tell by her tight body language she has no intention of letting me in the house. "Oh, thank you. We really appreciate that. Have a good evening."

She moves to close the door and I'm still struck by the abruptness of it all before I hear Liam's voice call out, "*Mom!*"

Her facial expression doesn't change though she does open the door back up. Liam appears behind her and makes his way past to wrap me in a hug. I make sure she can see my face as he does and I catch her slip just a bit as he wraps his hands around me. If she wants to play this game, so be it.

"Hey," he whispers in my ear which makes me break eye contact with the woman.

"Hey," I say back. "How are you feeling?"

"Better now that I'm out of the hospital," he replies. He *sounds* better too. "But Mom insists on babying me."

"What else is a mother supposed to do?" Mrs. Coll asks, feigning innocence.

"Did you get my texts?" he asks.

He lets go and I step back. "Texts?"

"Yeah, I was trying to figure out if you wanted to eat here for dinner."

I shoot a glance at Mrs. Coll who isn't letting anything slip in front of her son. "Oh, no. I mean, I can get something in town." I check the time on my phone. "It's only...eight...thirty." Most places in Stillwater will be closing up by now. And now I see a batch of texts from Liam all come through at once. Right. Stillwater doesn't have the best cell coverage.

"I only made enough for three anyway," Mrs. Coll says. "We didn't know if you would be coming in tonight or in the morning."

She knows damn well when I was coming because I confirmed with them when we left the airport.

"We can make it work," Liam says. "I'm not that hungry anyway." He grabs the bag.

"Honey, don't you think Emily should take that for you?" Mrs. Coll asks as Liam lifts the bag.

"I'm not an invalid, Mom," he says and smiles at me. "C'mon. Might as well give you the grand tour."

"But we were just sitting down. It's been a long day and—"

"It'll only take a few minutes," he replies and motions for me to follow him in the house. I shoot an apologetic look at Mrs. Coll. While I don't mind pushing back when she comes directly at me, Liam isn't doing me any favors in her eyes.

On the right is a formal dining room, but there's no one at the table and the lights in the room are off. Instead, Liam's dad is in the living room, sitting in a large recliner with a tray of food beside the chair watching soccer on a large screen TV which takes up most of the opposite wall, even covering part of the brick fireplace.

The short hallway opens up to the living room itself and off to the left is a set of stairs that lead down to the basement. Liam carries his suitcase down the stairs as I hear Mrs. Coll close the door behind us. I don't dare look back, instead I follow him into the basement which turns out to be just another hallway, except with a row of doors, all on the left side as well.

"These were our rooms as kids. Apparently mine is the only one that survived as an actual bedroom." We pass the first door which looks in on a craft room. The second opens to an equal-sized room that's been tastefully decorated. A sliding glass door looks out into the darkness of the back yard. But I can also see there's a patio out there with an old grill and some chairs.

"In a house with boys, putting us down here was probably

the worst thing a parent could do," Liam laughs as he wheels the suitcase over and puts it on the bed. Lifting it causes him to cough a few times, but it's not nearly as bad as it was at the hospital.

"You could just come and go as you pleased, huh?" I ask, walking around the room. It's spacious, but I don't see any evidence that a teenage boy used to inhabit it.

"They tried putting a security system on the house, but Wes figured out how to bypass it pretty easily," he says, opening the suitcase. "But yeah, this is the room where I spent my formative years. But I'm pretty sure Mom threw out all my old stuff. She doesn't like clutter."

I shoot a glance to the door, expecting to see her there watching us, but it's empty. Just the wood paneling of the hallway beyond. "Look, I don't want to make this any harder than it already is. I know I'm a disruption here."

He waves me off. "It's good for her. My parents can be overbearing in the best of times. It's just nice to have another target for them to focus on."

"Gee, thanks," I say, taking a seat on the bed as he unpacks.

"Anytime," he replies, pulling out the rest of his clothes and putting them in the nearby drawer. "Everything okay back at home?"

I nod. "Wallace approved the time off, so I guess you're stuck with me for a few days anyway. I'll probably head back periodically to check on Timber though."

A sad sort of smile falls over his face. "Emily, you really don't have to stay here. I was only kidding when I told you not to leave me. I can handle my parents for a few weeks."

"Do *you* need to stay?" I ask. "You already look a lot better."

He shrugs. "It will help my mom feel better. She wasn't happy when I decided to join the FBI. I figure this is something of an olive branch to her. Then again, I can only take so much." He closes the top drawer just as Mrs. Coll's voice travels down the stairs.

"Liam! Your food is getting cold!"

He smiles at me. "We'll just see how it goes. Plus, now that we're both on PTO, maybe we'll finally get some time together."

I snort a laugh. "Yeah, that's not happening. Not in this house. Do I look like I have a death wish to you?"

"Did you take your medicine yet?" Mrs. Coll yells from the top of the stairs.

"Bri, quit nagging the boy, I'm tryin' to watch this!" Mr. Coll yells back.

Liam plasters a huge fake smile on his face. "You know what? Let's find somewhere else to eat."

Chapter Five

LIAM MANAGES to find the one restaurant in Stillwater that doesn't close at nine on a Monday evening. It's a little hole-in-the-wall Chinese place that I never would have found on my own, or without the help of a really good map. I have to remember this is his turf, he knows all the ins and outs of this town, and they know him. But at the moment I'm just grateful to get some food in my stomach. Mrs. Coll was right about one thing, it has been a long day, and I'm already exhausted from all the travel.

"You could have told me, you know," I say as the waiter brings out a large plate of steaming dumplings. "I mean, I get it. But still."

He takes a dumpling and dips it into the peanut sauce before taking a bite. "It's too embarrassing. Plus, I told you about my dad."

"You told me he liked soccer. *One time.* That was it." I help myself to my own dumpling. I barely taste the first one I eat it so quick. I am *famished.*

"I just don't think my family is that interesting. Plus we're not super close. I haven't seen my brother or my nephews in probably two years."

"Wes," I say, pointing at him with another dumpling before popping it in my mouth.

"Yeah. He's two years older than me and lives in Atlanta. But he's divorced now. He and Katy separated a year or so ago now. At least according to my mom."

I grab another dumpling and swish it in the sauce. "I know family can be hard to talk about. I mean, look who you're talking to." That produces a smile. "But you could have at least given me a little warning."

"You have to believe me; I had no idea they were coming to the hospital. I wasn't even going to tell them until after I'd recovered. That Dr. Riley was way too studious."

I finish my dumpling and swallow. "That might have been partially my fault. I gave him a lot of grief when I first got to the hospital about not notifying anyone when they brought you in."

He sits back. "I'm sorry you had to see that. I didn't want...I mean you shouldn't have—"

"Hey," I say, reaching my hand across the table. He hesitates a second before taking it. "I know. Okay? How many times have I had to see that look of horror on your face when you found me in the hospital? Something Zara reminded me of recently." My hand wants to go to the mark on my neck that I've been touching up with concealer all day, but I resist. I'm hoping he was so drugged up when he saw the bandage he doesn't remember that part.

Liam pinches his features. "I guess I owed you a few, huh?"

I give his hand a squeeze. "Just don't do it again. Got me?"

"Sure, no problem. I'll just tell the bad guys not to shoot at me next time because my girlfriend said so."

I try to kick at him under the table but he deftly avoids it. "Smartass."

"Em," he says, his voice turning serious. "We need to talk about it."

I let out a breath and slump back in my seat, knowing he's right. I can't put this off forever. "Hasn't this whole issue taken up enough of our lives?" I ask. "Do you really want to do this now?"

"Considering what someone just tried to do to cover up the truth, yeah, I do," he replies. "It's not just the letters anymore. This is bigger."

I grab another dumpling, making sure I take my time with this one. "The picture is in my bag in the car."

"Did you recognize anyone in it?"

I nod. "That's definitely my mom as a kid. I've never seen a picture of her younger than her early twenties, but I look a lot like her. It almost could have been a picture of me at six years old."

He nods, clearing his throat and suppressing a cough. I furrow my brow, wondering if he's trying to play off how much his lungs are still bothering him. But I have to trust he's telling me everything. This can't work otherwise. "I know it's insane. But I *saw* her. At least, I think it was her."

"Where?" I ask.

"I'd just gotten through the cellar door and was scrambling to get away from the fire as fast as I could, crawling on all fours away from the house. And I saw this figure in the distance—a woman. She was staring at me and her eyes were...I don't know...*wild*." I glance up from the plate of remaining dumplings, watching him describe this woman. "She was staring right at me and then she just took off running off in the opposite direction. She had to have been the one who set the fire."

"Did you tell that to Detective Michaels?"

He nods. "But I remember those pictures of your mom from your apartment. Emily, the woman looked just like her, except maybe a little older."

I shake my head. "That's not possible. My mother is dead."

"I know," he says, like he's heard it one too many times. "I'm just telling you what I saw."

"Maybe you were dizzy from the smoke," I say. "A lot was going on. And you said she was at a distance. Maybe she just looked like my mom."

"Maybe," he replies, though I can tell he's not convinced. "But what about—" He stops as the waiter brings us our food. Vegetable Lo Mein for him, and orange chicken for me. Both look amazing.

We both wait until the waiter is out of earshot when he leans forward. "But what about the room I found?" His voice has a slight rasp to it, which I'm sure is a byproduct of the smoke. Though it only really comes out when he whispers.

"The room in the basement. With the TV, the chair, and the desk."

"And the same paper your letters are written on. Whoever was doing it, did it from there."

"But there wasn't anyone down there, right?"

"No. Though I felt like I'd walked in on someone's private space."

I put down my chopsticks. There's a big part of me that feels compelled to return to Millridge right now and lead the investigation into the house fire. It's so strong it almost feels like a magnet, pulling me. There's no telling who could be behind this, or what kind of influence they have.

I close my eyes, forcing the memories away. This isn't like the Organization. There is no grand conspiracy. This is just about *me*. Whoever this woman is, *if* she's responsible, she wants *me*.

"Em."

I open my eyes to find Liam staring at me. "There's one more thing. And I didn't tell the detective because I didn't know if you would want me to. But there were all these newspaper clippings and pictures downloaded from the internet. And all of them were of you. Pictures of you from press conferences, pictures that looked like they were taken from video stills. I wasn't sure what do to."

Further evidence that whoever is behind this wanted me in that house and not Liam. "I should have just gone myself. Then maybe all of this would have been over and finished by now."

"If you had, you might not have come back. I'm not getting the warm and fuzzies from this person. My first impression is she wants to kill you."

"No. I know what it feels like when someone has a target on me. This is something different. She wants something *from* me, that much I'm sure of."

"So why the cryptic letters?"

"I can't say yet. I want to wait and see what Detective Michaels finds. See if he manages to pull any evidence from the rubble. Then I'll go back and see what I can make of it."

Liam finally begins working on his Lo Mein. "Are you going to tell Wallace?"

"Not if I can help it."

"I wish I could have found out more. Or at least gathered some of the evidence before it burned up," he says, slowly eating some of the noodles.

"You did more than enough," I tell him. "I'm just sorry you got caught up in my drama. *Again.*"

"Hey," he says, putting down his own chopsticks. "It's *our* drama. Right?"

I smile. "Yeah." Part of me wants to broach the subject I spent the entire drive up here thinking about, but now is not the right time. He needs to heal first, and I think both of us would be better out of his mother's orbit before we go into more detail about our futures.

The rest of the meal is an enjoyable relaxation—something we've been missing from our meals together lately. We've both been so busy with cases here and there that we've barely had time to share anything other than a couple hours of sleep in the past four months. Sitting down like this and taking our time is a nice change of pace and I make sure to relish every moment of it.

After dinner, I drive him back home and despite his protestations, leave him there and head back into town to check myself into the only hotel in town. Last time I stayed at a much cheaper motel, but after my experience in Bellflower it's going to be awhile before I sleep anywhere that's not a few floors off the ground at least, even if I have to pay for it myself. The clerk doesn't look twice at my ID when checking me in, and instead seems more interested in the show on her phone.

Once inside I reflect on the last time I was in a hotel room in this city the floor was covered in different piles of paper, an organized chaos to try and find Gerald Wright. Little had I known he'd been right under my nose the whole time. At least this time while I'm here I can relax.

I take a few minutes to wipe down the room with Lysol cloths—an annoying habit Zara got me into after pointing out that every crime scene we've investigated in hotel or motel rooms always turns up more DNA than an orgy. After I'm satisfied it's clean enough, I take a few minutes to unpack my comfy clothes and get ready for bed. Not wanting to bother with my phone anymore, I switch on the TV instead, planning to go to sleep to the noise.

But I can't help but stop on the first channel I land on, which happens to be WLNK, the local Stillwater news station. A pretty young reporter stands in front of what looks like a trailhead, lit up with spotlights.

"...*locals say no one heard the shot. However, police are still looking for anyone who might have any information regarding the accident. Funeral arrangements are being prepared by Mr. Jordan's wife. The family asks that instead of flowers, donations be made to the Stillwater Nature Preserve or the Wildlife Society. This is Terry Baker, channel seven news.*"

The image flips back over to the man in the studio and for a second I catch the old graphic which says "Fatal Accident Claims One" before it switches to another story.

Fatal accident? With a gunshot?

Unable to help myself, I grab my phone and text Liam.

Hey, do you know anything about this shooting in the woods?

No, what is it?

Some local guy got killed it sounds like.

I can ask my dad about it. Apparently, he's temporarily back on the force. They're short-handed. Want me to check with him?

I pause. Do I want Liam's dad involved? Maybe it's better off if I leave it alone. But I can't just turn that part of my brain off either.

Yeah, but don't let him know I asked.

Lol. K, night crazy.

I smile and text back. *Night.*

Chapter Six

DESPITE MY ATTEMPTS TO sleep in, I'm awake early. Since I don't have anything better to do, I download a yoga video and try my hand at it, finding it more difficult than I expected. Zara's admonishment from yesterday has been bouncing back and forth in my head and I really need to start taking better care of myself. That probably means cutting out all the extra alcohol, getting a generous amount of sleep each night, and doing a lot more self-care in the meantime, which is something I've never been good about.

As soon as I finish the yoga program, I remember why I don't do this regularly. Taking care of yourself is a pain in the ass and it takes forever. Plus, by the time I'm finished I'm starving. I shower quickly and pull on some regular clothes, but I still keep my badge and weapon on me no matter what. After what happened in Bellefleur, I'm not about to let either out of my sight anytime soon.

Not wanting to face Mrs. Coll yet for the day, I head to the Early Derby, a place I enjoyed on my first visit to Stillwater. The food is still just as good and by the time I'm done I finally feel ready for the day. But as I'm getting ready to drive back to Liam's house to do whatever it is a good girlfriend does when their boyfriend needs to recover from almost having his lungs burned out of his chest, I spot the Stillwater Police Station down the street. The parking lot isn't too full and I have an urge to pop my head in.

I know it's probably irrational, but I really want to see what's changed ever since Chief Burke left. I'm sure it's not drastically different, but I remember marching that bastard down those steps in handcuffs all while he wouldn't quit telling me how much I'd be sorry.

Smiling at the memory, I let the urge win over and I drive down to the station, parking in the lot. I head inside and find myself staring at the same partition that was here when I first walked in over a year ago. A woman in her mid-thirties sits behind the glass partition, playing on her phone. She looks up and her eyes light up. "Agent Slate," she says, getting up with a smile. She's got that charming southern twang that's just light enough that it's not annoying. "Hang on a second, let me come around there."

She opens the security door on her side and makes her way around the partition and wraps me in a big hug before I even know what's going on. "Hi, Trish," I say. "How have you been?"

She releases me and steps back, beaming. Her cheeks are rouged with too much makeup, but her smile is genuine. "Oh, my God, I can't believe you're here! What are you doin' back in Stillwater? Not chasin' another serial killer, I hope."

"Oh, no, nothing like that," I reply, surprised by how happy the woman is to see me. I didn't even expect anyone to remember me. "I'm just here for...uh, personal reasons."

"It's cause of Liam, isn't it?" She wrinkles her nose when she says his name. "His daddy told us all about what happened."

"He did."

"Oh yeah. Barely a day goes by that Sean doesn't talk about Liam. Is he back in town yet? I'd love to see him again."

"Um...he is. He's staying at his parent's house."

"And you're here to help him get better," she coos. "That's so sweet of you."

"I mean...I guess," I say, still thrown by her exuberance. This is a lot all at once.

"Oh, I have got to tell the chief. He will be thrilled to meet you," she says, rushing back around and unlocking the security door again.

"Oh, no, that's not really necess—" I say before she's already on the phone.

"Chief Salazar? Could you come up front please? We have a very special guest."

I hold up my hand trying to indicate that she really doesn't need to call anyone, but she's already finished and has hung up before I can offer another word of protest. "He'll be right up," she says, leaning forward on her elbows which are perched on her desk. "Can I just tell you, oh my God, Emily, you don't know, but you are a saint."

I can almost see my own reaction, my mouth opening and closing without any words coming out before I finally force myself into action. "I'm sorry?"

"Oh, it's just that—" But before she can finish, the door to the back opens and out walks a man who is only about an inch or so taller than me. He's dressed in the chief's uniform, and has a tan complexion, like he spends a lot of time out in the sun, despite the fact it's winter. His green eyes light up when he sees me and it's like he's welcoming an old friend, even though I'm pretty sure I've never met this man before.

"Special Agent Emily Slate," he says, extending his hand as he approaches. "What a surprise. And an honor."

I take his hand and shake it, turning my gaze to Trish, who is beaming.

"Lee Salazar," he says. "I'm Stillwater's new Police Chief."

"So I gathered," I say when he finally releases my hand.

"They brought me over from Montgomery," he says.

"After the whole Burke debacle. Can I just say, you are something of a legend around here."

"A legend?" I ask.

"Oh, absolutely," he replies. "When I came in to take over, you do not know how much shit I had to sift through—how much corruption Burke had been imposing on this poor community for the past twenty years. The man was a menace. I continued to work with the Virginia Bureau of Investigation and your division to provide evidence for additional crimes. Didn't you hear about it?"

"I wish I had," I admit. "But they keep us pretty busy when we're out in the field. We don't do a lot of follow-up." Not to mention I was dealing with an assassin; the Bureau had been infiltrated by a clandestine Organization and now someone pretending to by my mother keeps sending me cryptic letters. "But I'd love to hear all about it."

"Fantastic," he says, beaming. "Though I'll have to get something on my schedule. We've been a little short-handed ever since the shake-up. We had to get rid of some bad apples that Burke had been protecting."

"Really?" I ask.

"There's always more than one," he replies. "But talk to Trish here, she runs the schedule for most of us in the department. I'd be happy to treat you to lunch or dinner."

"Liam's here too," Trish says, grinning.

"Great. Then we can make it for three. The two of you really turned things around for this department. And we would love to say thank you."

I'm speechless. I mean, I know we did a good thing by getting Burke out of here, but I can't believe Salazar is *this* appreciative. He's acting like we cured cancer or something. Though I have to admit I wouldn't mind hearing more about how long Burke is going to be in prison and what additional charges they found against him. "That sounds great."

"Perfect." He points a finger gun at Trish. "Can you get

that set up for us?"

"Absolutely. Be happy to," she replies.

"Great, and in the meantime—"

"Agent Slate?" I turn to see Sean Coll walking through the doors of the station, a concerned look on his face. "What are you doing here?"

"Ah, Sean," Salazar says. "I was just thanking Agent Slate here for her good work on helping rid the town of Burke. And I hear your son is in town too."

Coll gives me a hard eye, ignoring Salazar. "So that's what Liam was talking about this morning."

"I'm sorry?" I say, doing my best not to raise my defenses just yet. But Coll's energy isn't giving me the warm and fuzzies. He's holding himself tight, like he's gearing up for a fight.

"I was wondering why Liam was so interested in that accidental death from this weekend. It was because of you, wasn't it? You want information on the case."

I set my jaw. "No. I mean, yes, I asked him about it last night, but just because I saw it on the news," I say. "I don't want on anything. I was just curious."

"It's a terrible tragedy," Salazar says. "A man was killed by a stray bullet in the middle of the woods. Freak accident."

"A stray bullet?" I ask.

"It *is* small game season," Salazar reiterates. "And the area where they were camping borders a designated hunting region. We figure a hunter got lost and found himself in the wrong place."

"Are you sure it was an accident?" I ask, alarm bells going off in my head.

"We performed a thorough check of the area," he replies. "There was nothing suspicious about it. These things happen sometimes. But no one has come forward yet. Which is why we released the information to the media. We're hoping someone can give us a lead."

"And we don't need additional help," Coll replies.

I want to reiterate that I hadn't offered any, but Liam's father seems like he wants to pick a bone with me regardless.

"Well, now, hang on," Salazar says. "We have been short-handed for a while now. Weren't you saying the other day how you couldn't wait until we hired a few more hands so you could get back to putting your feet up?"

Coll scowls at the man. "It's nothin' we can't handle on our own." There comes that thick Irish accent again.

Salazar holds up his hands. "If you say so, Sean." He turns to me. "Apologies. Some of us don't have basic manners around here."

Coll grumbles something under his breath as he heads off, though I don't think it was anything that would have scored him any points with his temporary boss. He comes across to me as a proud man, and the last thing I want to do is step on any toes around here. I'm in up to my neck with Liam's mother already. I don't need a repeat performance with his father.

I give Salazar a sheepish look. "Maybe it's better if we leave that dinner for another time. I think I might be ruffling too many feathers here."

"Oh," the chief says, his gaze following Mr. Coll. "That's too bad. I don't want to put you in a difficult position."

The man has no idea. "Pleasure meeting you."

Salazar smiles. "Likewise."

I nod to Trisha. "Great seeing you again. If you'll excuse me." I quickly head back out of the station and find my car in the parking lot. I've only been here one day and already I'm just making things worse. Maybe staying here while Liam heals wasn't the best idea. I can be of more use if I head back to D.C. and dive into my caseload. That way I won't be in anyone else's way, and I won't need to stay somewhere I'm clearly not wanted.

Now all I have to do is break the news to him.

Chapter Seven

BECAUSE I'M NOT a coward I head back over to the Coll house, ready to face Mrs. Coll again and what is sure to be a barrage of promptings about me going home and leaving Liam here. I know he said he didn't expect me to stay—not really, but I can tell he really doesn't want to be left alone here. I still don't have a good handle on his relationship with his parents, but I could always suggest he just come back to D.C. with me. I'm sure that would do *wonders* for my relationship with his mother. He is an adult, after all. Last night, when we were texting, I felt like I was fifteen again, sequestered in my house while my *boyfriend* was in his.

It all felt so…juvenile.

I take a deep breath as I drive up to the house, though I'm surprised to see a Lexus in the driveway. I know Mr. Coll is at the station, seeing as I just left from there, but I don't see Mrs. Coll's vehicle anywhere. As I pull up to the house behind the Lexus I shoot Liam a quick text.

In the driveway. Okay to come in?

He sends a reply back almost immediately. *Yes, come on in.*

I raise my eyebrows at the strangeness of the situation, though it seems like the coast is clear for now. Maybe it's better that way. I can just have this conversation with Liam without his mother listening in and I can be on the road to D.C. by this afternoon. And his mother will come home to find me gone. At least that will be one battle I don't have to wage any longer.

I make my way up the steps and knock on the door twice before trying the handle. "Hello?"

"In here," Liam calls from somewhere in the back of the house. I let myself in and notice just how quiet the house is without Mr. or Mrs. Coll around. A raucous laughter erupts from somewhere in the back of the house causing my ears to perk up. I make my way down the short hallway and around the living room before reaching the kitchen, which doesn't look like it's been updated since the eighties. Off the kitchen is a sunroom that looks out on the back of the property, and must sit directly above the bedrooms below. Liam is seated in a chair situated around a breakfast table that's in the middle of the sunroom, while another man stands close by, leaning up against the kitchen counter. He's the same height as Liam, though his hair is a little darker and he has the same hazel eyes and devilish smile as Liam, which he turns on when he sees me.

Before anyone says a word there is no doubt in my mind this is Liam's brother.

"Em!" Liam says, getting up. He wraps me in a quick hug and I catch the smell of coffee and what I think is Kaluha on his breath. "I'd like you to meet my brother, Wes. This is Emily."

Wes's smile only widens as he holds out a hand. I take it, giving his grip as good as he gives me before he pulls me into a hug. "It's about time I met you," he says as I'm trying to process being bear-hugged by this man. He releases me quickly and beams at me. "I've been tellin' this asshole for six months you needed to come down to Atlanta. At this rate I was thinkin' the first time I'd meet ya would have been at the wedding."

"Wedding?" I ask.

"Wes," Liam warns and it hits me.

"*Ohhh*, waitaminute," I say, taking a step back.

"Em, he's just teasing," Liam says, taking my arm. When Liam turns back to his brother there is a scowl on his face like I've never seen before. "Right?"

Wes just bursts out in laughter before taking a sip from his own mug. "Sure, yeah. Of course," he replies before shooting me a wink. "God damn. He wasn't kidding though. You are absolutely gorgeous."

"*Wes*," Liam says, more forcefully this time.

"What? I can't compliment her? She is! Look at her!" He holds both hands toward me like he's trying to showcase me. Frankly, my mind is still back on the whole marriage comment.

"Can you just be civil for one minute?" Liam asks.

Wes puts on a serious face, turning to me and taking my hand in his. "It is my utmost pleasure and privilege to meet you, Ms. Slate. You have been the subject of many a conversation between my brother and I and it has been my lifelong wish to make your acquaintance."

Liam drives a fist into Wes's shoulder, causing him to drop my hand. Wes gives him a punch back and for a second I'm afraid they might actually get into an actual fistfight before I catch the smile on both their faces.

"Just ignore him, he never learned how to talk to people," Liam says.

Wes just raises his mug in solidarity with the comment. "Which is why my wife left me and took the kids. And honestly, can you blame her?"

"I...uh," I say, unsure how to respond. This is all very strange and I'm not quite sure what to make of Wes, but at least he's friendlier than either of Liam's parents. "Did you just get in?"

"Yep. Mom called up in arms that Liam was practically dying so I figured I'd better at least show up for the funeral. But since this dumbass refuses to die, I don't get a chance to try out my new suit."

"Very funny," Liam says, taking his seat again. "Sorry, Em. I told him to behave."

"If you told her anything about me then she should have already known that wouldn't happen." He winks at me again, though it seems more in solidarity than anything else. "I mean, he practically walks around with a stick up his ass. I'm just hoping you can help remove it."

"That's right, keep it up," Liam says. "Dig yourself deeper."

"Oh, come on," Wes replies. "I drove up here thinking you were in a coma or something. Honestly you don't even look like anything happened." He turns to me again. "*Did* something happen? Or did this big crybaby just want his mommy?"

I suppress a smile, unsure if I want to encourage Wes. Like his parents, he's a lot. But for the first time, none of that energy is directed at me, thankfully. He's so different than Liam. If it weren't for the physical similarities, I wouldn't have believed they were related.

"No, it really happened," I say. "He could have died."

Wes takes another sip from his mug. "Guess I would have gotten the house, then."

"Like you need it," Liam replies.

"You don't know, bro," he replies. "Alimony is a bitch." He turns to me. "Excuse my language."

"How long have you been divorced?" I ask.

Wes's eyes go wide, then he turns to Liam. "She doesn't *know*? I figured you would have spilled the beans a long time ago."

"We've had a lot going on," Liam says. "Our jobs don't allow for a lot of downtime."

"Yeah, yeah," Wes says. "Making sure justice is served and all that. Darling of the family. Meanwhile, I'm over here kicking ass in the financial sector and no one says boo."

"That's because it's not heroic to earn money," Liam says, taking a sip of his own mug. It's very interesting watching the two of them go back and forth. I wonder if they've always been like this. Liam really hasn't ever said very much about his family. I knew he had a brother and I think he told me once his name, but other than that I know virtually nothing about the man. Same with Liam's parents. Knowing Liam, he probably held off talking much about family because of all of my own personal issues with mine. But at the same time, we've only been in an official relationship for two-and-a-half months. And given our schedules and how much we've both been out of town, it's no surprise we haven't gotten this far yet.

"I'm tellin' you, baby bro, you should have forgotten all this cop nonsense and come to work with me. You could have been living large in your own penthouse apartment by now."

"A penthouse in Atlanta is still Atlanta," I say, finally feeling like I've caught up.

Wes turns to me, then chuckles. "You're not wrong. Would I prefer New York? Or Miami? Sure, but then again, I'm only thirty-three. Give me another five years."

"Wes likes to think the world begins and ends with money," Liam explains.

"Oh no, I'm not letting you bait me into this again," Wes says, crossing his arms with his mug still in one hand. "I want to hear all about you two." He changes his tone to a higher pitch. "How'd you meet?"

"We met here, actually," I say. "A little over a year ago. I was working an unidentified person. A woman had been found with her eyes sewn shut and shoved into a small box.

About fifteen miles…" I turn, orienting myself, then point back toward the front of the house. "That way."

Wes sets his mug down. "And that qualifies as the grossest thing I've heard this morning. Continue."

"Yeah, she'd been in that box for what, eight years?" Liam asks.

"Something like that. And her pelvis had been shattered where the killer had basically broken her in half to get her in there."

Wes's face has gone slightly ashen and his lips seem to have gone dry. "So…uh, you guys what? Hit it off over a dead body?"

I share a look with Liam. "Not exactly. But we solved the case together."

"Of course, we really didn't get together until later," Liam says. "After I finished training and moved to D.C."

Wes nods, swallowing hard like he's glad to be done with all the "body" talk. Another interesting difference between them. Liam has a strong constitution. It seems his brother does not. "I'm telling you man; you stirred up some shit when you left. Mom just about had an aneurysm. For a while I thought they might try to move down with me."

"Thank goodness for small favors," Liam says.

"Yeah, no kidding," he replies. "If I'd had to live with them, you guys would have been investigating a couple more homicides for sure."

I've decided I like Wes. He's brash and cocky, but in a sort of charming way. He feels to me like the big brother I've never had, though I have no idea if that's appropriate or not. Growing up without siblings, I've never quite understood that kind of relationship. And while I had close friends, none of them ever filled the same role like a sibling would. Which was why I was so glad when I got married I gained a brother and a sister. But given how that whole situation played out, I'm not

sure what I felt was ever real. Or if it was, it wasn't recip-
rocated.

But Wes has a way about him which makes him seem
easygoing, but also fierce about his family. It's obvious through
their interactions both men care for each other, though I
doubt either one of them would admit it to the other's face.
Still, it's a nice reprieve from the rest of Liam's family.

"So Liam tells me you're here to keep an eye on him and
make sure he doesn't run into any more burning buildings for
a few weeks," Wes says, draining the rest of his mug and
placing it in the sink.

"That's the plan," I say.

"Please tell me you're staying here." He grins.

"Mom really *would* have an aneurysm then," Liam says.

"I'm holed up at the Jefferson Hotel, in downtown," I say,
then turn to Liam. "Which was actually what I came to talk to
you about. I went over to the station this morning. Trish says
to tell you hi."

Liam raises his eyebrows. "Oh. How's she doing?"

"Good. And I met the new chief. Much friendlier than
Burke. But your dad came in while we were talking and
things...kind of spiraled."

"Ah shit," Wes says. "If there's anyone who can ruin someone's day just by looking at them, it's da."

"What did he do?" Liam asks, his voice full of concern.

I shoot Wes a look. I'd rather do this in private, but I
might as well get it over with. Any second I know Mrs. Coll is
going to walk through that door and I'd rather be out of here
when that happens. "I think maybe it's just better if I go back
to D.C. You don't need me here and I'm just getting in the
way."

"Wait, no, you can't do that," Wes says. I'm surprised he's
the one to interject before Liam. "You can't let them beat you.
Trust me, we dealt with them for years. Don't back down, it's

exactly what they—what *she* wants." He says the last part in a hushed voice, like the ghost of Mrs. Coll will hear us.

I wince. "You probably have family obligations that keep you here for a little while, but I think I'm only making the situation worse. I don't want to come between you and your family."

"No. You do, you absolutely do," Wes says, turning to Liam. "Right?"

"I don't want Emily to do anything where she doesn't feel comfortable," he replies. "I don't want you to stay because of me. If it's too much, then I completely understand."

"Oh, come on!" Wes says. "Have a spine! You don't want her to go, so say as much."

I turn to Liam. "Is that true?"

"Wes. Shut. Up." Liam growls. "You don't have all the information, okay?" Liam is doing what he always does, he's putting my needs above his own. He probably thinks there's something else going on under the surface, that all of this family time is bringing up some bad memories for me. But that's not it at all. I just don't want to be the problem in the middle of all...this. If Liam and I are going to have a long-term relationship, then I'd rather not have a contentious one with his parents. Tensions and emotions are high right now. And this isn't the best of circumstances for all of us to be cramped together like this.

"Liam," I say. "What do *you* want?"

"I'd love for you to stay, of course," he replies. "But not at the expense of your mental health. Trust me, if you need to go back, it's okay. I'll be back in a week or so."

"But the doctor said two weeks," I reply.

"I can always spend a week here and then a week back at home," he replies. "In fact, I'm not sure I can take two weeks here."

"Yeah," Wes says, having crossed his arms again. "Blow your brains out, man."

"I think that would be a better plan for everyone," I say, then shoot a glance at Wes who just seems to be watching the whole situation.

"Oh!" he finally says. "You want time alone to say good-bye. Right. I'll just…" He hooks a thumb behind him. "Great meeting you Emily." This time it actually sounds genuine.

"You too," I say as he heads back out.

"Catch you later," he calls to Liam. "We'll go out later, yeah? Saturday night?"

"Sure," Liam calls after him. When he's finally gone, he reaches for me, taking me by the hips and pulling me closer. "Sorry about him. He's always been a mess."

"It's strangely charming," I say.

"That's what his wife thought too, until she had to live with it a few years," he replies.

"You *have* to tell me that story."

"When I get back to D.C.?" he asks.

"Deal."

He pulls me in for a kiss and I relish it. From now on, I have no choice but to relish them all.

Chapter Eight

"HEY, EMILY!"

I turn to see Wes getting back out of his car as I close the door behind me, having given Liam a proper—if not short goodbye. Even though he's only going to be two hours away, I feel like it's farther, maybe just because his parents feel like an impenetrable wall.

"Have you been sitting out here waiting for me?" I ask as I make my way to my car.

"I had a conference call," he says. "But I wanted to make sure I caught you before you left. Liam—well, I'm sure you know he takes on a lot."

"Tell me about it."

"Yeah, and I was thinking, if something happens to him, like his symptoms get worse, he might not tell you. And mom *definitely* won't. Do you want to exchange numbers just in case?" He holds up both hands. "Promise to only use it in an emergency."

I'm still not sure about Wes. But he's right. Liam will most likely hide or downplay if his symptoms worsen. And his mother will outright lie. His brother might be my only lifeline once I go back to D.C. "Yeah, okay," I say and we exchange numbers quick.

"Thanks," he says. "I feel better knowing I can get hold of you if something happens." He looks back at the house. "Also, I was wondering what you were doing at the police station. Are you helping with a case?"

"Definitely not," I say, reaching my car. "Your dad almost popped a blood vessel when he saw me in there."

"You learn to ignore it after a while," Wes says. "At least, I have. It's all in one ear and out the other."

I get the feeling he wants to say something else, but it's just the two of us staring at each other and it's starting to get awkward. "Well, nice meeting you, I guess. Have a safe trip back to Atlanta."

He cracks a crooked smile. "Sorry if I came off a little brash. It's one of my defense mechanisms. Liam just talks so highly of you it's hard not to be intimidated, you know?"

I have to admit I'm surprised. It seems he and his brother are more alike than I assumed, it's just that Wes hides his vulnerability under a heavier mask. "Intimidated by me?"

"Are you kidding? Of course! He keeps telling me about all these cases you solve and how you helped stop that whole thing with the FBI and how many people's lives you've saved. I mean, the way he describes you it's like you're a superhero."

I can feel my cheeks redden, though I am going to have to talk to Liam about that. "No more than anyone else. And no more than your brother. He's done his fair share too."

"I know he seems like he's fine, but I can tell. This whole thing really scared him," Wes says. "I'd really appreciate it if you would stick around. Not to mention it would really get on my parents' nerves." He grins that mile-wide grin again.

"Oh, would it?" I ask.

"If you think I'm intimidated by you, it's nothing compared to my mother. She sees you as taking her place in his life. That he won't need her anymore because he has you."

"That's ridiculous," I say.

"Have you *met* Brianna Coll?" Wes says. "The woman defines ridiculous."

I chuckle. "I guess that's true. But I'm just getting in the way here. I don't want anything to interfere with Liam's recovery. And I think it would be better if I try and build a relationship with them when tensions aren't so high."

Wes shakes his head. "Nah. They're always like this. There's always a crisis in my mother's life and an inconvenience in my da's. Might as well pull the band-aid off now and get it over with."

"I don't know," I say, hesitant.

"C'mon, what case were you talking to my da' about? The one that really got him pumping?"

"Oh, it's nothing. It's just this local hiker that got killed by a stray bullet."

"Oh yeah, I heard about that last night when I was driving in," he replies. "Do they know who did it?"

"As far as I know no one has come forward yet. But I'm not about to get involved in the case. I just went over there because I was curious."

"You're just like my brother, you know? No wonder you two fit so well together."

"How so?" I ask.

"Never mind. Just…hang around for a few hours, huh?" He heads back for the house.

"Wes," I call out, wanting to ask him what he means and why it's so important I "hang around". But he's already back inside the house. I don't want to have to go back and say goodbye to Liam all over again, and there's still no telling when Mrs. Coll will be back, so I just get in my car and back out of the long driveway.

Thankfully, I don't pass the woman in the neighborhood, and I take my first breath once I'm back out on the main stretch, headed for my hotel. I don't know if Wes is right or not, but sticking around here to butt heads with their parents over and over is not my idea of time off. Plus, this way I can get back home, get Timber back where he belongs and try to settle into my routine again before Liam comes home.

It will be better this way. For everyone.

~

"You mean you're just going to tuck tail and run? That is so not like you."

"I'm not running," I reiterate as I finish shoving my clothes in my bag. "I'm removing myself from a toxic situation."

"Psssh," Zara says, completely exasperated. "The Emily I know doesn't back down from anyone. Why are you letting these people get to you?"

"Because they're *his family*," I say. "How is it going to help anything if I steamroll them?"

"It's going to show them you don't take shit from anyone," she replies. "That they can't push you around and expect you to just roll over."

"I don't know," I say. "It's always messier with family."

"That's the thing about you," she says. "You have no problem showing people who is boss in any other situation, but when it comes to *family*, yours or otherwise, it's like you go back inside your shell." It's hard to hear, but she's not wrong. And I don't have a defense for it.

"You need to march your ass back in that house, sit those two people down and explain to them how it's going to be. That's *your* house now," she says. "Emily's house. Emily's rules."

I stare at her face on the screen and she is dead serious. "I'm not going to go over and take over their house," I say.

"The hell you're not. I forbid you to come home until you

have all those people under your heel. The brother sounds interesting, though."

I smile. "I'm sure the two of you would get along famously. No, I need to let Liam deal with…whatever this is and stay out of it."

"Emily." There's that tone. I hesitate a second before finally turning to the phone so she can see me. "Do you want a long-term relationship with this man?"

"Yes," I groan.

"Then you are going to have to deal with his family eventually. It's better to show them who they're up against now, otherwise you're gonna be running for the rest of your relationship together." She takes a deep breath and lets it out again. "It's like when you go to prison. You have to establish dominance early. Show them who's the big bitch in the yard."

I practically bust out laughing. "You're insane. So the advice is to go beat up Mr. and Mrs. Coll."

"Metaphorically, yes," she replies.

"Let me get right on that," I say, shoving the last of my toiletries in my bag before I zip it up.

"I'm serious Em. You run from this now, you're never gonna stop."

"Maybe we just have one of those relationships where I don't interact with his family. Those exist, right?"

"If you really think that's best," she replies. "But you know my vote."

I smile, getting close to the camera. "You have made it crystal clear."

"Good. At least now I'll be able to say I told you so in about…oh, I'd say eight months. Holiday time. You know, families around the table and all that?"

"Eight months of peace might be worth it," I tell her. But before she can say anything else there's a knock at my door.

"Who's that?"

"I don't know," I say, reaching for my weapon on the side

table. Given my experiences with strange people in my rooms, I don't take chances anymore.

"You want me to stay on the line?"

"Yeah, hang on just a second," I say and make my way to the door. "Who is it?"

"It's Wes."

Wes? What the hell is he doing here? And how did he even find my room? "What do you want?"

"Who is it?" Zara asks. From the phone's position on the bed all she can see is the ceiling.

"I have something for you," he replies, and it feels strangely ominous. Like he's here to deliver a message from a mob boss.

"What?" I ask.

"It's a surprise. Geez, what's with all the questions? Are you going to open the door or not?"

"Em? You still there?" Zara asks.

"Yeah, hang on Z," I say. I keep the chain on the door and open it just enough to see Wes's figure on the other side.

"I guess it pays to be paranoid in your line of work," he says, flashing that smile of his again.

"How'd you find my room?" I ask.

"The dude who runs this place is an old-school chum of mine. I just asked him where the FBI agent was."

So much for a hotel being more secure. I let out a long breath and close the door again. "Hang on." I unhook the chain and open the door, stepping back and making sure there's enough space between me and him so that if he rushes me, I can deflect it. Not that I expect Liam's brother to actually do something, but I don't do great with unexpected visits.

"Em, *who is it?*" Zara asks.

"Who is that?" Wes says, pointing to the phone. He's carrying one of those old brown fold-over file things in his other arm, the kind that have the string clasp to keep them closed.

"This is my friend, Zara," I say picking up the phone. "Z, this is Wes, Liam's brother."

"Oh, the rich guy from Atlanta," Zara says as I show her to him. "What's he doing there?"

"That's a good question," I say, setting my jaw as we both stare at him.

He gives us a nervous chuckle and sets the folder on the nearest table. "Didn't mean to intrude, I just thought you might want to take a look at this." His gaze flits to my packed suitcase. "Considering you're about to take off."

"What is it?"

"The police file on that hiker that died," he replies, grinning again.

My eyes widen. "Where did you get that? That's confidential information."

He shrugs. "It was in my da's office. He always keeps physical copies of all the cases he's working on at any given time. Always has."

"Oh, I like him," Zara says.

"Shush you," I say and toss the phone back on the bed.

"Hey," she yells and I grab the file from the table.

"You need to return this to the house before he knows it's missing. I'm not about to get in the middle of a case I'm not even working."

"Aren't you just a little bit curious?" he asks.

"Does Liam know you did this?" I say.

"Of course not, he was already back downstairs in his room when I went back in. But you said you were interested in the case and I thought maybe if you took a look, you might not be in such a hurry to leave."

"Yeah, open it up and look at it!" Zara yells. "You said there was something fishy going on."

"I don't need the two of you ganging up on me," I say, the folder tucked securely under my arm.

"I disagree," Wes says.

"Did *you* look at it?" I ask.

"I might have taken a glance," he replies. "You know, just to make sure it was the right file." I curse under my breath.

"We need to get this back, right now."

"Oh, stop being such a goody and look at the damn file already," Zara says. "You know you want to."

"I think your friend has a point," Wes adds.

Dammit. I have been wanting to take a look at the file ever since earlier this morning when I learned it was a hunting "accident". Something like that is more likely to happen during deer or turkey season. Neither of which is happening right now.

"Fine. If the two of you will shut up about it," I say, opening the folder and pulling the file out.

"Nice," Wes replies.

"Peer pressure, it gets her every time," Zara calls out.

"Oh yeah? What else?" Wes asks, a little twinkle in his eye.

"Not another word or I'm hanging up," I tell Zara. I flip through the preliminary reports of the case. The victim was Josh Newsome, a resident of Stillwater with his wife, Marnie Scrofano. They have different last names, interesting. The report says they were out for a hike, made camp and while the two were stargazing, a stray bullet pierced Josh right through the chest, killing him instantly. The wife reports it occurred after dark, which means no hunter should have been out at that time.

Were they serious with this? "Something isn't right," I say, going back over the information again.

"What does it say?" Zara asks.

"It's been classified as an accident, but none of the evidence lines up to support that theory," I say. "The man was killed around nine o'clock at night. Do you know any hunters who are out there in the pitch black, creeping around the woods looking for 'small game' to kill? It doesn't make any sense."

"Maybe it was someone hunting illegally," she offers.

"Maybe, but if that was the case, they should have seen the big fire the wife reported the couple building before they began stargazing." I shake my head. "Something about this doesn't pass the smell test."

"So what are you going to do?" she asks.

I shoot Wes a look, and he's still wearing what I'm going to have to start calling his trademark smile. "I need to talk to the chief."

Chapter Nine

AFTER MAKING it clear to the clerk at the front desk *not* to give out my location information to anyone else, I head back to the police station, leaving Wes and his old friend to catch up. My plan is to explain how I came to possess the file to the chief, but also to raise my concerns about the investigation. Even though I'm taking a step in this direction, I am *not* working this case. Nor do I want to. I just want to make sure everything is on the up and up. Especially after my last experience here in Stillwater. There's no point in getting rid of the old guard if the new one is just going to come in and repeat the same mistakes.

"Emily! You're back," Trish says as soon as I walk in the door.

"I need to speak with Salazar, is he in?" I ask.

"Sure, he's right back—oh, well you know. It's back in… uh…Burke's old office."

"You mind buzzing me through?" I ask, I hold up the folder as if to show her I have something to share with him.

"Sure, go on back. I'll let him know you're coming." She buzzes the door and picks up her phone at the same time.

Walking back through the back portion of the station is

strange to me, and familiar at the same time. The place doesn't seem to have changed at all, and at yet it's completely different. None of the departments are in the same place as they were before. I pass by the office where Liam and I were set up when we were hunting Gerald Wright only to find it's been turned into a small cafeteria of sorts, filled with vending machines. All the old desks are gone.

When I reach the bullpen, I see it's been reoriented and is facing a different direction. But the way it has been laid out looks a lot more efficient than before. A couple of officers mill about, but no one seems to pay me any attention. I don't recognize anyone. Looks like Trish might have been one of the only ones spared when the department was restructured under the new chief.

The only thing that looks like it's the same is the location of the chief's office. The door is open as I approach, but I knock anyway.

"Here she is right now," Salazar says, the phone to his ear. He motions me in and hangs up. "Didn't think I'd get to see you again so soon. It's been what…four hours?" He checks his watch, exaggerating the move in a comical manner.

"I needed to speak with you," I say, placing the folder on his desk. "This was brought to my attention. I don't want to get anyone in trouble, but I need you to know I didn't go looking for it."

He gives me a funny sort of smile as he takes the folder, unlatches the string, then looks at it a moment. A dark shadow comes over his face. "Agent Slate, would you mind getting the door?"

Here we go. I stand, and close the door, cutting off the rest of the department.

"Where did you get this?"

"As I said, it was brought to me. But I think the bigger question is do you really believe this was an accident? Because from what I'm reading in that file, there's no way Josh Newsome was killed by a stray bullet."

"No," he says, setting the file down. "That's the cover story we're running with at the moment. The truth is we don't know *what* happened. It could have been an accident, but you're right. Given the evidence that doesn't really seem to be the case."

"So...what? Someone is out there hunting people?" I ask. "Have there been any other cases like this?"

He gives me a brief shake of his head. "Nothing. It's the first, so we're trying to take our time. But given this town's history—well, you know. You worked the Wright case. I don't know if we're dealing with something of a copycat here or something else entirely. It doesn't help matters that we're short-handed. After Burke was arrested everything fell apart. Half the force quit in solidarity and by the time they brought me in, the town was in something of a crisis without enough officers to fill the need. I've done the best I can in what little time we've had, but we've also had to make sacrifices. I've brought in people like Sean Coll to help fill in the ranks, but still..." He holds up his hands like he's fighting a battle he can't win.

"You'll get there," I say. "It will just take time. I just wanted to make sure everyone else was seeing what I was seeing. I guess after my last experience here—"

"—you were understandably concerned," he says, nodding. "I get it. I would have done the same thing in your shoes." He stares at the file for a minute. "What's your assessment?"

"I'm sorry?"

"You've seen the case file. What do you think we're working with here? I wouldn't mind having some FBI expertise thrown in the mix."

"Oh," I say, holding my hands up. "I don't want to get

involved. Like I said, I'm headed back today. Not looking to ruffle any feathers."

Salazar smiles. "You mean Sean. Don't mind him, he's that way with everyone. I've only known the man a few months now and I can tell you that's his default setting. It's not you."

"Still," I say. "I don't want to interfere where I don't belong."

"Then call it a professional courtesy. You have experience a lot of the rest of these officers don't have. And I don't need to tell you we can't afford to screw this up. The town hasn't seen anything like this since Gerald Wright. I'd really appreciate your help."

I let out a long breath. Obviously I've already formed my own opinions about the case, but this is a local matter. And I'm supposed to be on break. But didn't I just tell Zara I was coming back to work? So it's not like I'm chomping at the bit for more time off. A case to occupy my mind is exactly what I want…but not *here*. The whole point was to get away from Liam's parents so I don't have to deal with them anymore.

I give the chief a resigned sigh and hold out my hand for the file. He smiles and hands it back to me and I take a minute reading over all the information collected so far. "No one has done a follow-up with the wife yet?"

"As I said, short-handed. We also didn't want to alarm her if we could prove it was an accident, which we haven't been able to do. I'll admit I've been dragging my feet on that end. Back when I worked in Montgomery, nine times out of ten the story broke when we began talking to witnesses. Everyone loves the opportunity to be on camera."

"Not everyone," I say under my breath and continue looking through the information. "You have a single shot, taking place at night, shooting through a well-lit area. In my mind this was an execution. The shooter would have clearly seen the couple by the light of the fire, and no hunter would be out that late trying to shoot for *small game.*" I flip back through the pages. "Ballistics?"

"Waiting on the report from the coroner," he replies.

"According to Marnie, he was dead instantly," I read from the initial report. "And they were three miles from the nearest trailhead or public area. It's too much of a coincidence."

"Then it's your opinion he was murdered."

"My opinion is we don't have enough information to make a judgement call yet. You need more evidence. I'd really like to get a look at the bullet, if it's still in his body. And I'd want to do a follow-up with the wife, immediately."

He rocks back and forth in his chair a few moments, as if he's evaluating me. "Care to stick around for a few days? Help us out on this one?"

I wince. "I really need to be getting back. My dog—"

"From the way Sean was talking you were planning on staying here at least a week or better."

"Well, I *was*, but I think maybe now it's better if I just get back home. Let Liam heal in peace."

Salazar leans forward. "Agent Slate. Don't make me beg. We're short-handed and no one on this force has the kind of experience you do with these kinds of cases. Now I can either keep Coll and Hubbard and Viejo on it and they'll do a pass-able job...or I can give it to you. From what I know of you I'm pretty sure once you get your claws into this one you won't let it go until you've closed it. *If* your reputation is to be believed." He gives me a snarky sort of smile like the dig is an intentional test.

"I don't know if anyone has told you, but I don't like my competency being questioned."

He holds up his hands in defense. "No offense intended. I've just heard how good you are, you have a reputation around here whether you like it or not." He turns a bit in his chair so he can look out the window. "'course I could always just call up the FBI and formally request their help. And seeing as you're already here..." He lets the words hang in the air.

This feels like blackmail of sorts. Does he really not believe in his own people to get the job done? But then I recall Zara's admonishment about not running away. Taking on this case would no doubt enrage Mr. Coll and probably put me right back in the crosshairs of Mrs. Coll as well. Do I really want to be the kind of person who leaves when things get hard? Maybe working on a case will help provide a distraction that allows me to stay without needing to interact with them so much.

Two birds. One stone.

"Alright, Chief," I finally say, standing. "You win."

Chapter Ten

"SLATE FOR FLETCHER WALLACE," I say, holding my phone to my ear outside of the Stillwater Police Station. After agreeing to take the case, I confessed to Salazar where the file came from, though I didn't name Wes as the person who brought it to my attention. He said he would get it back to the senior Coll, and he provided me with access to their systems so I could keep an eye on any updates as they came in. He also gave me full authority to work the case as I saw fit, and to pull anyone I needed if necessary.

I didn't ask if he was planning on putting Coll and the others on different cases, because I'm sure I will hear about it from *someone* before the day is up.

"This is Wallace," my boss says on the other end of the phone.

"Slate reporting in," I say.

"Slate. You're on leave."

I take a deep breath. "A situation has developed in Stillwater. They're requesting my assistance. I thought it would be best to clear it with you before I began working the case."

"What sort of case?" His voice is flat, emotionless, like his attention is focused elsewhere. I give him the rundown of everything I have so far, but I don't really feel like he's listening, though I don't know why. Still, we have procedures to follow and after what happened in my hometown, I think it's best if I keep him in the loop on this one.

"What's your call?" he finally asks as I finish explaining the basics.

"I think we're looking at a murder. Maybe even a hit, though I'll need to look into the victim's history to figure that out. There's not a lot here, maybe if I dig for a couple of days I can uncover something substantial."

"It's your call," he says. "If this is how you want to spend your free time, I won't stop you."

Wait. "Free time?" I ask. "I'm on the clock here. They've formally requested my assistance."

"Until I see the order come across my desk this is a personal matter," he replies. "Unless I need to remind you that you have at least five cases on your desk right now. Cases you've actually been *assigned*. Not ones that you've stumbled into."

"But, sir," I protest, trying to communicate to him that someone needs to be here to make sure this case is investigated properly. It's not lost on me that not more than twenty minutes ago I was as hesitant to take this case as he is to give it to me, but now that I have it, I already feel that sense of protection I get about any case I begin working. It's like once I start, I can't stop.

"No buts, Slate. You're on leave. Work a local if that's how you want to relax. But I expect you back here in no less than eleven days, when your time is due to end. Understand?"

Every time I feel like I'm making progress with this man, it all blows up. It's one step forward and ten back. "Do I have operational authority?"

"Has your badge been revoked or suspended?"

"No."

"Then you have authority under the local jurisdiction.

Good hunting, sounds like you really want to get this one." He hangs up before I can say anything else. I want to slam my phone down in frustration, but I shove it back in my pocket instead. Pigheaded bastard. Why the FBI ever decided to bring him on is a mystery to me. He doesn't run operations well and he's always concerned about the bottom line, nothing else. How am I supposed to work under a man like that?

I reach into my pocket again, fully intending to call Janice and just go over his head. I've done that before and it didn't leave a good feeling in my stomach. It's the same thing as leaving because the Colls are difficult people to deal with.

Fine. He wants to play it this way, we can play it this way. I *will* do this on my own time, but he can bet when evaluation time comes up, he's going to be number one on my list.

I take a deep breath, close my eyes and crane my neck to the gray sky. Now I just need to tell Liam.

AFTER AN UNCOMFORTABLE PHONE CALL WITH MY BOYFRIEND where I tried to explain why I'm not leaving after all but it's not because of *him*, I decide to dive into the details of the case if for no other reason than to give my mind a distraction.

Damn Wes. If he'd just let well enough alone, I would have been back in D.C. by now, back with Timber, with Zara and working the cases on my desk like a good little soldier.

No, *fuck that*. I'm glad I'm here. Wallace can shove it up his pencil-thin ass for all I care. I'd rather be here, trying to help this community than be back there under his thumb while he keeps an eye on my every move.

I've decided my first stop is going to be that of Marnie Scrofano, the victim's wife. Her statement from the night is understandably erratic and I'm not sure the officer taking the information got everything. There are obvious gaps, such as when the incident happened versus when the police first arrived. Being that far out on the trailhead must have been terrifying for her, especially after seeing him shot like that.

When I pull up to the modest home, I notice there is a pile of mail at the door. Careful not to disturb it, I knock a few times, but no one answers. There's no car in the driveway either. Sighing, I head back to my car and start looking for any local family Scrofano has. The file mentions something about a mother who also lives in Stillwater, but I have to call Trish so she can find me an address. By the time I reach the elder Scrofano house, it's bordering on late afternoon.

This time, however, when I knock, the door is answered almost immediately. Before me stands a short woman, probably around five-two, with graying hair and an apron wrapped around her waist. Her thick glasses magnify her dark brown eyes. "Yes? Who are you?"

I show her my badge. "Special Agent Slate, with the FBI. I'm looking for Marnie Scrofano?"

"What does the FBI want with my daughter?" she asks.

"I'm here in regards to the incident in the woods the other night."

The small woman shoves a finger in my face. "Are you going to dismiss her too? Because if you are you're not stepping foot in this house."

"Dismiss her? No, I'm here to ask her what happened. I want to try to find out who killed her husband."

The woman regards me for a minute, then takes a step back. "Go easy on her. She's not doing well."

I nod, taking a tentative step into the home. I feel like any second Mrs. Scrofano is going to smack me with a wooden spoon for not taking my shoes off.

The house is compact, but clean. Right inside the door is a small sitting area that doesn't look like it's been used in twenty years. Beyond that is the actual living room, where a woman who looks to be about my age is on the couch, covered up to her head with a blanket. A small tray sits off to the side with a cup of what I assume is tea, though it looks untouched.

"Marnie?" I ask, treading carefully. "I'm Agent Emily Slate with the FBI."

Her eyes are open and her gaze flicks to me, but then back to the TV she was watching. The volume is already so low I can barely hear it, but that doesn't seem to matter to her. "I was wondering if I could ask you some questions about Saturday night." She doesn't move or respond so I know I'm going to have to be careful with this one. She's no doubt still processing the trauma.

"Is it okay if I take a seat?" I ask, indicating one of the sitting chairs across from the couch. She doesn't give me any indication that I shouldn't, so I gingerly sit down, keeping my face neutral. "They've brought me on to look into your husband's case," I explain. "I was hoping you might be able to fill in some holes about what happened that night."

I feel the presence of Marnie's mother behind me. "C'mon Marn, she's here to talk to you. The least you could do is sit up."

Marnie glares past me at her mother, but I keep my attention focused on her. She can lie down, sit up, stand on her head for all I care. I just want to know what happened.

Finally I see some semblance of movement as she pulls the blanket back and pushes herself up into a sitting position. Her hair is matted on one side from lying on it for so long, but she doesn't seem to notice. "What about it?" she asks, her voice raspy.

I'm very aware that sometimes these sessions can trigger a re-trauma of the event itself, which is the last thing I want to do. Instead, I hope I can tiptoe around the event without making her experience everything all over again. "I'm just going to ask you a few questions. And you let me know if anything gets too heavy, all right?"

"Why is the FBI here?" she asks, wiping at her eyes.

"I was brought on to assist the Stillwater Police," I say. "And I have a lot of experience with cases like this. They're kind of my specialty."

"Okay," she says, pulling her knees up to her chest. "Go ahead."

"First, can you tell me how long it took for the police to arrive?"

She pulls her features together. "I—I'm not sure. After… after…" She takes a deep breath. "I just started running. I had a light on me, and I knew it was possible I could get lost, but I thought…I thought maybe—"

"Someone was coming after you," I finish for her.

She nods. "I wasn't sure what to do. And I didn't have a signal up there. I thought I would get tired, but I just kept going until I reached the parking lot where our car was parked. And I got in, and locked the doors."

"And that's when you called the police?" I ask. She nods. "How long did it take you to get back to the parking lot?"

"I'm not sure. Maybe an hour? I didn't stop the whole way down, even when I fell a couple of times. I just felt like…like they were right behind me."

"And did you go back up to the campsite after the police arrived?" I ask. She shakes her head vehemently.

"Did Josh have any enemies? Anyone who might have been holding a grudge against him?"

"No one that I know of. Josh is—*was* an easygoing guy. Friendly, kind to everyone." She wipes her eyes again. "Even when people weren't kind to him."

"Who wasn't kind to him?" I ask.

"Me, for one," she replies. "I didn't want to go on the stupid hike in the first place. I didn't see why we couldn't just go to a nice hotel somewhere, or take a drive. Why did we have to be out hiking in the middle of the woods?" She takes another deep breath. "I was upset about it, and complaining.

Maybe too much. But he didn't say a lot about it. He just let it roll off his back."

"Did you happen to see anyone else out there that night?" I ask, looking back at the notes I've already made on my phone.

"It was pitch black. We couldn't see anything. Except the stars." She leans her head back, like she's looking up at the sky as we're talking now. "They were so pretty. It was so clear, I finally started to see what he had been talking about all these years."

I might be losing her. Sometimes victims will retreat into their memories, looking to hold on to the last good thing they can recall with a person who is no longer here. Some people get so obsessed with it, they regress until they can't live their lives forward anymore. They're stuck in the past.

I should know.

"I still think it was that guy we passed on the trail," Marnie says. When I look up I find she's staring directly at me.

"Guy?" I ask.

"The one I told the other officer about, the one with the rifle."

Wait, a second. I mentally flip through the case files in my head. I don't remember seeing anything about a man with a rifle. "Where did you see him?"

"On our way up to the site," she replies. "We passed him as he was coming back down."

"Was he the only person you saw?"

She drops her knees. "No, there were a few people coming off the trail as we were making our way up. But he was the only one who didn't say anything to us as we passed. Just kept his head down and kept on walking. I think I smelled alcohol on his breath as he passed, but I couldn't swear to it."

Shit. Somebody screwed up big time. "And you told one of the other officers about this?"

She nods. "That night, in the parking lot when they were trying to calm me down. I know I was a mess, but I saw what I saw."

"Could you describe this man with the rifle?" I ask.

"He was dressed all in beige camo," she replies. "And had a green trucker hat pulled down so I couldn't really see his face. But I saw the rifle slung on his back. I even told Josh that it made me nervous but he said there were hunters in that area all the time and it wasn't anything unusual."

"Did you happen to see what kind of rifle it was?" I ask, hopeful.

"It was in a case. I didn't see the actual gun."

Still. This is a huge break. "If I could have you speak to a sketch artist, do you think you could describe this man to us?"

"I don't know," she replies. "Like I said, I didn't see much of his face."

"What about any other details? Tall, short? Fat, skinny? Hair color?"

"Um, tall, I guess. Kind of on the husky side. Dark hair, pretty short. Wasn't much sticking out of the cap."

I write down all the details in a list. I'll need to get back with Salazar's people, find out who interviewed Marnie Scrofano and who missed a huge detail like this. I ask a couple of follow-up questions to make sure I have all my bases covered, but I've already had a huge break. By the time I'm done, Marnie seems stronger and more alert than when I arrived.

I thank both her and her mother for their time, then head back out. I've got some skulls to crack.

Chapter Eleven

By the time I'm finished with Marnie Scrofano it's too late to head back to the station and do any good. But I'm going to need to have a frank discussion with Chief Salazar about who interviewed her and how they could have missed such an important clue. So far, the new Stillwater Police isn't doing a lot to instill confidence that they're better than the people that had been working under Chief Burke.

But given how the day started, I can't really complain. I've already had a major break in the case, so I'm hopeful it will continue to go smoothly. It's possible Salazar's people are so overworked they just missed it, but even so, it's a big miss.

Despite making progress, I'm anxious when I pull back up to Liam's parent's house. Both their cars are in the driveway, telling me it'd be better if I don't step a foot in that home. Instead, I text Liam to let him know I'm outside. Again, it feels like we're teenagers again and we're doing everything we can not to get his parents involved in our relationship.

"Hey," I say as soon as he gets in the car. "How are you feeling?"

"Better now that I know you're not back in D.C." he replies, but I can hear the accusation in his voice.

"This isn't all about the case, you know. Zara gave me a good talking to before I even went to see Chief Salazar. She told me I shouldn't be scared of your parents."

"You're not scared of them," he replies.

"No. I just don't want to deal with them. It's—"

"*A lot,*" we both say at the same time, causing me to smile.

"I guess I don't understand why you're even doing this. You're clearly not sick enough to need someone watching over you twenty-four-seven. And you could rest as much as you wanted back home."

"I guess—" He hesitates before looking out the windscreen. "She's watching us. Third window from the right."

"*Dammit,*" I say and back the car back down the driveway and hopefully out of Brianna Coll's eyesight.

"I guess it's because I left so abruptly. Before I met you I'd just gotten out of another relationship here in Stillwater. I'd been living here my whole life, was settled and I saw my parents if not every week, every other week. When I could, between cases. But then you came along and—"

"Oh no," I say. "Don't put this on me. Your mother would never forgive me."

He chuckles. "Okay. Still. You came along and *inspired* me to do something more with my life. I'd been working under Burke for so long I'd become complacent, and I felt like I needed a clean break from everything to start over. So I really kind of cut them out for a while there. Not because I didn't want to see them or because I didn't love them anymore—"

"But because you needed a fresh start and they were a tether to your old life," I say.

"That's it. Exactly. And once I felt like I established myself in D.C. with my new job, new life...*you,* I could slowly start integrating them back into my life as well. So I guess what I'm trying to say is I feel guilty. For leaving them behind."

"And now you're trying to make up for it by letting your mother take care of you all the time."

He gives me a sheepish look. "It's what she loves. I've always been the youngest, so she babys me. But it gets damn annoying quick. When they showed up in the hospital I thought maybe now would be a good time to try and repair of some of the fences I'd broken. But I can only take so much. What I thought was going to be two weeks is already down to a week. And if she doesn't let up soon, I'll be going back to D.C. even sooner."

He turns to me with a huge grin on his face. "You might end up being here longer than me."

"Ugh," I reply. "Wouldn't that just suck. I could always just hand the case back to Salazar."

"C'mon. We both know you won't do that. No one can get you to let go of a case unless they pry it from your cold, dead hands."

I can't help but laugh because he's right. I don't let things go easily. "Well since you're not doing anything other than being pampered all day, how about an assist? I've already got a statement from the witness that Salazar's men—aka your *dad* missed. Even if you don't want to help you can at least run interference for me. I think you owe me that much."

"Sure. Anything to get me out of the house a few hours a day." He turns back to me, smiling. "You know, I thought when you left this morning I wasn't going to see you for another week at least. And even though I know you're not staying for me, I'm glad you're here." He holds out his hand and I take it.

"You're wrong. I *am* staying for you. But I'm also staying for this case. It's like Zara said. I can't run forever."

~

THE FOLLOWING MORNING I'M UP, SHOWERED, AND READY TO go by seven. Because I don't have a massive wardrobe, I ended up packing a few work suits for lack of anything else to wear, so I at least look a little more professional today. I dropped Liam off after a nice dinner last night and got back to the hotel early, where I informed the clerk I'd be staying through at least the week. He also assured me he wouldn't be telling anyone else I was staying there, though I think that was probably because my gun was on display.

It's a gray, overcast day and it makes me think of the kinds of days when you like to stay indoors and enjoy a nice cup of tea. Funny how when I finally have something to do, I start thinking about doing nothing. And when I have nothing to do, I can't stop myself from finding any excuse to keep from sitting still.

Instead of heading straight for Salazar and a confrontation that I'm sure won't move this investigation forward, I instead make my way to the coroner's office, hoping to get a look at the body of Josh Newsome. If I recall correctly, the Stillwater coroner was a stickler for details, which is probably why her preliminary report is the only thing in the file so far.

When I reach her office, the door is already open and I catch sight of the woman's familiar short, silver hair, though her back is to me as she's working on her computer.

I knock quickly. "Doctor Crowley?"

She turns and catches my eye, her eyes wide and bright. "Agent Slate. Surprised to see you back here." She stands and offers her hand, which I return with a hearty shake.

"I kind of got roped into this one," I say. "The Newsome case."

She nods. "I was just finishing up my notes. I'd hoped to get this done yesterday, but I had to send the bullet off to the lab as I wasn't familiar with it."

"Mind if I take a look?" I ask.

"Not at all." She motions for me to lead the way to Still-water's single examining room.

"You survived the cut, huh?" I ask, pushing through the

swinging door. "Looks like most everyone else that was here last year is gone."

"The mayor was adamant about weeding out the bad elements," she replies, that no-nonsense tone of hers seeping through. "But because I was never technically on the force, I wasn't under any pressure to leave. Not to mention try to find a coroner willing to work in a small town like this when D.C. is just a few hours away. More prestige, larger paychecks."

"But not for you," I say.

"What can I say? I'm a simple woman." I remember working with Sybil Crowley on the Wright case. She struck me as a sharp, capable woman who was working under very difficult circumstances and constraints…namely Chief Burke. I'm glad to see she's still here and free to do her job as she sees fit.

She heads over to the wall of coolers and opens one of the five drawers, revealing the washed-out body of Josh Newsome, who is completely naked. His skin has taken on a waxy sheen, and there is a large Y-incision on his chest that has been stitched back up. Right beside the incision is a large, gaping wound where the bullet must have entered.

"Holy shit," I say, staring at the wound. "Right to the heart?"

She nods. "As clean a shot as anyone could take. If it *was* a hunter, they must have a wall full of deer heads."

"Pass through the body?" I ask.

She pulls on a pair of gloves and gently lifts Mr. Newsome over so I can see the exit wound. "Straight through. Notice how the wound on this side is at least twice as large as the entry wound."

"The bullet shredded him on its way through," I say.

"Exactly. Which means it was a large caliber. Something big enough to take down an elk, or even larger."

"Bear?" I ask.

"Probably." She pulls off the gloves and heads over to another station where a couple of plastic bags sit. In one of them are bits of brass fragments. "This was what they pulled from the lean-to, which was directly behind him when he was shot. It took ballistics two full days to reconstruct it."

"What type is it?" I ask.

"A six millimeter Creedmoor," she replies, reading off the tag on the bag. She hands it to me. "In other words, a big ass bullet."

"Not something someone would be hunting small game with," I reply.

"If they were, they'd obliterate whatever they hit," she says.

"Match on the weapon?"

She walks over to another station. "They're still working on that part. We do know it's a high-caliber rifle. Something pretty big. My guess is it has a range of about a thousand yards."

I let out a low whistle. "So you think someone perched a thousand yards away and executed Josh Newsome?"

She replies with a sly smile. "I'm just looking at the evidence."

I make my way around the room, looking at the evidence so far, and taking another peek at Josh Newsome. There don't seem to be any other marks on him. If this man *was* killed on purpose, and his wife fled the scene, then would the killer have been bold enough to inspect his kill up close? Or would he have just left the area, the job done?

"Anything else you can tell me?"

"It was clean," she replies. "One shot, dead on impact. He probably didn't even feel it. Though due to the speed of the bullet, there was some blood splatter. Have you taken a look at the crime scene photos yet?"

I nod. "They were in the file. But didn't see anything that wouldn't have been consistent with what you've told me." I stare at Newsome. It just doesn't seem to make sense. Why would someone target him? "Anything else in the autopsy?"

"For all appearances he was a strong, young man," she replies. "Maybe a little extra fatty tissue around the midsection, but no more than average. Healthy, non-smoker. No indication of any illness or disease."

"And no other evidence left on the body."

"Not that we could find, no." She puts the bullet fragments away. "I don't envy your job, Agent. Seems like they always give you the tough ones."

I scoff. "It would be nice if just once they came along with a signed confession."

"Unfortunately we didn't find that while we were looking," she replies. "Let me know if I can be of any other help."

I nod. "Thanks. I'll take a look at the full report once you've uploaded it, but I think I have all I need for now. If you find anything on the weapon—"

"Don't worry," she replies. "I know just who to call."

Chapter Twelve

I HAD PLANNED on driving out to the trailhead to take a look at the scene of the crime, but as soon as I leave the coroner's office the sky is as dark as I've seen it and the snow begins before I can even get the engine started. It comes down fast, and by the time I'm on the road it's already blanketed the grass. Any hope of getting out to the trailhead today is probably off the calendar. Instead, I head back to the police station, hoping I can get an answer as to why no one picked up on this "hunter" Marnie Scrofano saw in the woods.

When I get back inside Trish is at her desk, but fielding what looks like a bunch of calls all at once. I'm sure the roads are playing havoc with people. Stillwater is set deep in the mountains, which is going to make most if not all of the roads treacherous. My guess is there are a lot of officers out trying to do their best to keep people from getting stuck.

She waves me over and buzzes me through without me asking, for which I'm grateful. I make my way back to Chief Salazar's office, but the lights are off and the door is closed. The rest of the department seems mostly empty as well. It's as I assumed. The weather is going to play havoc with people.

I type out a quick text to Liam.

You staying safe in the snow?

Lol, yeah. Mom's making chicken noodle soup in case the power goes out. Where R U?

At the station. Empty tho. Probably gonna head back to the hotel until it blows over.

I'd tell you to come here, but Dad was on the warpath last night. Wasn't too happy about Salazar pulling you in.

Figures. LMK if anything changes.

I prepare to head back out to my car. I better get moving if I don't want to end up stuck here at the station. I would brave the drive to Liam's to see him but I *definitely* don't want to get stuck there. And maybe some time to myself would give me a chance to work through this case a little more. I have my laptop with me, so there's no reason I can't do a little more research into Josh Newsome while I wait for things to clear up. I can at least figure out if anyone was trolling him online.

As I get ready to head out, I catch sight of one officer coming in from the front I *do* recognize from my last time here. She's on the other side of the bullpen, fighting with the coffee machine and her shoulders still have bits of snow on them.

"Sergeant Hubbard," I say, approaching.

The woman turns. She's tall, with dark brown hair pulled back in a ponytail and sharp features.

"Agent Slate," she replies, wiping her hand on her slacks before shaking mine. "I heard you were back in town."

Sergeant Jill Hubbard was the one officer Liam told me we could trust back when Burke was running things. And it seems like she wasn't culled with most of the rest of the force. But I already knew she was one of the good ones. If not for her, we never would have caught up to Gerald Wright in time. "Just temporarily. Salazar roped me in on your murder in the woods."

"Yeah, he likes to get people to do him favors," she says,

smiling. "Far better than the last choice though. You making any progress?"

"Some," I tell her. "Do you happen to know who interviewed Mrs. Scrofano on the night of the incident? I just spoke with her and she had a lot of information that wasn't in the report."

"Really?" she says, screwing up her face. "That's odd. I think Liam's dad took her statement, but I couldn't swear to it. I haven't been working on the case."

Ugh. Of course. Which now means I have to have an uncomfortable conversation with Mr. Coll at some point. I could just let it go, submit my own report and not reference the oversight, but that would be negligent. Whether Coll intentionally left out the details from Marnie or not, Salazar needs to know about it.

"Have you worked with him on any other cases?" I ask. "Salazar kind of just dumped it in my lap and I'm playing catchup."

She pinches her features and turns back to the coffee machine, which is sputtering as she gets a semi-clean pot under it. "Not personally. I know him, of course, back from when Liam and I were kids. But we haven't been assigned any cases together since he came back part-time."

My mind flits over her comment about her and Liam as kids. Liam often talks about the relationship he got out of right before he met me and I have a strong suspicion it was with Sergeant Hubbard here. Not that it matters. We both do our best not to get too deep into each other's pasts. And I'm certainly not one to judge, considering the shitshow my life has been.

"Okay," I tell her. "Thanks for the info. Be careful out there. Salazar got you working traffic?"

She nods. "Just until the snow lets up. Just pray we don't lose any of the power lines. Appalachian Power takes forever to get them back up for us out here."

I nod. "Good luck."

She lifts an empty coffee cup in my direction. "You too."

As I head back out, I find the snow is falling faster than before and already starting to stick to the roads. I'm not sure my two-wheel drive chevy will be able to make it back to the hotel, but I'm sure as hell going to try. The car slides a little as I'm backing out and thankfully there are no other cars near me in the parking lot. I take the drive slow, which means what should be a five-minute drive ends up being almost twenty before I reach the hotel. Thankfully the traffic is light; it seems like people know better than to be out in this kind of weather. Though I do catch a couple of large trucks with chains on their tires driving by.

Once I'm back in my warm room I shake off what little moisture remains on my coat and text Liam that I've made it back safely. When I pull back the curtains, I'm greeted with a beautiful view of the mountains surrounding Stillwater, all covered in white as the snow continues to fall. The weather app on my phone predicts the snow will last until the evening, before tapering off. Tomorrow should be warmer, but probably not enough to melt everything.

Still, I want to get out to the site of the murder before too much time passes.

Since I seem to be stuck inside I go about doing as much recon on Josh Newsome as I can. From all outward appearances he seems like a normal guy. He doesn't have a particularly exciting social life from what I can see, though from his IG handle I notice he had an affinity for outdoors activities. Probably why he and his wife were on a hike in the middle of winter. But there's nothing to indicate anyone was upset with him, or that he had any negative encounters.

I dive into Stillwater's system and start pulling financials on the man. Maybe there's a secret money trail somewhere. You never know what some people are hiding behind the veneer of "normal". But when I look back at all his bank accounts, nothing stands out. Average balances, average debt. No large deposits or withdrawals. No charges that seem suspicious.

Nothing.

I sit back in the single chair in the room and stare out the window, watching the snow fall. It's peaceful, like the world has been tucked under a white blanket to go to sleep. Why would anyone want to kill someone who for all intents and purposes seems like an ordinary, pleasant person? What prompted something like this? Obviously it wasn't a crime of passion. It wasn't like Josh Newsome insulted someone on the street and they pulled a Glock on him. This was targeted.

Which brings up another question. If he *was* targeted, then why didn't the killer take out Marnie as well? They certainly had the equipment to do it.

I'm starting to see why Chief Salazar wanted me to take a look at this. He must have come to similar conclusions already. Maybe he's just looking to hand off his difficult cases so he can fudge his department's numbers a little, make them look shinier than they actually are after coming out from under Chief Burke's shadow.

But even if that's the case, it doesn't help me with my immediate problem. I'm even more bothered by Marnie's assertion of this hunter out there on the hiking trails. Even if he wasn't responsible, why was he out there? I've already checked the designated hunting areas for Stillwater and while yes, one of them butts up against the trails, someone would have had to have been pretty deep in the brush to come out on the trail side. Not to mention they would have had to scale half a mountain to get there. Marnie said the man was on the way down. So either he went out to hunt in the woods, made his way all the way across and up the side of a mountain and was coming down, *or* he hiked up that direction.

I suppose maybe an enterprising hunter might think they could find some game on a side of the territory that isn't normally used. But again, with a rifle like Marnie described I doubt he was out for small game. Maybe he was out there illegally tagging deer and Josh Newsome witnessed it.

It's thin, but right now it's all I've got. I'll need to talk to Marnie again, see if perhaps Josh went off by himself at any point during the hike.

Frustrated I'm not getting anywhere, I pull my chair over to watch the snow from the window. The whole town has gone silent and all I can see are the orange streetlights reflecting off the fresh powder. Even though it's barely noon, it feels like almost eight at night. I have the urge to find a cup of coffee and a book.

But before I can begin the hunt my phone dings with a message. I grab it, thinking it's probably Liam but I'm surprised when I see who it's from.

Hey, it's Wes, Liam's brother.

Why is Liam's brother texting me?

Wanted to give you a heads-up. Mom is fixing a big family dinner Friday night. Guess your invite got lost in the mail. Be there at seven. Sharp.

What is this guy playing at? As soon as I think I have Wes Coll figured out, he goes and does something like this. Is he just *trying* to start something between me and his parents? And why am I hearing this from him and not Liam?

Dinner on Friday night with the Coll family. I'm not sure I'm ready for that. But before I can even dismiss it, I hear Zara repeating her little mantra in my head. I'm here. I'm working a case. What's one more thing added to my plate? Maybe I can even confront the elder Coll about his apparent oversight in the case. Really stir things up.

I think about how proud Zara would be as I send him a text back.

I'll be there.

Chapter Thirteen

I ENDED up hanging out in the hotel for the rest of the evening while I watched the snow fall, making little progress on Josh Newsome. As predicted, it tapered off in the evening, and by the time the following morning rolls around, the plows have already done their jobs and most of the main roads are clear.

I opt for a quick coffee at the Early Derby before trying my luck getting out to the trailhead. Though before I make the trek, I have to stop in one of the local stores to pick up a couple of essentials. Namely, thicker boots for hiking in the snow. But as I'm shopping my phone vibrates in my pocket and I rush to grab it.

"Slate," I say, checking the size on the nearest pair of black boots.

"Hey," Liam says. "Where are you?"

I pause, looking around for any store signage. "Um… Packers," I say. "They have boots. Why, where are you?"

"At your hotel," he replies. "Knocking on your door with a bag of biscuits."

"Oh," I say, setting the boots down. "I didn't realize— sorry, I'm working the case."

"Guess I shouldn't be surprised you're up so early; though I was hoping to catch you."

I sit down on the small bench where you try on shoes. "How did you get to my hotel?"

"I borrowed my mom's Subaru," he replies. "I had to get out of there, she was driving me nuts."

I check the boot size again and pull it on. Feels like a good fit. "I can be back over there in ten."

"No, I'll come to you. What's on the schedule today?"

"I was going to head out to the scene of the crime," I tell him. "Take a look around."

"In the snow?"

"Hence the boots."

"Sounds good. I'll tag along."

I furrow my brow as I stand, checking the feel of the boot as I walk around. "I'm not sure that's such a good idea. It's an hour-and-a-half hike. Up half a mountain. Aren't you supposed to be resting your lungs?"

"I feel fine," he replies. "Plus, I'd much rather spend the day with you than listen to another minute of my mother droning on about how she doesn't have a grandchild yet."

"That bad, huh?"

"You have no idea. I'm starting to think I can just live with the guilt. Three days is enough, right?"

I chuckle. While I wouldn't mind having another pair of eyes on this case, I'm not confident Liam should be trudging through the snow less than a week after being in that fire. "You can come, but you're staying in the car while I go check out the site."

"Fair enough," he replies. "I'll pick up a couple of warm coffees and meet you over there. Mom doesn't need to be driving in this stuff anyway."

I smile. "See you in a few." As soon as he hangs up my smile drops. I didn't want to bring it up over the phone, but he and I need to talk about Wes. And this *dinner* tonight.

Why can't anything ever be simple?

～

BY THE TIME I'M CHECKING OUT WITH MY NEW BOOTS AND A few other supplies, Liam is already waiting in the parking lot, sitting in the driver's seat of his mother's car. He sticks his head out. "Let's take this up to the trail. I think it has a better chance of getting out if we get stuck."

"You okay to drive?" I ask.

"Liam Coll, professional chauffeur at your service," he beams.

I shake my head and grab my stuff out of the back of my car before getting in the passenger side of his mother's car. The faint smell of her perfume hangs in the air.

"You sure you're okay not racing us up to the trailhead?" he asks. A fresh cup of coffee sits in one of the cup holders and there is a small bag from a place called *Diana's* on the center console. As soon as I open it, I'm smacked in the face with the smell of fresh-baked biscuits.

"I think I can let you have this one," I tell him as I pull a biscuit out. My batting average with remembering to eat breakfast has improved since we started dating, but I still forget half the time. My mouth practically waters before I take a bite.

Thankfully Liam knows the way so I can focus on the case while he drives. We spend most of it in silence as I can't quite pull my gaze away from the picturesque view of the freshly fallen snow as I think, rolling the facts over in my mind again and again. Thankfully the entrance to the trail where Marnie and Josh were camping isn't more than fifteen minutes outside of town.

"Talk about the worst place for something like this to happen," Liam says as he pulls the car into the unplowed parking lot. While the roads might have been cleared, little else has been. And given the snow coverage, no one would ever know a murder took place not far from here.

"Depends on your perspective," I say as Liam pulls into the lot. "From the killer's view, this was the perfect place. Remote, away from anyone who could call for immediate help. And if it was someone who knew these woods, as I suspect they were, then they could plot an escape route easily enough."

"Do you think that's why they didn't shoot the wife? Cover so they could escape?"

I pause, thinking. "Unlikely. If they had shot her, *no* one would have found their bodies for days. Maybe longer with how quickly this storm rolled in. He would have had ample time to get away. In fact, by not killing Marnie, he put himself on the clock."

"But why do that?" Liam asks. "Unless it really was an accident. Could he have been shooting at something else instead? That's what my father seems to think."

I scoff. "Yeah. I bet he does." I don't mention the fact that he neglected to include the witness statement on the report. "All I know is Josh Newsome was shot straight through the heart with a bullet big enough to kill a bear. And unless I'm mistaken, bears are in hibernation right now."

"Then there is no doubt in your mind. It's murder."

"Not only that," I say as I pull on my new boots, relishing the warmth from the car as long as I can get it. "I don't think it's this killer's first."

"What makes you say that?" he asks.

I point to the trail entrance ahead of us. "It was clean and professional. Low risk, high probability of success. And that it happened at night tells me he was probably using a night vision scope. Crowley told me she thought it was a thousand-yard range rifle. I want to test that theory."

"Test it? How?"

I pull my heavy gloves out, slipping them on my hands. "I want to trace the path of the bullet."

"In the *snow?*"

"I can't afford to wait," I reply. "The longer we wait the more likely something changes or gets destroyed and the longer that killer is out there." If this is what I think it is, we might be looking at a killer who has done this multiple times. Perhaps even dozens or more. Either Josh Newsome was incredibly unlucky, or we may have a professional killer on our hands.

"You sure you're good to go out there on your own?" Liam asks.

"*You're* not hiking it, I know that much," I tell him. "Not in your condition. But if I'm not back in three hours, call someone to come get me."

"Yes ma'am," he replies, smiling.

I lean over and give him a quick peck on the cheek. "Stay warm. I'll be back in a little while." Even though I know service is bad out here, I take my phone anyway. Along with a few other tools I've gathered. With my new boots, extra socks and two layers under my heavy coat, I feel ready enough to tackle this mountain. It's been a minute since I've hiked, so it takes me a little while to get the feel for it again. And even though the ground is covered in snow, the trail is still clearly visible due to its width and relative flatness.

About fifteen minutes in I can no longer see the parking lot, even though the snow on the ground makes it extremely easy to get the long view of the woods themselves. Everything is completely silent and the air is calm and smells only slightly of distant pine. Even the birds have hunkered down.

I find with a focused mind and a purpose; the hike moves quickly. There are a couple of steep grades where I have to watch myself going up and which will be treacherous coming back down in the snow, but I make great time. The entire way I'm thinking about all the cops and EMS techs who had to make this hike to reach Josh Newsome. This really is the worst place for someone to get hurt or die.

I see the lean-to about five minutes before I reach it. Coming up over a hill, it appears in the distance, not too far off the main trail. I hasten my pace and reach it quickly. The area is still marked off with police tape, though I can't imagine anyone would have been up here since. The fresh snow at least confirms no one has been here since yesterday.

There's little evidence anyone was here recently, though I spot a burned-out firepit, barely more than a mound in the blanket of white. I shuffle some of the snow about to see indentations in the dirt where a pair of fold-out chairs sat before they were taken into evidence. The bullet went right through Josh, through the back of the chair and embedded itself in the lean-to. The second chair was removed because it was covered in Josh's blood splatter.

I take a cursory look at the scene, everything seems normal. Pulling my phone out, I inspect the piece of wood that was removed from the lean-to: a circular hole about three inches in diameter. I pull out the industrial strength laser pen I purchased at Packers along with my boots and set it up so the beam shoots directly off into the distance, in the direction from where the bullet would have come. This would be a lot easier at night, but I can only work with what I have.

The green light shines out across the campsite, but isn't strong enough for me to see much past where the site leaves the trail. Instead, I open the compass app on my phone and check the directions. One-hundred and fifty-one degrees south by southwest. I lock in the direction on the compass, grab the laser pen and start making my way in that direction. Because my GPS isn't working out here, I count my footfalls. My stride is about a yard and a half which means I need about seven hundred steps, give or take, to reach the location of the shooter.

It's a long shot, I know. But at the same time, I want to see if Crowley's suspicion about the rifle is correct. Unfortunately, the path heads deep into the woods, off any trail. However as long as I keep the compass I should be able to find my way back.

Watching my phone like a hawk, I make my way through the woods, careful not to over or under step, even though the terrain isn't clear. One thing I notice is there aren't enough large trees to completely block the shot, at least not yet. And the further I get into the woods, the more confident I become about my theory. There are no large drop-offs that would have prevented the line of sight. And no large obstacles which would have gotten in the way.

By the time I reach seven hundred steps, I find myself in a small clearing where a felled log crosses my path. I carefully dust off the snow from the log and there, in the top of the soft wood, is a small, rectangular indentation. Though there's no proof, mounting a gun on the damp wood for a long period of time for stabilization would create a pattern like that. I take detailed pictures of the log before inspecting the rest of the area. Because of the snow it's difficult to see anything else, but I think I have what I came for.

Just as I'm about to start back in the direction of the trail, I notice my phone has service again. And even though it's only one bar, it's enough for my map app to work. Pulling it up, I find I'm not more than a hundred yards from another trail that runs perpendicular to the one I came up.

I know I should head back to the first trail so I can get back to Liam, but my curiosity wins over. I'm still warm, don't feel fatigued, and still have plenty of water, so I head off in that direction. When I reach the small trail I notice it's a lot rougher than the more "commercial" trail from earlier. This one looks like the kind that's probably only used by hunters and I realize I'm probably in the designated hunting area.

Following the trail for about twenty minutes, I find it's not nearly as hard to navigate as the hiking trail. The slopes are lower and softer, though there are more branches in the way and I trip more than once trying to get down. Were it not for the snow, I probably wouldn't have had a problem.

But before I know it, I'm back down off the mountain and standing at the end of a bare pathway, blocked off by a large, metal gate that's chained in the middle. This looks like it could be private property or state-owned, I'm not sure. However, there are no trespassing signs posted.

I pull out my phone and check my location. I'm almost half a mile from where I left Liam, off a different adjacent road. But I have full cell service.

"Hello?" Liam answers.

"I need a pickup," I tell him.

"What? Where are you?"

"At the edge of the woods about half a mile from you," I reply. "I think I just found our killer's exit strategy."

Chapter Fourteen

"So you think he set up some kind of sniper position and just waited until they were in place, then left from this other lot?" Liam asks as we're driving back to Stillwater.

"I do. And I want to get Salazar's forensics team on the location to see if they can find anything from a vehicle that might have been there last Saturday."

"Em, that was almost a week ago. And there's snow everywhere. Not to mention it's nothing but gravel. What could they find?"

"I dunno, a shell casing, or maybe he dropped a glove or something."

Liam glares at me.

"Okay, I know. But I don't have a lot to go on here. And if you haven't noticed, I'm running out of leads to follow."

He nods. "I get it. Explore every avenue. So then what's the call? A contract kill?"

"I don't know," I tell him. "But now I'm sure Josh Newsome was not this man's first victim. That was no accident and it was no lucky shot. He was perched. Waiting."

"How did he even know Newsome would be out there?" Liam asks.

That I can't answer. And usually a contract kill has something to do with money. But there's nothing in Newsome's financials that indicates anything strange. *Someone* must have benefitted from his death. I just need to figure out who. As soon as I can do that, I can find our shooter. I grab my phone and call into Crowley, but it's already past five and I don't know if she works weekends.

"Hey, Sybil, this is Emily Slate. I know it's the weekend, but I'm following up to see if anyone has found anything about the weapon used. Thanks." I check the time on the car's dash. "Shit."

"What?" Liam asks.

I turn to him, my face serious. "How come you didn't tell me about your mother's dinner tonight?"

"How do you know about that?" he asks.

"Wes sent me a couple of texts. Which is another thing. Why does he have my number?"

Liam shrugs. "He asked, I didn't see the harm. I mean, technically if you want to get to know my family my brother is probably the least annoying among them. But I didn't tell you about the dinner because I figured you didn't want to deal with it. Considering yesterday you were ready to head back home because of them."

"Maybe I was, but I've had a change of heart," I tell him. "And I'm not letting them win."

He smiles. "Good. I don't know why I've been letting them —or more precisely *her* walk all over me too. Maybe I was just feeling so guilty and thought I deserved it."

"Or maybe you were in a life-threatening situation and you're just now starting to deal with the trauma of that. No one would blame you for having brain fog over the past few days. A week ago you couldn't even talk."

He rubs his throat, though it looks like an unconscious move. Though I notice he's rubbing precisely where the scar runs across my neck. I haven't let him see my neck without it being covered up yet, and I don't plan to. Not for a while, at least.

"Yeah, you could be right. Maybe tonight will be a good chance for us both to clear the air."

"Sounds like a plan to me," I tell him. "But I need you to swing back by so I can get my car. I want to head back and freshen up first." Even though the hike wasn't very difficult, I was still sweating most of the time due to the extra layers of clothes. If I'm going to confront his parents, I'd rather not do it smelling like a gym locker. *Again.*

Thankfully the roads have dried and are mostly clear, though there are still some patches of black ice. Liam drops me back off at Packer's parking lot and I head over to the Jefferson for a quick shower and a change of clothes. By the time I quit messing with my hair it's almost seven and I head back out in hopes of passing a grocery store on the way.

Finding a Piggly Wiggly—which, will have to do—I get a text on my phone as I'm perusing the wine section.

Nothing on the gun yet. Still looking. Have a good weekend. -Syb

"Damn," I say to myself. Even though I expected as much I still held out a little hope. But that bullet was shattered, and no casing was found, which makes matching the exact weapon more than difficult. Almost impossible. If we had a complete round where it had stopped in his body, then *maybe*. But this thing was a monster and a couple of inches of flesh wasn't slowing it down.

Having chosen a cheap brand of wine, I make my way over to the Coll house. My phone dings again on the way over and I catch another text from Wes.

I know you're not standing me up.

What is it with this guy? Is he *flirting* with me? I am terrible at knowing when people are flirting—at least when it comes to myself—so I just ignore the text. If he is, I'm going to need to shut that down right away.

Just keep on piling it onto the Emily plate. Why not? Let's see how much more I can handle before I crack.

I pull into the driveway at seven-oh-seven. Wes's Lexus sits right behind his mother's Subaru and Sean Coll's Explorer. All the lights are on in the house.

Damn, Z. Where are you when I really need you? I take a deep breath, step out of my car and catch my reflection in the windshield. Jeans, a loose sweater, and a black coat. Not exactly formal wear, but then again I don't do formal. Unless I'm at work, and then I've got a suit. But that's as far as it goes. In my off time I like to be comfortable.

Wine in hand, I step up to the porch and ring the bell. A half second later the door opens to reveal Wes, a big grin on his face. "I knew you'd come," he says, then his eyes go to the wine. "For me?"

"*No*," I tell him, walking past quickly. "It's for your parents."

He follows me down the hall. "Well, Mom doesn't drink and da' only likes scotch so—"

"Emily," Mrs. Coll says, catching sight of me from the kitchen. "What are you doing here?"

"I invited her, Mother," Wes replies. Mr. Coll is still in the living room, watching soccer on the large TV while Liam stands close to his father, his arms crossed. As soon as he sees me he comes over and wraps me in a hug.

"Thanks for coming," he says. "But watch out. She's already on the warpath."

"I understand you and my son went out this afternoon," Mrs. Coll says, wiping her hands on her apron and coming to meet me in the living room.

"Yes, I'm working a case," I tell her. "I needed to see the scene of the crime." From his chair, Mr. Coll just scoffs, though it's loud enough that no one could have missed it.

"Do you really think it's a good idea for Liam to be out in

this kind of weather? Isn't that something you could have handled on your own?" she asks.

"Mom, we've been over this. I volunteered to go out with Emily. I didn't even get out of the car," Liam says.

She brushes him off like he hasn't said a word. "That's not a very responsible thing for a federal agent to do, is it? Take a civilian with her to a crime scene?"

"Okay, Mom, that's enough," Liam says. "Emily isn't responsible for my injuries and she's not to blame for anything that happens to me, okay? If you want someone to blame, blame me."

She looks at me a second longer, then turns to her youngest son. "If I could, I would." Then she returns to the kitchen.

"What the hell did that mean?" I ask, looking at Liam, then at Wes. Neither of which seems to want to meet my gaze.

However, Liam takes the bottle of wine. "Thanks, I'll put this in the kitchen."

"Like soccer?" Wes asks, seeming to reset himself and guiding me to the living room couch. "It's a cardinal sin in this house if you don't."

The older Coll looks over at him. "Don't you have somewhere else to be?"

Wes just smiles. "There's nowhere I'd rather be than here with you, da."

"Uh," I say, trying to cut the obvious tension. "Who's playing?"

Sean turns to me. "Are you blind? It's right there on the bottom of the screen. I thought you were supposed to be observant."

Okay, we're going to get this out the way right now. I'm not going through this entire night stepping on eggshells. "Look, Mr. Coll," I say. "I didn't ask for the Newsome case; Chief Salazar practically begged me to take it. He said your department is overworked and under—"

"We could have handled it without your interference," the man replies.

"Yeah? Because I spoke with Marnie Scrofano yesterday and she told me she provided information about a man hiking down off the mountain with a rifle on his back. We've already identified the round came from a rifle. So why wasn't that information in the file when I received it?"

Coll doesn't reply, he just stares at the screen.

"You were the one who took her statement, weren't you?"

"Dad?" Liam says from behind me. "Is that true?"

The man turns back to us, his eyes burning. "I am trying to watch this. Is it too much to ask to let a man watch a game in his own home? Or does he have to be subjected to the third degree whenever we have a guest?" His accent goes super heavy and "third" comes out like "tird."

"I need to know Mr. Coll. If you intentionally omitted her statement it could be seen as conspiring to cover up evidence. We could have—"

"*I don't remember! Christ,*" the man yells, silencing all of us. We sit there in silence, Liam's father glaring at all three of us. There's something in his eyes…shame maybe and I realize that I might have called this thing wrong. His gaze flits up and he opens his mouth before closing it again. "Bri…I…"

I turn to see Mrs. Coll standing behind the couch, her hands folded in front of her. Her lips are pressed tightly together and if the woman was a rubber band, I would say she's about to snap. But she calmly takes a breath before she speaks. "We were going to wait until it was just the family, but you might as well know." As she says it, she levels her gaze at me for a moment too long. "Your father was diagnosed with dementia three months ago. Rapid onset."

"What?" Liam asks.

"I didn't want anyone to know," Coll replies. "Didn't want anyone treating me different."

"Jesus, Dad. Really?" Wes asks. "After everything this family has been through?"

I shoot a look at Liam. *What has this family been through?* He just looks away. It seems he has as many skeletons in his closet as I do.

"I'm…very sorry to hear that," I say.

"I'll tell Salazar Monday," Coll says, still staring at the screen. "He'll let me go, but he'll be gracious about it. And then you can have the case all to yourself."

I get up and walk over to Mr. Coll, kneeling in front of him. "That isn't what I wanted. I only agreed to help because Salazar made it sound like the department needed it. Despite everything, I don't want to see the same thing happen to Still-water again. This place…it's kind of where I turned my life around. I owe it for that."

"Aye," he says. "It's a good town. Good people. Always has been."

"I won't mention anything about Scrofano's statement in my reports," I tell him. "There's no foul. She gave me the information again."

Mr. Coll's face softens. "Thank you. You're a good lass." I nod, happy that I can do that small amount for him at least. He's got some battles ahead of him. The whole family does.

"Dinner's ready," Mrs. Coll says. "Wes, come help me prepare the table."

I look over to Liam, sitting on the couch, looking like his world has been crushed. His face is drawn, and he's staring at the floor without really seeing it. He's just received devastating news, so I don't blame him. As someone who has lost both their parents to disease, I know the battle he's facing. And I plan on being there for him through all of it. I can't ease the pain all of this will cause, but I can at least be there for him as he goes through it.

I walk over and take his hand, giving it a small squeeze. "C'mon," I say. "Let's eat."

Chapter Fifteen

MOST OF THE TIME, I know what to expect out of life. There are very few times when I'm surprised. However, *this* is one of those times.

As we reach the dining table that sits in the sunroom looking out on the back of their property, I can hardly count all the different plates and bowls of food. It's enough to feed at least a dozen people, even though there are only five of us. A plate of fried chicken sits in the middle, surrounded by meat-loaf, two different kinds of potatoes, vegetables, what looks like some kind of roast, rolls, salads, a cranberry sauce that looks homemade and an entire rump of ham at the far end.

"Holy shit," I whisper as I take in all the food. I half expected a couple of microwaved meals and maybe a bowl of chili. But this is like a Thanksgiving feast.

"Emily, I've set you a place there, next to Liam," Mrs. Coll says as we all gather in the room.

Wow, second shock of the day. "You guys do this every Friday?"

"We do this when our sons are in town, which isn't very often," she replies.

"It looks amazing. Thank you."

The woman doesn't respond to the compliment, instead busies herself with making sure everything is on the table correctly and everyone has plates, glasses, and drinks. "Is there anything you need—"

"Sean, get in here," she says, interrupting before I have a chance to finish. I should have known better than to offer any help. I look to Liam to maybe share one of our glances, but he's still in shock over the news about his father. I rub his shoulder gently as we sit down and he seems to come back into himself a bit. Everything smells amazing. Despite the fact the entire table is full of food, there is still enough room for my setting. Honestly, I had figured that by showing up I would have either been asked to leave or I would have been relegated to a stool in the kitchen while everyone else ate at the table.

Maybe Mrs. Coll doesn't dislike me as much as she pretends to.

Mr. Coll lumbers into the room, taking a seat at the head of the table. How he's not absolutely gob-smacked by the size of this meal is beyond me. I can't imagine people actually living this way all the time. I turn to Liam. "I guess now I know where you get it from."

"He's cooking for you, isn't he?" Wes asks, taking a seat on the other side of the table while Liam and I sit on the side closest to the kitchen.

"If I didn't she'd never eat anything other than takeout," he replies. I smack him playfully on the arm, but he's not wrong.

"You don't cook?" Mrs. Coll asks.

"I never picked it up," I reply, knowing she's just looking for something else to dig her claws into. "Plus, with my schedule I've never really had the time."

"How long have you been in the FBI?" Wes asks.

"About five years," I reply. "Ever since I got out of school. It's all I've ever wanted to do."

"No shop talk at the table," Mrs. Coll says. I raise my eyebrows but avert my gaze so Mrs. Coll doesn't see it. Strict house. No wonder the boys snuck out whenever they could.

I know better than to begin reaching for things on the table, so instead I watch everyone, waiting for the social cues that will tell me the best way to navigate all this. Mrs. Coll is the last one to take a seat at the far end of the table, closest to the ham. I feel like she's watching me out of the corner of her eye, waiting to see if I'll make a move, but I stay completely still. I'm like prey being stalked in the jungle. If I just don't move, she won't be able to attack.

"Emily, since you're our guest tonight, would you mind saying a prayer before we eat?" Mrs. Coll asks.

So much for that theory.

"Uhhh…" I stammer. "I'm…not Catholic."

There is the smallest hint of movement at Mrs. Coll's mouth, but she doesn't betray her feelings, not openly. Instead, she turns to Wes. "Will you take over then?"

"Be happy to," Wes says, giving me a wink before bowing his head. I follow suit and Liam squeezes my hand under the table. Wes rattles out the fastest prayer I've ever heard.

"God above, hear this line,
Guide us through life's twists and time,
With each passing day,
Keep worries away,
In your light, may our spirits shine."

When I raise my head again and look at Mrs. Coll, a scowl has formed over her face. Wes, however, looks perfectly pleased with himself. And even Mr. Coll chuckles once before clearing his throat. *Was that a limerick?*

"Okay," Liam says. "Dig in."

Everyone begins piling their plates full of food, passing either plates or dishes around so everyone gets a taste of each item. By the time my plate comes back around to me it's packed high with more carbohydrates than I think I've eaten in a solid month.

"This looks amazing," I say, my mouth watering. "Thank you."

"It was nothing," Mrs. Coll says. "We're glad you could join us." She says it as I'm about to take the first bite and from the look she's giving me my paranoid brain screams out that she's somehow poisoned my food. But that's ridiculous.

Everything I taste is an explosion of butter, sugar, grease or fat, or some combination of all of it and it's amazing. If I thought Liam's cooking was good, this is next level. For a long time the entire table is silent as all of us focus on our plates.

"So," Mr. Coll says, being the first one to break the tension as he cuts into a large slice of the ham. "What's your thoughts on the case?"

"Sean, what did I just say? Not at the table," Mrs. Coll says before I can respond.

"Oh let the girl speak, Bri. I'm jus' askin' how she's gonna handle it. Is that a crime?"

Mrs. Coll huffs, but doesn't protest again.

I finish chewing and swallow, wiping my mouth with my napkin. "Well, I can't go into too much detail," I say, shooting a glance at Wes and Mrs. Coll. Because they're not in law enforcement I technically shouldn't be revealing anything about an active case to them. I really shouldn't be revealing anything to Liam either, considering he's on leave.

"I don't need the specifics," Mr. Coll replies. "Just curious how you're going about it."

"I have a couple theories which I'd like to test out tomorrow," I tell him, turning to Liam. "I've got some driving to do. Might have to stay somewhere else overnight."

"You're going back to D.C.?" Mrs. Coll asks, the hopefulness in her voice unmistakable.

"Not D.C., no," I say. "I'm looking for a pattern and I'd like to see if any of the surrounding towns have similar cases."

"That's interestin'" Mr. Coll replies. "I hadn't thought of that."

I nod. "I had a case a few months back where someone was driving to a different town every weekend to take a victim. In that case it was because they were being targeted and each of the victims was living in different areas. I'm wondering if something similar might be going on here."

"I'd be happy to tag along," Liam says. "If you want the company."

Mrs. Coll slams down her silverware on her plate, breaking the plate in the process before the entire room goes silent. She takes another deep breath. "Excuse me," she says before gathering the bits of her plate and heading back into the kitchen.

I shoot a glance at Liam, but he's only staring at Wes, who is looking away. I turn my gaze to Mr. Coll who seems to be ignoring the whole thing and is continuing to eat. "Is she okay?" I ask.

"Mom's under a lot of pressure," Wes says before leaning in. "And to be honest sometimes she can be a little dramatic."

"Careful boy, that's your mother you're talkin' about there. I won't have you disparagin' her at the dinner table."

"Da', come on. We all know——"

"Enough," he says. "It's not dinner conversation."

I give Liam's hand another squeeze under the table. Whatever is going on here I want him to know he can talk to me about it if he needs to. But I don't want to get in the middle of what is clearly a family issue.

"Emily, tell me more about this old case of yours," he says. It seems Mr. Coll has warmed up to me, for now at least. "How many victims are we talking?"

"I'll be right back," Liam says, leaving me and Wes with Mr. Coll. The older man smiles at me for what is probably the first time. I smile back. A win is a win, and I'm going to do everything I can to salvage what's left of this evening.

"Well, it's actually a really interesting case," I begin. But even as I relate the tale, my thoughts can't help me to drift back to whatever is going on in the kitchen.

Chapter Sixteen

I DIDN'T SEE Mrs. Coll for the rest of the night. And dinner went smoothly after that. Liam returned to the table, but he wouldn't say anything about his mother and Mr. Coll pretended it hadn't happened at all. Eventually, once we were all done, I helped clean up and then headed back to the hotel for the night.

I didn't ask Liam what was going on, and I don't plan to. I'm going to leave it up to him to decide to talk about it if he wants, but it's killing me not knowing what is going on with his mother. She has to be one of the most cunning people I've ever met, and she wields that cunningness like a sharp blade. I must consider the possibility that her outburst last night might have been nothing more than a ploy on her part to throw me off. Then again it might not have anything to do with me at all —which I sincerely hope is the case.

The following morning I'm up early and grab some snacks from the vending machine before heading out. After last night's feast, I don't think I'll need a full meal for a solid month. Liam again reiterated his willingness to come along with me this morning. I'd much rather spend a few hours in the car with him than be alone, and it might be a good opportunity for him to open up if he wants.

After grabbing a couple coffees I swing by his parent's place to find him outside already, despite the fact it's barely above freezing. He's sitting on the porch, watching his breath when I pull up. When he gets in the car he shivers once before pulling off his gloves and placing them close to the heaters.

"Hey," I say as soon as he's in. "What were you doing?"

"Trust me, it's just easier that I was outside," he replies. "Mom is on the warpath this morning."

"Don't forget you have reduced lung capacity," I say. "I don't think it's the best idea for you to be sitting out in the freezing cold. You're supposed to be healing."

"Listen, I'm sorry about last night," he says. "Wes is right, Mom is overdramatic. I mean, there's good reason sometimes, but she more or less threw a tantrum right there at the dinner table. If either me or my brother had done that when we were kids, she would have taken a stick across our backsides. Not literally, of course."

"I don't know," I say, backing out of the driveway. "I could see her going out and pulling a switch down off a tree."

"She's been like this for…a while now," he sighs. "Part of the reason why I knew I needed to make a 'clean break' from them when I moved to D.C. was because of all this."

"You don't have to talk about it if you don't want to," I tell him as we get back out on the main road. "We can focus on the case."

He chuckles. "It's funny. Last night, after you left, Dad confessed to me that he was glad you were taking over. He said he didn't trust any of those idiots down at the station not to 'cock it all up'."

I laugh. "I'm glad one of your parents likes me at least. And all it took was revealing a devastating family secret." I reach out to him with my free hand. "How are you doing with all of it?"

He shrugs. "It's not exactly a surprise. I've noticed in my conversations with him lately that something has seemed off. My mother seems to forget I've been an investigator for nearly half a decade and still likes to think of me as a little boy. I could see the signs. If you'd been around him another week you would have seen it too. But really I'm more worried about Wes."

"Wes?" I ask. "Really?"

"He acts like he's got it all together, but he hides a lot too," Liam says. "His divorce devastated him. He loves those kids, and the fact she got them and he only gets to see them periodically is killing him inside." He lets out a long breath. "It doesn't help matters that my mother continued pressuring him for more grandchildren when she barely sees the ones she has."

"I guess that's one thing I've never had to deal with," I say. "That generational pressure."

"Dad's not too bad about it, but I swear, you'd think the world was ending because Mom didn't have a half dozen grandkids to dote on. And it's not just him, that decree extends to me too."

This is tricky territory. Liam knows how I feel about kids, better than anyone. He's seen how I don't fare very well around them. We've had a few conversations about it, but if we're going to take this relationship to the next level, we need to be on the same page.

He turns to me, grinning. "I can see the terror in your eyes already."

"What do you mean?" I ask, trying to play innocent. "There's no terror."

"Emily, you are petrified at the idea of having children," he says. "But here's a secret. So am I. It's not something I've ever wanted. If I did it, it would be out of guilt to them."

"You can't—" I begin.

"Oh, definitely not," he replies. "I just meant if I wasn't

the emotionally mature person I am today I might accidentally fall in that trap."

I glance over, unsure if he's kidding or not. But then he
places his hand on my knee. "Don't worry. I don't see that as
part of our future. I just want to be with *you*."

My heart, which had unexpectedly began beating faster
without me even realizing it, begins to slow. "Yeah? Don't
need little Liams and Emilys running around?"

"Not even a little," he says. "There are enough people out
there. Why make more?"

I snort a laugh and find myself relaxing. "Won't your mom
be disappointed?"

He shrugs. "She'll get over it. And if she doesn't, who
cares? It's my life. *Our* life."

God. Just when I think I couldn't be any more attracted to
him. If we weren't out hunting for a killer I'd pull this car over
and demand a repeat performance of the first time we were
together.

"So tell me your theories on this case. Why are we driving
out to…where are we going?"

"Charlestown, Maryland," I say. "It's about an hour
outside of Stillwater. I want to check with the local departments to see if any of them have cases which match our
killer's M.O."

"But wouldn't they have been classified as accidents?" he
asks.

"Exactly. Which is why we need to do a deep dive into the
surrounding areas. See if anything was overlooked. If he's
making his kills look like accidents everywhere, then there's a
good chance he's been able to operate unchecked."

"And you still think he's done this more than once?" he
asks.

"After what I saw out there in the woods along the trail,
I'm certain of it," I tell him. "I don't think it's just a coinci-

dence they happened to be that far up on the mountain, or that he had another trail close by where he could leave the area undetected."

"So then you think he planned it," Liam says. "He had a grudge against Josh Newsome."

"It's the only thing that makes sense," I reply.

"Well, since I'm just a passenger here, I look forward to watching you in action," he teases.

I shoot him a smirk. "Good, maybe you'll finally see how real detective work is done."

CHARLESTOWN IS ON THE OTHER SIDE OF ONE OF THE Appalachian Mountain ranges, which means we are driving over a lot of back roads that go up and down and up and down again. Because of the recent snow I have to keep the car to a lower speed than I'd like, as the possibility of black ice isn't worth the extra thirty seconds it would save.

But it makes the drive arduous and by the time we're on the downslope headed into the town, I'm ready to be out of the car.

"Hey," Liam says as we begin to pass the first couple of houses that mark the edge of the town. He's been quiet for the rest of the ride. I thought maybe it was because he was trying not to get carsick as he loves to remind me even in bad weather I tend to take things a little too recklessly. "I just want you to know what happened last night with Mom…that wasn't about you. It was about me."

"I just wish I could figure out what I needed to do to get on her good side," I say.

"Stop being such a bad influence." He smiles as he says it, but I can tell there's some truth behind the words.

"Is that what she really thinks?" I ask.

"Keep in mind her idea of a bad influence is someone who encourages people to do anything that's contrary to her own view of how someone should live their life."

Ah, that makes sense. "So in other words, find a stable job, a nice girl. Get married, settle down and go through the whole 'plan'."

"Exactly. And do it all within throwing distance so she can come along and be there the whole way."

"I knew she was upset you joined the FBI; I just didn't realize how deep the hole went," I say.

He pauses. "Well, it's more than that. Ever since what happened to my brother she's been...different."

"What happened to Wes?" I ask.

He gives me a small tilt of his head but doesn't look directly at me. "Not Wes. My other brother, Gerry."

I raise my eyebrows, though I keep my focus on the road. *His* other *brother?*

"I know what you're thinking, but it's just not something we talk about."

"Hang on," I say and I pull into the closest parking lot, which happens to be of a Dollar General. I put the car into park and turn all the way in my seat so I'm staring at him. "You have another brother?"

"Had," he emphasizes. "Gerry was about two years older than Wes. He'd be almost thirty-five by now."

"What happened?" I ask.

Liam sits back, his head against the headrest while he stares up at the ceiling of my car. "Gerry was the first one to follow in Dad's footsteps. But he didn't want to stay in Stillwater. Thought it was too small-time. He went to the academy, graduated, and started as a patrol officer up in New Jersey."

I can see the pain on his face as he speaks, this is something deeply personal to him. Being an only child, I don't know what it feels like to lose a sibling, but I imagine it was probably close to what I felt when I thought I was losing Zara. And that was the most gut-wrenching feeling I've ever felt in my life. Something I wouldn't want even some of the worst offenders we catch to feel. The pain of losing someone so close...of knowing that connection is gone forever. Even as he's speaking I feel the tears prickle my eyes.

"The worst part of it was that it was all so senseless," Liam says. "It's not like he died trying to save a building full of people or that he jumped in front of a bullet for someone. He was just...caught in the crossfire between two gangs. Took a bullet to the chest, died instantly. And that was it."

"Liam," I say softly. "I'm so sorry."

He takes a deep breath. "Gerry was...he was like a compass for me. The oldest brother, kind of like our leader. He was a role model. And he had all these expectations on him too, I know they weighed on him. But he never let it show. He was strong for everyone, even when we weren't always there for him."

"Did they ever find out who did it?" I ask.

"Never enough evidence," he replies. "Not that it would have mattered anyway. He wasn't the target; he was just collateral damage. Best we could have hoped for was manslaughter."

"Are you sure?" I ask. "Because it could have been—"

"Em," he says, his voice serious. "I know you have theories about stuff like this, but trust me when I tell you, it was senseless. No one was gunning for him. Not him personally, anyway. Maybe because he was a cop they weren't worried about him getting in the crosshairs. But he wasn't the only one hurt that night. A woman lost her eye from bullet fragments. One person was permanently handicapped when they caught a bullet in the spine. And there were some arrests made, but none of them could be tied back to that specific bullet." He lets out a long breath. "Pointless."

I let the silence stretch out before speaking again. "Thank you, for telling me," I say softly. "I know that can't be easy."

"I didn't bring it up before because I didn't want it to get in the way of...everything else. You have enough going on that you don't need to add my drama into the mix."

"Hey," I say, grinning. "I'm always happy to add your drama." We sit in silence for a moment as I ponder what he's told me. "Were you already on the force when he died?"

Liam nods. "He was the one who helped inspire me. Him, and Dad and Grandpa. But after he died I promised my mother I wouldn't do what he did. I wouldn't go become this big city cop."

"And then you met me," I say, finally understanding the full weight of the situation.

"I realized I'd become too entrenched in the small-town pettiness that had taken over Stillwater," he says. "And to be honest, I'd gotten sick of being stuck there. I didn't want my whole life to revolve around that town. I wanted—"

"—to make a difference," I say. "But from your mom's perspective...ugh. No wonder she hates me."

"She doesn't *hate* you; she just feels like you're the catalyst for putting me in the same position Gerry was in. And she's already lost one son to the job."

My eyes go wide. "Wait, did you tell her what happened with Camille? When she took you hostage?"

He barks out a laugh. "Are you *insane*? I don't tell her ninety percent of what goes on at our job. She thinks I sit behind a desk most of the time. And honestly, that's what I need her to believe. For my own sanity."

"That's probably smart," I say. "And that's good to know on my end too. At least that way I won't accidentally slip and say something I shouldn't."

He smiles. "I appreciate that."

"Hey, after everything you've done for me, it's the least I can do." I pause a moment. "Though, now I know where all that cooking skill comes from I might start expecting five-star dinners."

He laughs. "Whoa there. Slow the horse down. Maybe we'll just start with desserts and go from there."

"Sounds perfect to me."

Chapter Seventeen

LIAM and I spend a good three hours going through their records to find any deaths that could have even been marked as suspicious that had yet to be explained. And while there had been a few hunting accidents in the past year, including one fatality, the shooter in that case had come forward immediately. It had been a fourteen-year-old girl who had been out hunting with her father. A stray bullet had gone awry and entered the abdomen of a nearby farmer who was out tending to his cattle. He died a couple hours later but there had never been any question about where the bullet came from and the pattern didn't match the one established in Stillwater.

I'm not being so narrow-minded as to think the killer can't vary up his style every now and again, but framing a little girl for your kill is going a bit far. I didn't think we'd hit pay dirt on the first town, but still, it's disappointing.

We head on to another nearby town of any size: Davis, West Virginia. It's a coal-mining town, like a lot of the others in this area of the country and doesn't see a lot of activity. But the people are friendly enough and the sheriff gives us full access to his records.

Again, Liam and I spend a couple hours going back a

couple of years, but there's not much in the files and nothing that would suggest anything close to what happened in Still-water. I know Liam's not completely on board with my theory yet, and unfortunately none of this is helping my case.

"Agent Slate," the sheriff says just as we're packing all the files back up and preparing to leave.

"Yes?"

The sheriff is a gruff man of in his sixties, sporting a full beard and moustache and not an ounce of hair on his head. But he's got one of those faces that you can tell smiles a lot, just based on his demeanor. "I called down to my friend Sheriff Cook down in Strasburg and told him about your theory. He thinks he might have a case that fits."

"Really?" I ask, hopeful for the first time.

"Yup. But it's a couple hours' drive down there," he replies. "I could have him send the info up here, if you like."

Strasburg is only about thirty minutes from Stillwater, just in the opposite direction of Charlestown. "Thanks, but we're headed back in that direction anyway. That way we can inspect any details in person if we need to. But thank you for reaching out to him. That really helps us a lot."

"Hey now, if there's a killer out there who's just picking off people one at a time, I want them caught as much as anyone. I'll keep my ear to the ground in case I hear anything else. You can be damn sure he's not gonna kill any of my citizens."

"I appreciate that, Sheriff. Thanks." We nod and head back to the car. When I put the address in my GPS I let out a groan. "Two more hours. At least we'll be close to the hotel."

"Bet you wish Zara was here now, don't ya," Liam teases as he pulls on his seatbelt. He pulls out his prescription inhaler and takes two deep breaths with it.

"If she was she'd just insist on listening to nineties the whole way," I tell him. "Is that thing helping?"

"I don't have to take as deep of breaths when I use it," he says. "I just hope it isn't permanent."

"It won't be," I say, though I can't be a hundred percent sure. "Remember I went through something similar."

"You never feel short of breath?" he asks.

"Not really." What's really been bothering me lately has been my delayed reflex time. It almost got me killed in Louisiana. As soon as we get back to D.C., I'm hitting the gym hard. I can't afford to slow down, not now. Maybe I'll even be able to rope Zara into some sparring sessions.

He looks at the inhaler for a moment before putting it away. "Yeah, you're probably right. I just want to make sure I'm healed as fast as possible. I don't want Wallace benching me because he thinks I need more downtime."

"I hear that," I say, pulling out of the police parking lot and heading back out of town. It's already four o'clock and I'm starving. But I'm not sure I can wait until we get on the other side of the mountains. "I need to eat."

"How does lard for dinner sound?" Liam asks.

"*Lard?*"

"I doubt you're going to find a vegan restaurant anywhere close to here."

"I'd settle for Greek," I say.

"Got one," he replies. "Forty-five minutes away."

"Works for me," I tell him.

AFTER A HEARTY MEAL WE'RE BACK ON THE ROAD TO Strasburg, though by the time we reach the town it's already getting dark. *And* it's a Saturday night. I'm not hopeful, but I don't want to put this off any longer than necessary, so I drive us up to the sheriff's station, which only has two other cars in the lot.

"Yeah, it was a strange one," the deputy, who is named

Orellio, says as she meets us at the door. "Happened a few months back. Hunting accident." She leads us down a set of stairs that head into a back section of the office where the records are kept. "At least, that's what we thought until we got the call from Davis. Said you folks were looking into any deaths that might have been deemed suspicious but hadn't otherwise been investigated."

"*Did* you deem it suspicious?" I ask as Orellio heads down a row of files and pulls one from the top.

"Not really. Accidents happen, especially out here. We've got a big hunting community. Figured someone would fess up to it eventually. Then, o'course, you get busy with other cases, it starts to slip your mind."

"All of which might have been on purpose," I tell her, taking the file and looking through it. "Victim was out turkey hunting?"

"Yep. Bill Crease. Big turkey hunter round here. He even used to run a class for the young'uns. Teach 'em how to hold a rifle. How to shoot. You know, simple stuff."

I exchange a glance with Liam, thinking back to the four-teen-year-old who killed that farmer. Flipping through the file I see a lot of similarities with Josh Newsome. "It says here he wasn't found for three days?"

"Well, it was the holiday season, and best our examiner could tell he was shot on Christmas Eve or Christmas Day. Bill didn't have a wife and his kids are off living in other parts of the country so no one came lookin' for him until he didn't show up to church on Sunday."

"Where's the ballistics report?" I ask, anxious to get a look at the bullet.

"Didn't do one," Orellio says. "Sheriff didn't see any point in it. Said someone would come forward eventually."

"Damn," I say, closing the file. "Then we're going to need to exhume him."

Orellio checks her watch. "At seven o'clock on a Saturday?

Agent, this isn't New York. We don't have those kinds of resources here."

"How long?" I ask.

"Best we can do is Monday mornin', I'm afraid."

I hand the file back to her. "Schedule it. We'll be back."

Orellio lets out a long breath. "All right," she says, hesitant.

"What's the problem? I thought you said he didn't have any family close by."

"He doesn't, but…know what? Never mind. We'll take care of it. FBI needs to look at the body, I ain't gonna argue."

"I'll get a warrant if I have to," I tell her. "But I'd rather not."

She grumbles. "That won't be necessary. We'll get it done. Monday morning."

I give her a sweet smile in return. "Thank you."

Chapter Eighteen

"BACK TO STILLWATER?" Liam asks as we head back to the car following our conversation with the deputy.

"Sure," I tell him. "Not like we have anything better to do." I make an exaggerated face looking in the back of the car. "And I see you brought no overnight bag, so I guess I'm dropping you back at home."

"Don't want to share a toothbrush?" he teases. "I'd much rather spend the night with you than one more night in that house. Mom will just have to deal with it."

"I think we can come to some sort of arrangement," I say, pulling out of the parking lot. A nice, quiet night together would be a pleasant change of pace, since we're obviously stuck until Monday before we can determine if our new victim matches our first.

"Dammit," Liam says as I get back on the interstate headed north. He shoots me a look as his phone buzzes in his hand. "Wes. I forgot." He puts the phone to his ear. Even from my position in the driver's seat I can hear the noise coming out of the other end.

"Baby bro where the hell are you?" Wes yells.

"I'm working on the case with Emily, we're headed back to town," he replies.

"Good. Get you and your missus's asses over here as soon as you're back."

"Over where?" I ask.

Liam gives me a sheepish look. "Remember? Wes asked me to go out with him tonight." He covers the speaker end of the phone. "I was hoping I wouldn't be here so I wouldn't have to do it."

"Yeah, I did!" Wes yells on the other end, oblivious to the second part of that conversation. I can tell he's already trashed.

"Do we need to go make sure he's okay?" I ask. "Make sure he gets back to his hotel safely?"

Liam grits his teeth. "I suppose."

I roll my eyes as we head back north to town. Playing babysitter this evening hadn't been on my agenda. By the time we reach Stillwater it's almost nine-thirty and I head straight into downtown, following Liam's directions as he takes us to whatever club Wes has found himself in. While I typically don't deal with drunk people, I'm being a bit more lenient than normal here because this is Liam's brother. And because different people deal with grief in different ways. Knowing now what I know about their brother, and the revelation about their father last night, I guess I need to cut Wes a little slack. But my patience only goes so far. If he's blitzed, I may just throw him in handcuffs and let him sleep it off in the drunk tank.

We end up parking half a block away and make our way to the entrance of the bar-slash-club where a bouncer sits on a stool outside. It looks like the kind of place that probably only has bouncers on the weekends. Before we even get up to him, I have my badge out and visible so he can see. If he's surprised to see an FBI agent walking into his place, he doesn't show it. He lets us through without a word.

Inside the club is a cacophony of light and sound, at decibels so loud I can barely hear myself. The place is packed, and the dance floor is already jammed up with the weekend crowd, all of them moving and jumping to the music.

Wow, people in Stillwater get the weekend party started early.

"Where is he?" I yell to Liam who is trying to look over the crowd.

"Bar!" Liam yells, pointing toward the back of the building. A second later I spot Wes leaning over the bar saying something to a bartender with a low-cut t-shirt on, though it doesn't look like he's getting anywhere.

Liam and I make our way through the crowd, though there are so many people in here it's hard to navigate. I wouldn't have thought Stillwater had a large enough population for a place like this, but then again it is Saturday night. The air is thick with fog, scattering the lights from above. I haven't been in a "club" atmosphere in a while and find the whole thing...too much. Too much noise, light and *way* too many people. Zara would love it in here, though.

I don't get places like this. I mean, I understand people need to get out and let loose every now and again, but I just don't see the appeal. Shoved shoulder to shoulder with a hundred other people, sweating your ass off to overhyped music that drowns out any possibility of conversation and paying twice as much for drinks all while guys feel you up all night long? No thank you.

As if on cue, I feel a hand along my backside and in an instant I have a wrist in my grip and I twist.

The man the wrist is attached to yells out, dropping his drink and falling to his knees as people move away from us. His face is pinched with pain and as he reaches up to try and remove my grip with his other hand, I twist a little more, causing him to cry out again and collapse even further.

I pull out my badge and make sure he can see it as I yell

over the music. "Touch anyone else again in one of these places and you'll be in a cast for eight weeks. Get me?"

He nods, shaking his head violently and I let go. He cradles his sore wrist as he sits on the ground. Douche.

"You should have just broken it," Liam yells.

"Didn't want to deal with the paperwork," I call back. He smiles as the crowd parts, allowing us to reach the bar. Fortunately it seems like most of them witnessed the event and aren't willing to get close to us.

Wes, however, is completely oblivious, still trying to talk to the bartender who has moved on to the other end of the bar.

"Wes!" Liam yells, getting his brother's attention. The man turns around and his face lights up. He wraps Liam in an enormous hug, patting his back with his free hand. His other hand holds a clear drink of sorts, and part of it sloshes on the back of Liam's shirt.

"You came! I knew it!" he yells. He lets go of Liam and before I can stop him, wraps me in a similarly powerful hug. "Hell yeah. *Now* it's a party."

"Wes, are you okay?" Liam asks, though I see him wince.

"'course. What can I get you?" he tries to flag down the bartender again but it looks to me like she's actively ignoring him.

"Wes," Liam says. "Let's go get some coffee or something."

"What? Are you crazy? You just got here!" He sets his drink down on the bar and starts waving with both hands before the bartender finally relents, though I catch her roll her eyes as she comes over.

"Yeah?"

"My friends here will have two long islands," he says. "Heavy on the island."

"No, that's okay," I say, giving her a subtle shake of my head. "Can we just close out his tab?"

"Em! You're not going to kill my buzz this early, are you?

It's Saturday for chrissakes. I thought you were *cool*, man." He says it in a sort of sarcastic fashion, but I can also tell there's real intention behind it.

"No, I'm not," I reply. "I'm very uncool." I turn back to the bartender. "Close him out."

"Wow, what bug crawled up your ass?" Wes asks as he downs the rest of his drink in one swallow.

"Okay," Liam says, taking him by the arm. "Let's go."

"Get off me," Wes yells, wrenching his arm back. "You don't want to hang out, fine. But leave me here."

"C'mon," Liam says. "You don't want to do this. Not now." I see that wince in his face again. It's brief, but it's there.

"Really? If not now, when?" he asks. "We just found out Dad's losing his mind. You know that shit's genetic right? It'll happen to you. And me. Hell, maybe it even happened to Ger. Who knows?"

"All right, that's enough," Liam says. "We'll talk about this later, when you're not doing this."

"Are you deaf? I said leave me alone!" Wes yells, adopting a more defensive posture. He's winding himself up, just looking for a confrontation. It's something I'm very used to seeing. I slowly position myself behind him, ready to provide backup if Liam needs it.

"Wes—" Liam begins, reaching out for his brother, but Wes is so hot he tries to make the first move. In an instant I have Wes's arm behind his back, pinned in such a way so that if I apply the right amount of pressure, he'll crumple like tinfoil.

"Hey, what—ahhh!" Wes yells as I apply the smallest amount of pressure to his arm, causing his whole body to go slack. Much like the guy on the floor, Wes is completely helpless.

I look over to Liam, but his face has gone red and it looks like he's having trouble catching his breath. I look up to all the fog in the room from the damn machines. "Everybody *move!*" I yell out, holding up my badge. "You, get outside now," I tell Liam.

He nods and most of the people in the bar have either stopped dancing or are at least giving us a wide berth. I escort Wes out, keeping him under my control as I let Liam lead the way. The whole time he's covering his mouth with his sleeve and coughing. I should have known better than to let him into a place like this.

"Hey, what's wrong with him?" Wes asks as I feel his body relax. We reach the door and Liam is first outside, his cough only getting worse.

"Where's your medicine?" I ask. Liam points in the direction of the car. *Dammit,* half a block away.

I lean closer to Wes. "I'm gonna let you go. Watch your brother, I will be right back. Can you do that?"

"Yeah, yeah, I got him," Wes says. Any hint of drunkenness is gone from his voice and while I know there's no way he could have sobered up, the adrenaline flooding his system will keep him okay for a minute or so. I let Wes go and he tends to Liam while I sprint back to the car, running as fast as I can. The ground is still slippery in some places, but I remain focused and return to the two of them quickly. Liam is sitting on the ground, still coughing when I hand him his medicine.

After three full puffs, he finally stops. "Thanks," he croaks out.

"Shit, man, I'm really sorry," Wes says, before turning to me. "To both of you. I didn't even think about it."

"No, I didn't either," I say. "It's not all your fault."

"You're too nice," he says, before he pitches forward, his hands on his knees. "Oh, man. Not—" Before he can finish the thought, he retches all over the freshly shoveled snow.

"That's nice," I say, my hands on my hips.

"Shouldn't have had three long islands in an hour," Wes replies, a sheepish look on his face. I stare at the both of them,

Liam sitting on the ground with his head between his legs and Wes leaning on his knees like he might collapse at any second.

"You two are a pair."

Wes sits down beside Liam on the wet pavement. "I just wanted to hang out and get to know you better. I never get to see family," he says, rubbing his brother's back. Funnily, now that he's thrown up, some of the color has come back in his face.

"Maybe next time we just do dinner," Liam says, his voice still hoarse. "*Without* Mom and Dad."

"Yeah, sounds like a good idea."

FIFTEEN MINUTES LATER I PULL MY CAR INTO THE HOTEL parking lot. Liam is in the passenger seat while Wes is in the back, lying across the seat with his arm over his eyes and moaning slightly. Surprise, surprise, Wes is staying at this same hotel. Which makes sense, I guess, since he knew the clerk.

"Sorry about all this," Liam says as we help Wes out of the back of the car. He seems to have regained his breath but for a few seconds I was afraid I might have to rush him to the closest hospital again. I keep forgetting he's not at a hundred percent. And if I'd thought about it, I never would have let him into that foggy, smoky bar.

Wes mostly walks under his own power, but sways a lot, which means I have to keep him hoisted up until we get to the third floor where his room is. We get him inside and deposit him on the bed.

"Just…wanted…fun…night," he murmurs, though he's mostly out of it. I'm content to leave him as he is; he'll probably be okay.

"So," I ask Liam once we're back out in the hallway. "Want me to drop you off too?"

"I'd much prefer to stay over," he says. Then he gives his

chest an exaggerated rub. "I'm not sure it's a good idea I stay alone tonight."

I smirk. "Come on."

As we head down one floor to my room, Liam takes in the hotel. "You know, this is one of the nicer hotels in town. Wallace approved this?"

"Wallace can deal with it when I submit my expense report," I reply. Though I'm not about to tell Liam the real reason I won't stay at a one-level motel anymore. Even though I know it's ridiculous to think that something like what happened in Bellefleur could ever happen again, I just can't get the image of that knife against my throat out of my head. I'm in for some long sessions with Dr. Frost.

But until then, it's buildings with more than one floor, and interior hallways. No exceptions. Wallace can bitch and moan about it all he wants; I'll pay it out of my own pocket if I have to.

Once we're in the room, we try to go straight to sleep, but it seems neither of us is really tired and we don't seem to be able to keep our hands off each other. Maybe it's because Liam just had another brush with his own mortality. Or maybe it's because we really haven't seen much of each other in the past month. Whatever the reason, I'm not complaining.

I have to be careful with him; I'm not able to use my typical fervor, but in some ways it's nicer. Slower. Still, I'll be glad when he starts feeling better. By the time we actually get to sleep it's close to midnight.

It strikes me just before I fall asleep that this is the most comfortable I've felt since before Bellefleur. And I don't want to let it go.

Chapter Nineteen

THE FOLLOWING morning we sleep in. I feel like Liam needs the rest and I'm not about to refuse a couple extra hours sleep. Not to mention the bed is really comfortable. By the time we're finally up and ready, I already have a dozen texts on my phone from Wes, apologizing for last night. He offers to take us to brunch, which I begrudgingly agree to but only if it's somewhere without bloody marys or mimosas.

Amazingly, Wes is sobered up and looks like a brand-new man this morning, sporting a clean pair of khaki's and a tasteful sweater over a collared shirt. Just what I'd expect someone of his stature to wear on a weekend. Brunch goes a lot smoother than any of the other interactions we've had and Wes admits he's probably been going a bit too hard lately. With all the news about Liam and now his father, I can hardly blame him. We all have our spirals. He admits thinking about coming back to the D.C. area instead to be closer to family. There are a couple of jobs opening up, though most require a pay cut. But I believe him when he says he'd rather be close to the people he loves than have a lot of money.

By the time brunch is over, I've changed my opinion about him. He's not a bad person, but he is an instigator. And he's going through a lot right now. Thankfully, we leave things on a high note. He promises to let us know about his decision regarding coming back to the area before heading back.

It's rare that Liam and I have some quality time together, so we spend the rest of the day relaxing. No talk about his mother or father, other than the fact that he needs to go back to pick up his stuff. We head back to the hotel and just lie around, watching TV for a while, which I have to admit is really nice. I'm not the kind of person who does well with a lot of time on my hands, but when I'm with Liam, I don't feel the same pressure I normally do to always stay busy. Instead, it's like I can finally relax into myself a little more. And while the case looms in the back of my head, I don't spend the entire day obsessing over it. It will be there when we're ready.

"You know," I say as Liam's legs are wrapped around mine and tangled up in the sheets at the same time. The TV is on, but we're not paying it any attention. It seems we're both a bit more starved than I'd given us credit for. "By the time our parents were our age they already had homes, kids, everything. They'd already made a lot of their big life decisions."

"Different generation," he says, staring directly into my eyes. "Don't tell me you're looking at settling down."

"Maybe not settling down, but I've been thinking a lot lately. I mean, I'll be thirty next year. It's kind of a big deal. And I'll admit I'm a little freaked out by it."

"All the reason more to enjoy your twenties while you can." He grins.

I've been thinking long and hard about this for weeks now, ever since he first brought it up back a month and a half ago. At the time, I felt like he'd broadsided me, just because I had been so focused on work and all the other shit that had been going on at the time. Not to mention we were dealing with an international terrorist. But here, in this bed, it feels like the rest of the world had melted away and it's just the two of us.

"I want to move in together," I say before I lose my courage to say it.

His eyes go wide. "Wait, really?"

"I should have said yes the moment you asked," I admit. "I was just…unprepared. But it's what I want. I want to make a home together with you. And Timber."

"Well, I mean it's going to be Timber's home," he says. "We'll just be guests in it."

I laugh. "Is that a yes?"

"You know, I should make you wait a week, see if I can't make you squirm a bit." But there's a smile playing on his lips. "But I'm too damn impatient for that. Yes."

I pull his face closer and lock my lips with his. It's a little more primal this time, like we're making a pact. One that can't be broken. "Okay," I say, breathing hard and reaching under the covers to get him going again. "Your place or mine?"

His breath hitches. "I think, somewhere new. A place that's ours."

"Yeah, I like that." I climb on top, never breaking eye contact with him. It *is* a solemn pact. Moving in with someone is a big deal for me, and Liam knows it. After everything I've been through, for the longest time I never thought I would take this step again. And maybe it's because I'm finally starting to learn more about his family and his history, and I understand him better. We're cut from the same cloth in many ways. We both have pasts that have defined our lives. And now, we're both taking the step forward to create something of our own, together.

Neither of us gets many more words out, but I see it all in his face. And I know he sees it in mine.

Our pact is made, signed, sealed and delivered. And it's delivered with a bang.

～

On Monday morning we're up early, still feeling that post-coital glow. I haven't taken a day like that in I don't know how long, but it was one of the best days I can remember. Just being with Liam, nothing on the schedule, nowhere to be and no one to save. We picked up most of his stuff from his parent's house yesterday, so we're both fresh and ready to go. We head back down to Strasburg, meeting Deputy Orellio at the station. She informs us that the work crew is already out at the gravesite.

When we arrive, it's not hard to spot the massive CAT machines working on the far side of the lawn. A couple of men in hard hats stand close while I catch sight of the sheriff and another deputy watching from not far away. As we approach, both of them turn.

"You must be the FBI agents," the sheriff says, extending a hand. "Tim Walsh. Sheriff. This is Deputy Taylor." The young deputy nods.

"Agents Slate and Coll," I say, shaking his hand. "We appreciate you doing this."

"Ol' Bill was a mainstay 'round these parts," he says, watching as the giant bucket digs into the ground. "Shame about all this. You really think he was murdered?"

"That's what I'm hoping to find out. I've called down the medical examiner from Stillwater to take a look. She should be here within the hour. She's familiar with the other case, so I'd like her to check for any similarities."

The sheriff holds up an open hand. "Whatever you want. Just as long as I ain't gotta do it."

We watch the giant machine dig into the ground some more in silence, the only sound the machinery as it hums and rumbles along. Finally, it hits the casket.

"Hook it up!" one of the workers calls out and another jumps down into the pit, attaching wire cables to all four sides of the casket.

I happen to glance over and see a woman standing not

very far away, watching us. At first I think she might be nothing more than a passer-by. But every time I turn, she's still there, watching it all unfold. "Sheriff," I say. "Do you know who that is?"

He turns and his face falls. "Ah, shit. What's *she* doing here?"

"Who is she?" Liam asks.

"That's Bill's girlfriend, Tanya," he says. "They broke up a couple weeks before he died. Or was killed, I guess. She tried to get her hands on his insurance money, but that went to his kids."

"What does she want now?" I ask.

"Whatever it is, it prolly ain't good. Woman's nothin' but trouble," the sheriff replies. He heads off to talk with her. I notice her perk up as he approaches.

"Great, just what we need, another wrench in the works," I say.

The foreman motions for everyone to stand back as they lift the casket out of the ground. There's a deep rumbling sound before it lets go, but then it finally appears out of the hole.

"Ya'll want this back at the morgue?" Deputy Taylor asks.

I nod. "We'll be as quick as we can."

"Yeah, she's pissed," Sheriff Walsh says, walking back over. "Thinks she should have been consulted. Said she had rights because they were together for so long."

"How long?" I ask.

"Maybe about eight years," he replies.

I look back at the woman who is glaring at me with a scowl. "Any idea why they broke up?"

"Nope. And I don't care to know either. Not my business."

"Even if the man was murdered?" I ask.

Sheriff Walsh just grimaces before directing the casket over to the nearby flatbed. I motion to Liam. "Come on. Let's get back so we can meet with Sybil."

~

BY THE TIME WE GET BACK TO THE MORGUE WITH THE BODY not far behind, Sybil is already there, setting up her equipment. Even though usually I'm a glutton for punishment, I can't be in the room when she cracks that box. There are some smells that once they get in your nose, they never let go. I've been around more decaying bodies than I care to admit, so I'm more than happy to let her do her job without me hovering over her. Instead, Liam and I sit out in the waiting area waiting for her to finish.

"What do you think, apartment, townhome? Something else?"

I turn to him. "Okay, moneybags. How much can you afford?"

"Eh. I'm sure we can make something work. It won't be huge, but it'll be enough for us to live in. It's not like we spend a ton of time at our places anyway."

He's not wrong there. The job takes up a lot of our time, and usually I tend to use my apartment for sleeping and little else. Occasionally I'll have a day where I can sit and relax, but those have been few and far between lately. Except for yesterday. "I want something that either has some green space close, or maybe even a balcony. Timber is going to need somewhere to run."

"You know, the sooner we buy a house the better. Better to pay on a mortgage than pay rent."

"I guess," I say. "If you want to deal with all the maintenance. I can't imagine you up under a sink on a Saturday morning, trying to fix a leak."

"You never know," he says, giving me a gentle push. "I'm pretty handy."

Would Zara freak out if she knew what I was thinking about Liam's hands while there was a body being dissected not more than thirty feet away? Probably.

I clear my throat. "It might be worth looking into Bill Crease's girlfriend."

I catch the sly smile on his lips telling me knows I'm changing the subject on purpose. "You really think she could have murdered him?"

"Even if she didn't, she might have some information we could use. If they were together for eight years, she might know someone who had a grudge against him."

"But we still don't have a suspect for Josh Newsome," he replies. "We couldn't find anyone who was angry enough to murder him."

"I know. We're still missing a big piece of the puzzle."

"Agents," Sybil says, coming through the double doors in her white bodysuit. Her face is covered by a breathing mask which she removes, then proceeds to remove her gloves as well. She takes a deep breath once they're off. "You'll be glad to know the bullet is still in there. Thankfully it's mostly intact. And it's a match to our other case. Same caliber and design."

"Which means there's a very good chance we're looking at the same killer," Liam says.

I knew it.

"*Now* I think it's time to talk to the girlfriend."

Chapter Twenty

I KNOCK hard on the flimsy screen door, though it just rattles under my hand. We're standing outside a double-wide that sits by itself in a large field, surrounded by mostly dead grass. The snow that made Stillwater so beautiful didn't come this far south, and the entire area looks old and decrepit. Weird how different a place can look based on just the weather.

"Tanya?" I call out, knocking again. "This is the FBI, open up."

An old Civic sits in the gravel driveway, behind a beat-up truck that probably hasn't run in twenty years. The yard is also full of junk or old children's toys, but again, it doesn't look to me like any kids live here anymore. Maybe a decade ago.

A woman opens the door, though the screen still stands between us. She's got a pronounced chin, and deep-set eyes and her face is covered in wrinkles that belie a hard life. It's the same woman I saw earlier at the gravesite. "What the hell do you want?"

"Are you Tanya Cox?"

"So?"

"We'd like to ask you a few questions about Bill Crease."

Recognition dawns in her eyes. "You're the people that

dug him up this mornin'." She spits. "Ya'll had no right to do that. Law says I get a say in what happens to his remains."

"If you were married, yes," I reply. "But we checked. There's no marriage certificate on file. And without that legal right and no other next-of-kin, we have jurisdictional authority." Most of this is b.s., but right now I don't feel like arguing with the woman. I need to find out who is going around killing people and trying to make it look like an accident.

"Well fuck you too, Mrs. high and mighty," she says and moves to close the door.

"Did Bill have any enemies?" I ask before she can. "Anyone who might have wanted him dead?"

The door opens back up. "Look, I don't care what you want or why you're here. I ain't givin' you nothin. Now leave me the hell alone." She slams the door before I can protest any further.

"Looks like the direct approach didn't work," Liam says as we step of the low porch.

"We'll keep her on the persons of interest list," I say. "Insurance fraud is a good motive. But whoever is doing this isn't careless. They're not going to put themselves on their victims' radar before killing them."

"Then how the hell are we supposed to find him?" Liam asks.

"*We're* not," I say. "But maybe someone else can."

"Hey there, enjoying your vacation?" Zara asks. "How are Liam's parents? Still a pair of pills?"

I clear my throat. "Z, you're on speakerphone."

"Oh, *hey* Liam," Zara says, recovering quick. "How are the parents? Nice and pleasant as ever?"

He chuckles. "No, I think your first assessment was dead on target. Though my dad is softening a bit."

"Good. Because the way Em described them she thought she might have to shoot at least one of them before it was all over."

"I think I can guess which one," Liam says.

I clear my throat. "*Anyway*, we're calling because we're working on this Newsome case."

"And you need my help," she says. "You know, I do have cases of my own I'm working on here. Did you know we've got a major counterfeiting operation that's running out of D.C.?"

"*What?*" I ask. "When did that happen?"

"Apparently while we were in Louisiana. Nadia found it. Wallace has the whole department working on it, trying to figure out the best way to bust these guys."

"Damn, I'm sorry I'm missing that," I say.

"It's no biggie. Just the largest counterfeit takedown in years. It's gonna look great on my record."

I chuckle, glad to hear she's regained some of her confidence. Before Bellefleur I wasn't so sure I'd ever see the old Zara again.

"Tell Wallace you need a raise."

She laughs. "Yeah, *right*. I don't even think that man gives *himself* raises. Tell me whatchoo got."

"I need that statistical brain of yours," I tell her, then outline the basics of the case. "I'm looking for patterns. But there's no way we can check every accidental death in the greater northern Virginia area. Is there any way to build some kind of database that can sort through all of these records quickly? Look for any commonalities. We already have two deaths that match. But I have a feeling we're going to find a lot more."

"Hmm," she says. "Basically, you want a system that would search through all the police records all across the country to find any deaths with similar circumstances."

My excitement drops. "Well, when you put it like that…"

"Yeah, sorry, Em, but nothing like that exists. And building it would take months, if not years. And then you have to get every police department to agree to upload their files and make sure they're all compatible. I know what you're asking for, and it's the same thing the federal government has wanted from local police since probably the FBI was invented."

I let out a long breath. "Yeah, I guess I wasn't thinking about it like that."

"Don't count me out just yet. Here's what I can do. Believe it or not, Elliot is like a math genius. I can get his help and maybe we can figure out how to a build a bot that can scour news articles about accidental deaths in the general area. We could probably apply a few filters to that and see if any patterns emerge."

"Really?" I ask. "How long would something like that take?"

"A couple hours. Maybe a day, depending on my work here. Oh, and I have another appointment with Dr. Frost later too…so. You know."

"I know," I say, fully in solidarity with her. "So you went with Frost, huh?"

"Well, you seemed to warm up to him, after a few months. I figured he was probably my best bet. But he annoys the shit out of me with that pen tapping of his."

"I know, it's the worst. And the way he always crosses his legs when he thinks he's asking you a profound question? You see it coming a mile away." We both laugh before I look over to Liam, who is also grinning. "I'm gonna get Liam to start going to him."

"Wait a second, how did I get roped into this?" he asks.

"Between the three of us I think we can make the doctor's head explode," I say.

"Oh yeah? Well, I guess you can't make a good FBI agent if you don't have some crippling trauma dragging you down," Zara jokes. "Welcome to the club, Liam."

"Thanks a lot," he replies.

"Em, I'll get right on this bot. But it may be a day or two, depending on my schedule. Unless you think Wallace would approve priority."

"Definitely not," I say. "He's still thinking I'm on leave for this. Apparently, I'm working this case on my own time, despite the chief specifically asking for FBI intervention."

"Are you *serious*?" she asks. "Go to Janice. There's no way she knows about this."

"I can fight my own battles," I reply. "Plus, I still need to figure Wallace out. And right now I think it's best if I keep a low profile. I'll go to Janice if it's necessary."

"You're a stronger woman than me, I just hope it doesn't blow up in our faces once it's all over."

"Me too. But in the meantime, I'd keep a low profile on the bot."

"You got it. I'll keep you updated."

I want to tell her about me and Liam moving in together, but I think that's probably a conversation better saved for a dinner over margaritas. "How is Timber holding up?"

"Restless. He misses you."

"Tell him I'll be home just as soon as we find this guy and kick his ass to jail."

"You got it, Em. Also, where's that hunky brother of yours Liam? Still causing trouble?"

"He went back to Atlanta already," Liam says, shooting me a confused look. "He had to go back to work."

"Too bad," she replies. "He was cute. But he was definitely a troublemaker."

I place my hand on Liam's arm. "Thanks, Z. I owe you."

"I'll add it to your tab," she says. "Be safe you two."

"How does she know Wes?" Liam asks after she's hung up.

"I was on the phone with her the other day when he came by my hotel room with your father's case file in tow. If it hadn't been for him, I probably would be back in D.C. by now."

"I'm pretty sure he was just trying to stir up my parents," Liam says. "Ever since Gerry, Wes has always kind of acted out in his own way."

"Yeah, I could tell," I reply. "Do you need to talk about it?"

"I mean, having him close wouldn't be the worst thing. But you've seen how he is. Sometimes he can get a little…rowdy. And now that he's lost Katy, I just don't know if he'll be able to keep things together."

"He'll have to figure it out," I say, putting the car back in gear. "You can't do it for him."

"You're right, I just…feel protective, you know? He sent me another email last night, apologizing again for the whole thing at the club. It was…sincere. Which is rare for him."

All of this talk of Wes makes me wonder what it would have been like if I'd had siblings too. Would it have been complicated and messy and difficult? Probably. But maybe it would have been worth it too. I can't help but think about that picture Liam brought back from Ohio. The one that showed my grandmother pregnant with another child. All this time I'd always thought I was like Mom, that we were both only children. And in that way I'd related to her better. But it turns out that was just another lie. And somewhere out there, I have an aunt or uncle. Wallace may not approve any additional time off, but one way or another I'm going to find them.

WE SWING BACK BY THE MORGUE ONE MORE TIME BEFORE heading back up to Stillwater with Sybil. She's learned just about everything she can from Bill Crease, so I give Sheriff Walsh the go-ahead to rebury the man. Because of the amount of time that's passed since Crease's death, I don't feel like it would be a good use of time to head out to the scene of the crime. The odds anything has survived three winter months is low, not to mention we have no idea *where* the shot could have come from, unlike with Josh Newsome.

But, once we're back on Liam's home turf, I want to see what I can find about Bill Crease. Maybe there's something else that links him and Newsome together. Something other than a bullet, which, despite Sybil's claims will have to go off to processing to verify it came from the same gun. But my hope is now with two bullets, one much more intact than the first, we'll be more likely to get an identification on the weapon used. In the meantime, I'm operating under the assumption the same weapon killed both men, three months apart.

When we arrive back in Stillwater it's already afternoon, but I'm beginning to feel the pressure of taking yesterday off, so we head back into the station. I offer to drop Liam back off at the hotel, but he insists he can keep going. He's been using his inhaler more often, which is worrying, but I'm not going to mother him about it. He'll tell me if things get too difficult.

As we're headed into the station, Trisha buzzes us through, and I almost run into Sean Coll on the way in.

"Oh, sorry there Slate, didn't see ya comin'," Mr. Coll says. He looks over at his son. "Missed you for dinner the last two nights. Your mother wasn't too happy about it."

"I'll talk to her later," Liam says. "We had the opportunity to sit down as a family and *she's* the one who left. That wasn't my fault."

"No, suppose not," he replies.

"Are you on your way out?" I ask.

"Jus' here lettin' Lee know about my...well, that I'd be goin' back to retirement, effective today."

I pinch my features. "I'm really sorry about that. I've heard nothing but good things."

He looks over at Liam, then at me again. "Here, come

with me." He turns and heads back into the back of the station. I shoot Liam a confused look but he just shrugs and we follow Mr. Coll back into the precinct. There's a desk with his name still on it close to the bullpen. About thirty files sit stacked on the desk, some on the verge of toppling off.

"I was thinkin' 'bout what you said the other night," he says. "About this guy makin' his kills look like accidents. So I came in early this mornin' and did some diggin'. Figured I'd at least get one more go in before formally turning over the keys. I was gonna leave all this for you, but I think it'll probably be more helpful if I give it to you now."

"What is it?" I ask, looking at the files.

"These are all the accidental deaths I could find from the surrounding counties, though I only looked for a few hours. I printed 'em all out. Probably cost Lee a fortune in paper. But I never worked well on those computers. Hurt my eyes too much. Anyway. I grabbed as many as I could find, the ones that seemed suspicious at least."

I stare at the stack, wide-eyed. "How did you do this?"

"When you've been in the job as long as I have, you make a lot of friends in other places," he says. "Hell, half the people I used to work with only live a couple counties away. And damn near every one of 'em owed me a favor."

"Holy shit, Dad, this is amazing," Liam says, staring at the stack.

"I may be fadin' but I'm not out for the count yet," he says before turning to me. "I was wrong to come after ya like I did. I hope you can forgive an old sinner."

"I'd like nothing more," I say, my heart swelling.

"Good. If you're as good a cop as my son says you are, I'm sure you're lookin' to dig into these so I'll get out of your hair." He puts a reassuring hand on Liam's shoulder. "Call your mother. For my sake, at least."

Liam chuckles. "Sure, Dad."

Coll gives us one more nod, then heads out. I stare at the

stack, unable to believe what Mr. Coll has managed to put together.

"You ready for a long night?" I ask.

Liam grabs the first file off the top. "I'll find a place where we can set up."

Chapter Twenty-One

"It's just up ahead," Liam says as the Virginia landscape rushes by.

I glance over at him, then tap the screen in the middle of my dashboard. "I know how this thing works, you know."

He returns a sheepish look. "Sorry, I just feel so useless here. You chauffeuring me around, me having to keep taking hits off this thing." He holds up the small inhaler as if to prove his point. "I could have gone to Staunton myself, saved us a lot of trouble."

"It was no trouble," I say. "You heard Jill, she was more than willing to help." I look for any reaction but don't see one. It's not that I would ever think Liam would go behind my back with someone he used to be involved with, I just like giving him a hard time. And if he was in a better mood, he would probably respond to it.

We spent the majority of yesterday going over the cases Mr. Coll had left for us, doing a deep dive into each one. I ended up losing track of time, though at some point Sergeant Hubbard appeared and given what I know about her, I didn't have any qualms about roping her in.

It actually turned out to be a good thing, because by the

time midnight rolled around, we'd identified two of the cases were highly likely to be related to our killer, based on the initial reports. But again, no ballistics. Sergeant Hubbard, or Jill, as she insisted I call her, volunteered to head down to Staunton, Virginia, to the site of a fisherman who died near a lake there. Meanwhile, we're headed to Warm Springs to look at the body of an older woman who was out on her porch and was clipped by a bullet almost two years ago. I'm thankful to have her help, as it cuts our work in half, and after I gave Salazar everything we'd found so far, he was more than willing to provide us with additional resources.

This entire time I can't quit thinking about how easily Wallace dismissed me when I told him Salazar wanted me on the case. He was so ready to send me down to Louisiana a few weeks back, how is this any different? I know it can't be a budgetary issue. Something like this wouldn't even register on the balance sheets. I'm one agent, in the field. Certainly nothing as large as the national manhunt that was organized for Simon Magus.

Then again, Fletcher Wallace works in weird ways. Despite having worked with him for almost four months now, I still haven't managed to figure him out. And that makes me uneasy. Especially given my history with people in the Bureau. I don't think he's a spy…but I do feel like something else is going on. I have a sudden urge to call Zara and make sure she's okay.

As I take the turn-off route 220, I catch one sign that says the town is up ahead. Like most of the towns that fall in the Appalachian Mountains, there's not much out here as far as infrastructure. I'd call it one of those "blink and you'd miss it" towns. Technically it's not even a town. Just a "census-designated area" which I believe is one step above pure wilderness.

The road narrows, and we come to a stop sign at a t-intersection.

"Is this it?" I ask.

"According to the map," Liam says. "We're in the middle of town."

Across the street is an older-style house, though it's well-kept. Looking left is what seems to resemble an old mill, and there's a two-lane bridge which crosses over a creek. To the right the road disappears into a thicket of woods.

"Where the hell are we supposed to meet this guy?" I ask. "I thought there'd at least be a post office or something."

"There," Liam says, pointing to the GPS on my car. "There's a county courthouse around the block." I drive down past the old mill, which looks like it's been converted into a restaurant or bed and breakfast of sorts, before taking the next left. Sure enough, there's a grand three-story courthouse right off the main road. Large white columns march across the front of the building and it even has a domed spire.

"Bath County Courthouse," I read across the front. "And there's the sheriff's office, right beside it." A smaller, two-story building sits in the same building complex. We park in the courthouse parking lot and make our way over to the sheriff's office. All of these buildings look like they were erected sometime in the late nineteenth or early twentieth century. Despite being brick, they have that kind of old-timey charm to them.

When I open the door to the sheriff's, an honest-to-God bell rings above my head. I can't help but look up in awe.

"Mornin!" A young woman in a deputy's uniform says. She's sitting behind a small desk that's just to the inside of the door. The tag above her badge says *Ryan*. "How can I help ya'll?"

"I'm Special Agent Emily Slate with the FBI," I say, holding up my badge. "This is Special Agent Liam Coll. We called earlier...about a—"

"Oh, yes, about poor Mrs. Havens."

"Yes, the woman who was killed on her porch."

"Well, we don't know she was killed," Deputy Ryan says,

standing. "But I guess that's what ya'll are here to find out, isn't it?"

"You said on the phone you had the full ballistics report?" I ask.

The deputy nods. "That's right. Ya'll follow me." She heads through a door in the back. "Hey there Jim. These are the FBI agents," she says, waving to an older man at a desk on the other side of the door. "Jim" doesn't reply, just goes about his business.

"You'll have to excuse him, he doesn't have the best of manners," the woman says, still chipper. She waves to another deputy. "Hey there Ronnie. This here's the FBI agents."

"Mornin'," Ronnie says, nodding.

We return the greeting. "Friendly bunch you have around here."

"Oh yeah. Most of us grew up together. Warm Springs born and raised." Finally we reach the back room where all the files are kept. There's one that's already out and on the only table in the room. "Went ahead and pulled it for ya. Take a look. I'd be happy to drive you out to Mrs. Havens's house if ya like."

"Maybe," I say picking up the file and flipping through it. "No one ever came forward to claim responsibility?"

Deputy Ryan puts her hands on her hips. "They did not. We'd hoped after that newspaper article someone would. I mean, we all know accidents happen. Just a few months back Derrick Poston fell off his combine and the thing damn near ate him up. Wasn't hardly enough to bury."

I try not to make a face at her casual mention of the man's grisly death and instead focus on the information in the file. "Just one shot?"

"As far as we could tell."

My face falls when I read the ballistics information. "Damn. Round isn't the same. This is a seven millimeter. Hornady."

"Yep," the deputy replies. "Common round used for deer hunting around here. Which was why we didn't think it was out of the ordinary."

"Have you had any other suspicious deaths?" I ask. "Anything, other than Derrick Poston, that might have raised a red flag?"

"Not really. Most people here are just hard-working and want to enjoy what life they can. We ain't the richest, nor do we wanna be. There's nothin' in Warm Springs worth killin' over."

I can't argue with her logic there. Any murder in a town like this would almost certainly have to be a crime of passion. The statistics just don't bear it out. The greater area doesn't have a population of more than five hundred.

"So what now?" Liam asks.

It's possible this is unrelated. Maybe it really was an accident. But I don't like the fact no one has come forward. "When was the last time someone was accidentally killed by a hunter's bullet? Before Mrs. Havens."

"Oh, hm," the deputy says, screwing up her elf-like face. "I'm not sure. Maybe fifteen years or better? I'd have to ask the sheriff. But unfortunately he's out for the week. Picked up a nasty bug."

"That's okay," I say. "Can you show us Mrs. Havens's home?"

"Absolutely," she says, sounding as excited as a cheerleader. "Follow me."

THE DRIVE TO MRS. HAVENS'S HOME IS SHORT, AND NOT FAR from the center of town. Her property is on a large lot, with the house set far back from the road. A for sale sign sits close to the end of the driveway, which is unpaved. What strikes me as odd as we drive up to the house is there are no woods anywhere close to the home. It's all cleared land, though it's overgrown from no one having taken care of it for a while.

"This is it," the deputy says, getting out and shielding her eyes from the sun. "Take a look around."

"Still for sale? After two years?" I ask.

"Not a lot of people lookin' for houses around here, I'm afraid," she replies.

Liam and I examine the property carefully, walking the perimeter. From every angle the entire house is completely exposed and open. The closest cover is at least five hundred yards away in any direction. When we make our way back around to the front I'm struck by just how many steps it takes to get up to the porch.

"Up there?" I ask.

Deputy Ryan nods. "Yep. Over in the right-hand corner. See those gables? She always kept plants throughout the year. A real horticulturist. Grew things even in the winter you wouldn't think possible."

I climb the steps to get a better look. The porch has obviously been cleaned and there are no blood stains anywhere on the wood. When I get to the right-hand corner I take in the view. Because the house sits on a small hill, I can see most of the property, even the road where we pulled off and the long, gravel drive.

"What are you thinking?" Liam asks, looking up at me from the lawn.

"I dunno," I say. "Just…trying to figure out how it could have happened." I turn to Deputy Ryan. "Any designated hunting areas around here?"

"Some. But lots of times hunters don't stick to those. It's why the sheriff figured no one came forward. Didn't want to lose their license and their weapons from hunting in a non-designated area."

I shake my head at the stupidity of it all. "That and they would have been charged with manslaughter, correct?"

A frown frames her face but quickly disappears. "Yes, of course."

"Right," I say, uneasy about this whole situation. I head back down off the porch. "I think we've seen all we need to see."

"You sure? I'd be happy to show ya'll anything else if you think it'd help."

I survey the area one more time. "No, I think we have everything we need."

"So what's the verdict? Was it an accident or not?"

Liam and I head back to the car. "We'll let you know."

"ANYTHING ABOUT THAT STRIKE YOU AS ODD?" I ASK AS WE head back to Stillwater.

"Seemed to me like the town of Warm Springs has their priorities screwed up," he says.

I keep pondering Deputy Ryan's words to me. *Someone might be afraid of losing their license and their weapons.* Was that really their primary concern when someone had died?

"So that's a bust, right?" Liam asks. "Bullet didn't match. We can cross it off the list?"

"Not yet," I say. "I'm not willing to eliminate the possibility just because we have a different round being used. Who's to say he's not using different weapons each time?"

"Well, considering the one thing you had connecting Josh Newsome and Bill Crease was the bullet, *you're* to say. I mean without that, the whole thing falls apart. You're trying to connect cases that are obviously unrelated."

"I hear you," I say. "But look at the location. That house was *exposed.* There is no way someone could have shot her with anything other than a long-range rifle with a scope. Just like the one that killed Josh Newsome."

"And how many hunters use long-range rifles with scopes?" Liam asks.

"Probably a lot," I admit. "I know it's thin. But doesn't it *feel* like there is something more going on here?"

"Maybe you just want something more to be going on here," he says.

"What do you mean?"

"Just that generally you're used to working on cases where you're fighting against someone clever. Someone with a purpose. What if this guy has no purpose? What if he just shot Josh Newsome and that's the only murder he's ever going to commit?"

I shoot him a glance. "You know that's not what generally happens."

"No. But it *could*. We could be spending all this time looking for additional cases when no others actually exist."

"And the bullet that killed Bill Crease?" I ask.

"Could be a coincidence."

I have to admit, what we have is flimsy. Nothing anyone would ever stake their career on. But at the same time, I can't shake this feeling like there is something more going on here. Maybe he's right, maybe I'm making a mountain out of a molehill and I should just focus on Josh Newsome. The only problem is there's nothing there to focus on. He was a regular guy and unless someone is hiding a really big secret about him, no one had a reason to kill him.

"I just don't know," I say.

Liam's phone vibrates in his pocket. "Hang on, it's Jill." He accepts the call, then switches it to speaker. "Hey, Jill, you're on speaker. We're headed back to Stillwater."

"Find anything?" she asks.

"Not much," I admit. "Just an M.O. that might fit. But the ballistics were off."

"I wish I had better news, then," Jill says. "I have no ballistics on mine. Shot went straight through the man's head. Bullet was never found."

"Could they at least tell how large the round was?" I ask.

"Had to have been pretty large. I got a look at the photos from when they recovered his body from the lake. Gruesome stuff. But by the time they'd gotten to him, the fish had already started eating."

"Give me the whole thing," I say.

"Report says Willard Cummings was out on the pier fishing. Best the local police can tell the bullet caught him in the back of the head and he fell face-first into the lake. His pole and gear were also recovered. No witnesses. And the area is well-known for both hunting and fishing. The date of death was seven-fifteen-twenty-eighteen."

"Not nearly as recent as the others," I say. "Anything about it seem suspicious to you?"

"It was a headshot, so that automatically brings up some concerns. But the police did an exhaustive investigation and they never could determine if it was intentional or not. Cummings didn't have anyone looking to off him and there were no financial or personal motivations that anyone could see."

"So exactly like Josh Newsome," Liam says.

"And Bill Crease. And now Mrs. Willa Havens. I think the one thing that connects all of these victims is the fact there is no motive."

"Are you saying someone is out there just picking off random targets?" Jill asks.

"As much as I hate to say it, yes."

Chapter Twenty-Two

ON THE WAY back to Stillwater we stop at a cute little diner for a late lunch. After our call with Jill I've been lost in my own head, trying to figure out the specifics of this case. Liam has been quiet the rest of the ride too. But I wait until we're seated in a booth away from anyone else before I ask him what he's thinking.

"I guess I just don't see it yet," he finally says after I prod him for a good minute.

"You don't trust me."

"No, that's the problem. I do trust you. And I can't help but wonder what's wrong with me, why I can't see what you see," he says.

"It's not the most ironclad theory, I'll give you that," I say. "But there's just something about the way these kills have been orchestrated that is getting to me. None of them make sense... at least not in the traditional sense. What's the motive?"

"You said there wasn't one," he replies.

"But if that's the case, then what is this? A crime of opportunity? Someone who just gets off on killing innocent people?" The waiter comes over and drops off a pair of menus along with some silverware and I have to remember to temper my voice.

"If these all are the same person, he has gone to extreme lengths to make sure they don't seem connected. Which means we're not dealing with your average killer here. He's smart, and he's careful."

"Are you even sure it's a he?" Liam asks.

"Statistically, yes. Remember what they taught us in training?"

Liam nods. "Odds are he's male, white, middle-aged, and above-average intelligence."

"Right. I've never worked for the Behavioral Analysis Unit, but I know how they operate. And I know the statistics. I'd say we're looking for someone who is average in every sense of the word. Doesn't make waves, doesn't stand out. Because he gets all his thrills from this. This could just be an outlet for him or it could be what he lives for. Either way, we know he possesses little to no empathy."

"Family?" Liam asks.

"It's a toss-up. Some people can fake it well enough to keep a family as a cover. Others are more the loner type. It's difficult to say."

"Speaking of statistics, any luck with Zara?"

The waiter comes back over but I haven't even had a chance to look at the menu yet. "Two coffees, black," I tell him. As soon as he's gone I lean back in. "Nothing yet. I sent her all the cases your dad pulled for us, hopefully that will help. But from the way she was talking, finding some way to track this guy is going to be a long shot."

"You never know, she's resourceful."

"She's also doing it without Wallace's knowledge. Her and Elliott both. I just hope they manage to come up with some-thing. Otherwise, I don't know where to go from here."

"You mean you don't think poor Mrs. Havens had millions

of dollars socked away in her mattress that were worth killing over?"

"At least that would make sense," I reply. I hate it when I can't understand something. Not that I think I'm smarter than anyone else; of course there are subjects that are beyond me. Like quantum physics. But this…*this* I should be able to get, and I just can't wrap my mind around it. I've built a career on watching and observing people, understanding what makes them tick. And whatever is driving our unsub has thus far eluded me. Mostly I want to catch him just so I can shake the answer out of him, though given his level of intelligence, I doubt he'd tell me. He'd probably think it was all part of some game.

Who knows how long this guy has been operating, exploiting the fact that none of these departments ever talk to each other. Just going out every week—

"Hang on a second," I say. "What was the date of Cummings' death?"

"Uh…seven, fifteen, eighteen?" Liam says, trying to recall Jill's report.

"And Mrs. Havens?"

"September fourteenth, twenty-nineteen."

I think back. "Josh Newsome was on the twenty-seventh. And Bill Crease was twelve-twenty-six," I say, pulling out my phone. I check each of the dates against the calendar. "They were all on weekends."

"That's not too unusual, right?" he asks.

"But if I'm right, and this guy is average, it means he probably works a nine to five. Which means he typically has weekends off, freeing him up to go out do some killing."

"Yeah, that fits," he says.

The waiter returns again but I wave him off. I don't want to lose my train of thought. "If he's only killing people on the weekends, that means he's got more time to get it done. He doesn't have to be in a rush."

"Just like a hunter," Liam adds. "Some of them will sit in those blinds for twelve hours or better, waiting on the perfect kill."

"What if that's what he's doing? Just waiting until the perfect victim comes along? Say he finishes his workday on Friday. He spends the rest of the evening prepping for the weekend. Then he heads out early Saturday morning, on the hunt. That means he has the entire rest of the weekend to get his fix in. To get his 'trophy'."

"But none of the victims were missing anything. He's not taking trinkets from the bodies."

"No, he's not. It's in his head. He doesn't need a physical representation of the kill. It's the kill itself, the thrill of taking the life where he gets off. If he brought anything back it would only serve to incriminate him. And he's smart. Smarter than most."

Liam sits back in the booth. "Wow, Em. That's a lot."

"Tell me about it. But it fits, right?"

"I think it does. But then how does he determine where he goes?"

I furrow my brow, thinking for a moment. "If it were me, and I had a stable life somewhere, I wouldn't be hunting anywhere close to where I live. The weekend gives him some leeway to make it a destination trip. Maybe even an overnight or weekend trip. We need more data. We need to find more victims."

"But we already went through all of Dad's files. These two were the most likely candidates."

"I know," I tell him. "We might have no choice but to start going to each county seat and searching through the records ourselves."

"Em, that could take *months*. Wallace will never let us off the hook for that long. Didn't he say he expected you back next week?"

He's right. I don't have a lot of time here. It's not like I can just keep putting off my real job to try and solve this one case. Now if Wallace were to *assign* me to it, officially, then I could take as much time as I wanted. Not that I want to spend months in the Appalachian Mountains hunting for a hunter. But right now it's the only way I can see to narrow down his pattern. The more data points we have the better chance we can figure out where he's coming from. And if we go back far enough, maybe even figure out where he lives. My assumption is he's been at this a while, given how clean everything is. But there was a time when it was his first. And that one *might* have been close to home. Finding that needle is going to be near impossible, though.

"I gotta call Z," I say, pulling out my phone. "This might help her with her bot."

"Right now?" Liam asks, motioning to the waiter we're still not ready.

"Hey, you only get one day off a year and you used that up on Sunday." I shoot him a wink.

"Helloooo," Zara answers on the third ring.

"I have a theory," I tell her.

"Hit me with it." I go about explaining everything that Liam and I just talked through, along with all of the information we have so far from our four possible victims. Coupling that with the files Mr. Coll pulled, I'm hopeful some of this will help.

"Yeah, that's good info, Em, thanks," Zara says. "Elliott and I have been working on the bot as often as we can and we think we've got something working, but it's not going to be perfect."

"That's just unacceptable," I tell her, though I can't help but grin.

"Whaddaya mean it's unacceptable?" she bellows. "We just put this whole thing—oh, wait. You're messing with me. Emily Slate actually messing with *me* for once? Who *are* you?"

I shrug, even though she can't see it. "I dunno. I just had a really good weekend."

"I can tell," she replies. "Tell 'the weekend' hi from me. We're gonna test run this thing in the next few hours, I'll call you with the results."

"Thanks, Z. You're a lifesaver."

"I know it," she replies before hanging up.

"Okay," I tell Liam. "I think it's gonna help. *Now* we can eat."

"Finally," he says. "I'm starving."

Chapter Twenty-Three

AFTER GRABBING a bite to eat we head back to Stillwater and spend the rest of the afternoon pouring over the cases again. Jill arrives back and joins us, our hope being that with the three of us working we'll find an angle we hadn't seen before. We decide not to limit ourselves to the cases Mr. Coll found; those are just the tip of the iceberg and not all of them were viable options. I'm convinced there are more victims out there, it's just a matter of identifying them. And until Zara tells me her little experiment has worked, we need to do this the old-fashioned way.

Surprisingly, I actually like Sergeant Jill Hubbard a lot. She's competent, fair, and even-keeled. I do my best not to compare myself to her, but part of me can't help it. And I have to give Liam credit, he doesn't let their past relationship get in the way of the case. They're both more professional about it than a lot of people I know, which is never a bad thing. I've never had to work with an ex before, though I'm sure if I did, it wouldn't be easy.

By the time evening rolls around we're all beat without having made much headway. My eyes are blurry from reading so much text and Liam looks like he's about to collapse. We bid Jill a good night and are on the way back to the hotel when Liam starts feeling around in his shoulder bag.

"Shit, I think we have a problem."

"What?" I ask.

"I think I left my refills at my parents' house," he replies. "I thought they were in my bag here, but I don't see them."

"They couldn't be in your carry-on in the hotel?"

"I never put them in there," he says. "In case I needed them close. I thought I grabbed them the other day when I got the rest of my stuff, but I must have missed them."

I let out a long, frustrated breath. "Guess that means we need to make a detour."

"I'll be in and out in less than a minute," he says.

I grumble, then turn the car around and head back for his parent's house. It's already dark again, so all we're greeted by is the light at the end of the driveway and the ones on the end of the garage.

I pull up behind his mother's Subaru while Liam jumps out, headed for the front door. I tap the steering wheel nervously while I wait. Except, when the door opens again, it's not Liam. It's Brianna Coll, wrapping herself in a heavy shawl as she makes her way out to the car.

"Goddammit," I mutter under my breath. Should've known I couldn't get out of here without another encounter with the woman. I figured after her abrupt exit at dinner the other night I probably wouldn't see her again. But she's obviously interested in seeing me.

"Emily," she says before I can even get out of the car. It's chilly out, but I don't expect this will take long.

"Good evening, Mrs. Coll. Aren't you cold?"

"Am I to understand you're making Liam work while he's supposed to be on bed rest?"

This again. "No, Mrs. Coll. I'm not *making* Liam do anything. I'm working the Newsome case and I can't stop him if he wants to help." Though I can't help but think about how often he's using that inhaler.

"He really shouldn't be doing that. He needs to stay home and rest. Otherwise, he's never going to get better."

I let out a long breath. "Mrs. Coll, I understand where you're coming from. But I can't make Liam do anything anymore than you can. I can't imagine what you've gone through. I don't have kids, so I don't know what losing one of them would be like." She stiffens, her eyes going wide. "But I know it can't have been easy, and you probably live with that pain every day. But Liam is not Gerry. And you can't control him. You can't stop bad things from happening to people, just like you can't stop good things. People have to be allowed to live their own lives."

She is visibly trembling, though I'm not sure if it's from the cold or if it's from fury. Either way, it's probably not good. "How *dare* you speak his name," she growls. "You didn't know my son, don't try to use my loss against me. I only want my family to be safe, secure. How could I ever expect someone who has no family to understand that?" She turns and walks away as Liam is coming back out the door, a small bag in his hand. Though I barely notice it; my entire system feels like it's gone into shock.

"Mom, what are you doing?" Liam asks.

"Come with me, you're going to get some rest," she says, reaching for him, but he pulls away.

Then he sees my face. "What did you say to her?" he demands.

"Nothing I'm sure she hasn't heard a thousand times before," Mrs. Coll replies. It's as if I'm watching this whole scenario play out from somewhere above. Like I have left my body elsewhere and am a casual observer of the universe, detached from everything.

"Em," Liam says, rushing over. "What did she say? Are you okay?"

My soul slams back into my body and my breath hitches, but I keep it together. "It was nothing," I say, though it barely escapes my lips. "I…need to get back to the hotel."

"Dammit, Mom," Liam says. "I've put up with this long enough. Gerry's death wasn't anyone's fault. It was a freak accident. They happen. Stop trying to push your pain off on everyone else. We all miss him. Me, especially. But that doesn't mean I lash out at people I care about."

"Liam, you don't know what you're saying," she replies.

"No, I do. Maybe I was blinded before, in more ways than one. But I see everything very clearly now." He turns back to me. "Here, get in the passenger seat. I'll drive us back."

"*Liam,*" his mother admonishes. "Don't you dare leave me here like this."

I get in the passenger side, feeling like a zombie where I'm not fully in control of my own movements. Mrs. Coll's words have struck something deep inside me and I don't feel like myself at all.

"This is your own doing," Liam calls back. "When you're ready to act like a civilized person, you know how to find me." He gets in and slams the door shut before backing the car out of the driveway. "Are you okay?"

"Yeah…I…uh, I'll be fine," I say, though her words keep echoing in my head. *How could I ever expect someone who has no family to understand?*

Someone who has no family.

No family.

I turn, covering my mouth and doing everything I can to will the sensation back down. This shouldn't be affecting me like this. I've heard ten times worse from perps all day long and it doesn't bother me a bit. So why now? Why am I having such a hard time controlling myself now?

"Em…" Liam says, rubbing my shoulder, but I keep my face turned away from him, my features pinched together. I don't want him to see how much this hurts. "I'm so sorry about her. There is no excuse for whatever she said to you. She can be an extremely cruel person when she wants to be."

"It's fine," I manage to say, though it's taking considerable willpower not to crumple into a ball right now.

"It's not, but I understand if you don't want to talk about it. Just know that she doesn't really mean it; she's hurt and scared and is afraid she's going to lose everyone she ever loved because she can't control what we do. I grew up hearing that voice all the time. When you're ready, I'll be here." His hand moves off my shoulder and I hear him messing with something in his lap, then I hear the telltale sound of him inhaling his lung medicine.

I am being so selfish. Liam is the one who is in the middle here. And why should it matter what Mrs. Coll says to me? It's not like she's *my* mother. Maybe because I'm dealing with all these stupid letters it's just beginning to strike a nerve.

Wiping my eyes quickly, I turn back to face the road. "It's fine. Just got…overemotional there for a minute."

"Are you sure?" he asks.

I don't want him to deal with more of my shit; he's done enough of that in the past. Especially not when he still needs to heal. "Yeah. Don't worry about it."

Chapter Twenty-Four

AFTER A RESTLESS NIGHT'S SLEEP, we head back to the station again to keep up the search. Even though I tried taking something to help me sleep better, it was still broken and difficult. I kept waking up, thinking it was time to get up already. I know that means my mind is running too hot, that there's too much bouncing around up there.

After the confrontation with Liam's mother and the events of the day, I had hoped sleep would have come easily. But as soon as I was up, I knew it was going to be one of those days where I'm gonna need a couple extra cups of coffee just to make it through.

The good news is I feel more like myself this morning. I don't know *what* that was last night, but I never want to go through it again. Even though I'm tired, at least I'm still me. And I think continuing to focus on the case will be a big help.

As we're driving back to Stillwater's police station, my phone buzzes and I see it's Zara.

"Morning," I say, as her face comes up on the screen. I lock my phone to the dash so we can both see. "I hope you have good news."

She's right down to business. "Two things. First, Timber

kicked me in his sleep last night. Like he was running some-where. Never done that before so it was weird. Second, Elliott and I stayed late at the office last night after everyone else had gone home and ran the simulation based on all the data you gave me. Guess what? I think we've got something."

I pull the car into a nearby parking lot and throw it in park. "You're kidding."

"Not this time. Based on the parameters you set and using Mr. Coll's cases as a learning tool, we were able to program the bot to scour the web for any mentions of strange deaths that might fit the profile. I limited it to the states of Virginia, West Virginia, Maryland, and Pennsylvania. And, Em, you're not going to believe this."

"Don't make me beg," I say. "Just tell us."

She purses her lips. "*Someone* is grumpy this morning."

"*Someone* didn't get a lot of sleep last night."

"Oh, we didn't did we?" she asks, arching an eyebrow and shooting a glance at Liam. "I don't see how that's a problem."

"Z, come on," I say.

"Wow, you really *didn't* sleep well? Okay, here, look at this." Her face disappears from the screen and it's replaced with a map of the states she mentioned. There are red dots all over the map, though a large number of them are clustered around our area, including the places we've already visited. Staunton, Warm Springs, and Strasburg.

"Is that—" I begin.

"Yep, it's an anomaly," she replies. "No way this is random, and it doesn't match with any other geographical region. Someone has been using that area for their own means, it looks like."

"Can you send this to me?" I ask.

"Like you have to ask, it's already in your email. Along with links to each of the reported deaths on the map." Her face reappears. "Come on, admit it. It's impressive."

"Damn right it is, I can't believe you actually got it to work."

"Well," she says. "It's not perfect. I'd say you have about a ten to fifteen percent margin of error. So don't swear by it."

I shoot Liam a quick look. "Margin of error? That doesn't sound like the Zara I know."

"Hey! I don't think it's going too far to say the fact we got it to work at all—oh, wait. You're messing with me again." She turns so she's looking at Liam. "What have you done with my best friend?"

He laughs. "Honestly I'm a little scared myself."

"Maybe I'm just finally learning how to relax," I tell both of them, though the incident from last night flashes through my head again. I stuff it back down.

"Well, whatever the reason I'm not complaining," Zara says. "Also, I think you owe me for pulling this together for you. How do you feel about open mic night at the Roxbury?"

"Never in a million years," I say without hesitation.

"*There's* the Emily I know," she replies. "Just checking. Take a look at the data, let me know if you have any questions. Otherwise, good luck."

"Z, you're a lifesaver," I say. "Thank you."

"Don't worry, I'll find some way you can repay me." She winks and then the picture is gone. I pull my phone back off the cradle and check my email. Sure enough, there's the link for the file from Zara.

"Despite that sounding more ominous than it probably should have, I think this will really help."

"Do you think it will be more accurate than the files my dad pulled?"

"I hope so, considering we only found a few of those to be possibilities. But this could give us that extra data we've been looking for. A way to pinpoint him and figure out his patterns." I back the car up and return to the main road, headed for the police station.

"Do you still think we should leave Mrs. Havens's case in the rotation?" he asks.

"I know the ballistics don't match, but I don't want to rule her out just yet. Not until we get a look at these other incidents."

Five minutes later we're back at the station where I can sit down and go through Zara's findings in depth. The link she sent over leads to the same map we saw earlier. It looks as if she's copied over a live map and just plotted the data on top of it. And now that I can get a better look at all the individual incidents, we're looking at almost fifty different people who have died.

"We're right in the middle of the storm," Liam says, pointing to Stillwater on the map. Little red dots surround the county, though not in all directions.

"I wouldn't say middle, exactly." Instead of a circular area around any one particular town or city, which is what I would have assumed initially, the majority of the dots seem to follow along the I-81 corridor, clustering near the north, and tapering off at the south. There are plenty of other dots deep in the nearby states, though I'm not considering those right now. My focus is on the primary cluster.

"You said if it were you, you wouldn't be killing where you lived," Liam says. "Considering these deaths more or less follow a line, where does that leave us?"

I stand by my original statement. Why kill people around your hometown, especially if you were trying to make them look like accidents? That would only bring more suspicion. No, he's spread these out, but maybe not as randomly as he thinks. I point to Stillwater, where one red dot represents Josh Newsome. I then drag my finger down as the dots become more numerous before dissipating again, my finger following the interstate. I stop down where there are no dots at all.

"Here." The city of Roanoke sits right off the I-81 corridor. Further south is Christiansburg, and further than that, Pulaski. "I think he's coming from somewhere around here."

"But that's nowhere close to where the kills are taking place."

"Exactly," I say. "Look at what's *not* in this area. Red dots. That's as strange as a bunch of them being up in the northern part of the state. All things being equal, if these *were* accidents, there should be an even distribution across the entire area. But there are *two* anomalies here. A concentration in the north and an absence in the south. He's leaving his home turf clean. And in doing so, pointing an arrow directly at himself."

"So why keep going to the same area each time? Doesn't that make it more likely to be found out?"

"Not if the departments don't talk to each other. And keep in mind, this is over a five-year period. *And* there's a good chance not all of these are him. But I'd bet a lot are. The interstate provides quick and easy access to a different part of the state. It gets him out of his home area, and it allows him to do his dirty work and come back without the need to go too far." I almost have to chuckle. "Despite all his attempts, he's still a creature of habit." I was wrong about him. He's not unlike most other killers. He just happens to have much more patience than most of them. "We need to start looking at all these deaths." I glance over at Liam. "Okay with Jill helping out some more?"

"Doesn't bother me," he replies. I really admire that about him. If there is one thing for certain, Liam is not about drama.

"Great, let's find her and get started."

Chapter Twenty-Five

WE SPEND the better part of the day sifting through the information. Zara has done some good work, pulling all this together for us. Each of the dots on the maps corresponds with either an open case, or a news article. The hard part, just like with Mr. Coll's files, is sifting through them to find which ones are genuine articles.

Thankfully, Chief Salazar is more than happy to allow Sergeant Hubbard to continue helping now that the weather crisis has died down and we're making good progress. She's quick, thorough, and doesn't waste time on cases that aren't matches. But there's so much to sort through I almost want to ask Salazar to bring Mr. Coll back in, just to spread the work around.

Unfortunately, it's slow going and I find myself lost in the details of the work, looking for any commonalities between victims. More often than not we're working with incomplete information, so I spend a lot of time on the phone with other departments, trying to figure out how much they know. Even though we'd probably get more information driving to all these places and pulling the files ourselves, it's too much legwork for three people. It's like sifting through a mountain, looking for one particular rock that resembles a couple of other rocks you've collected. Sometimes rocks will look similar, but aren't really the same on the inside.

I think this is what the killer was counting on if anyone ever picked up his trail. Even with Zara and Elliott's work compiling all this information, it's almost too dense for three people to get through. We might as well go out and start randomly interviewing the populace, though I have to believe we're going to find what we're looking for eventually.

At some point in the afternoon, Jill leaves. But it doesn't register to me until she's been gone a solid hour and I haven't seen her back yet.

"Did we lose one?" I ask, looking over the report of a Mr. Robert Bulwarth of Winchester, Virginia.

Liam looks up and I can see his eyes are bloodshot. "Yeah, I guess we did." He checks his watch. "We've been going for almost nine hours straight."

I pull out my phone and check the time, partially out of reflex. "Damn. I didn't realize." It's already late afternoon, though the station is still buzzing with activity.

"Oh, here," Liam says. "She sent me a text about half an hour ago. She was getting a migraine, went to lie down and will be back when she can."

"Yeah, I'm feeling one of those coming on myself," I say, closing the window and going to the next file. It's a possible match, but there's so little information about the man's death that it's gonna take a few calls with Winchester Police to fill in all the holes. My throat is sore from talking on the phone so much and right now I just don't have the energy to make any more calls.

"Break time?"

"Why don't we go over what we have first, then take a break," I say. "We need an opening here somewhere. Something that points us to this man."

"Em, you know that's not very likely."

"Maybe not, but it's in here somewhere. He's out there causing all this. On purpose. That leaves a mark. Maybe it's buried under an ocean of paperwork, but there is a clue in all of this that will get us to him. We just have to find it."

"And if we can't?" he asks.

That's not something I like to consider. It's not like I have a perfect record on cases; far from it. There are probably two dozen cases back at the FBI with my name on them that are still open, pending further investigation upon the receipt of more information. But the sad truth is most of those will end up as cold cases, unless something miraculous happens. This could be one of those times as well, and I might have to leave Stillwater in the same state I found it: with a killer on the loose and no way to track them.

I'm not ashamed to admit that those cases I can't close eat away at me. I always think there was something more I could have done, something I missed when in fact, more often than not, there just isn't enough information for *anyone* to solve them. It's a hard reality of the job; one that doesn't sit well with me. Which is why I kill myself, or very nearly try, doing everything I can to make sure the cases I work are exhausted. I may have a bunch of unsolved that have come through my possession, but what I *don't* have is a record of other agents picking up the slack and solving a case I worked on because I missed something.

At least I can say that much.

Liam groans as he pulls his chair away from the desk and faces me, a stack of freshly printed papers in his lap. "Sometimes you can be torture, you know."

"Quit whining and give me what you've got," I tell him.

"Sixteen cases so far, though I only have complete information on about half of them," he says, shuffling through the papers.

"How many match the shooting style and M.O.?"

"All but two."

"Discard those two," I say. "How many of the remaining match the ballistics?"

"Four," he replies. "But one of them isn't sure because the bullet wasn't fully recovered and another couldn't confirm the coroner's work because the coroner had to be let go for drinking on the job." He hands the remaining two papers to me.

I scan them over quickly. As best I can tell they're a match. I stand up, head to the corkboard at the end of the room where we've put up a paper map, marking it with pins that we *know* belong to this killer. There's already one for Josh Newsome and Bill Crease. As well as Willa Havens. I put two more pins up for Liam's two victims in the locations where they were found.

Stepping back, I look at the map. It's a lot less impressive than the one Zara sent over. And so far, there's no pattern.

"So you have twelve more that are maybes," I say, still thinking about how odd Mrs. Havens's case was, even though the ballistics didn't match. "Do any of your remaining cases share a weapon type?"

He flips through the pages. "I've only got five more where they positively identified the weapon used," he replies. "Three of them were identified as a Browning X-Bolt."

I turn around, my hands on my hips. "That's odd, isn't it?"

"I'm not sure, I don't know anything about the gun," he replies. I screw up my features and head back to my computer, looking up the weapon.

"Says here it's not that common," I say, reading off the manufacturer's site. "Not a lot of hunters use it because it's expensive. But it gets the job done." I turn back to him. "According to them, anyway."

I return back to the map, grabbing a set of blue pins. "Give me the locations where those three were killed."

"Buena Vista, Glen Wilton, Montebello," he says.

I take a step back. "Did Bath County have a weapon type on the bullet that killed Mrs. Havens?"

"Hang on," he says, shuffling some papers as I stare at the map. The three blue pins stand out at me. They're not as far north as some of the other sites, and they have a relative cluster of their own.

"Just says Browning on here," Liam says. "Doesn't specify."

I take a blue pin and place it on Warm Springs, then step back again. The pins almost form a "V" shape, and the tip of the letter points directly south.

I head back over and scan my computer for the files that I've confirmed are our killer, using the ballistics match and the M.O. Returning to the map I place three more red pins.

"What do you see?" I ask, stepping back again.

"Looks like blue further south, and red further north," Liam replies.

I nod. There's not one red pin south of the blue ones. "He changed weapons. And when he did that, he started moving further away from where he lived. Get me the dates on all these," I say.

Liam pulls up the individual dates for each of the blue pins. All of them correspond to deaths that occurred more than eighteen months ago. All the red pins correspond to deaths that have happened in the time since.

"Mrs. Havens was his last before he switched," I say, tapping her pin on the map. "Something changed. Maybe he got spooked, maybe he knew he needed to switch things up before someone caught on. And he started operating in a wider area. While these are more tightly clustered…" I make a circle on the map around the blue pins. "…the rest are more spread out. He's learning as he goes, adjusting to make it harder to track him."

"How does that help us?" Liam asks.

"It tells us when he changed his weapon," I say. "And if it

was a Browning X-Bolt that killed Mrs. Havens, then we need to start calling some gun shops."

"You really think he would have sold it?"

I smile. "Remember, this guy is your average joe. He's not a millionaire. And if what I read on their website is true, this is an expensive gun. He couldn't afford to just throw it away or destroy it. Especially if he needed another one. My bet is he traded in for a different model."

"Then we're looking for a Browning X-Bolt," Liam says.

I nod.

He sighs in response. "I guess this means no break."

UNFORTUNATELY, I SHOULD HAVE LISTENED TO LIAM. AFTER calling over fifty gun stores in the area, we're no closer to finding our weapon than we were when we started. None of the owners had any record of anyone purchasing or selling a Browning X-Bolt. Even though I want to keep going, the stores have all closed and my stomach is rumbling so loud I'm sure Liam can hear it.

Once again, we're the only ones left in the station and after a straight day of nothing but investigation, my eyes feel like they're about to fall out of their sockets. I stand up, my body sore and aching; if it hurts this much now what's it going to be like in another ten years? No wonder so many agents retire early.

Liam looks more peaked, like he hasn't had enough to drink. Again, I've been pushing him too hard. And I know him well enough that he's doing it because he doesn't want to disappoint me and he doesn't want to admit he isn't capable. He might not be about some drama, but Liam does have a lot of pride in himself.

"Okay, I'm calling it," I say. "We need a hearty dinner and about twelve hours of sleep."

"I won't argue with that," he replies.

"Know of a good place for dinner?"

"How about somewhere with food to go?" he says. "I'm not sure I can stay awake for dinner."

I smile. "Yeah, works for me." Liam is too polite to say it, but that's his way of letting me know he is absolutely out of gas. Wasn't the whole point of me coming up here to help him recover and get better? And instead here I am running him ragged as we try to track this guy down.

Once we're back in the car with the heat going, I decide to broach the subject. "Tomorrow, I want you to take the day off. Stay in the hotel room, rest. Relax. I can handle this for myself for a while."

"But it will take you longer," he says.

"Doesn't matter. You're not doing yourself any favors by trying to prove to me how tough you are."

"Like you don't do the same thing," he says.

I furrow my brow and he brings one finger to my neck, just barely touching the mark hidden under a half-pound of coverup from my close encounter in Bellefleur. *Damn.*

"Were you ever going to tell me?" he asks.

"I didn't want you to worry," I say. "You were in the hospital, having almost died. The last thing you needed on your mind was my problems."

"How close was it?" he asks.

I let out a long breath, but decide not to answer.

"That close, huh?" He pauses a moment. "Emily, this isn't going to work if we can't be honest with each other. You are going to *have* to trust me to handle things. Even when they're bad things that happen to you."

I shake my head. "I just couldn't. There have just been so many close calls lately. That whole mess in Fairview where I nearly got my face caved in, Bellefleur and even the whole thing with the Organization. It feels like I'm in the hospital every other week. I didn't want you to deal with that again. I've already put you through enough."

"Maybe that should tell you something about how hard you've been going these past few months," he replies. "I remember you saying once the Organization had been dismantled you were going to start taking it easy. That things would calm down. But, if anything, you're working harder now than ever. When was the last time you even saw Timber?"

"That's not fair," I say. "We both just had a really nice day off on Sunday. Wasn't that me taking some time?"

"Were you thinking about the case while we were off?"

I bite my lip before responding. "Actually, I wasn't. For the first time, I didn't feel like I needed to."

We're quiet for a few moments. "You know, your tenacity is one of the things I love the most about you," he says. "But it's also what drives you to push yourself harder than necessary."

I try to smile, but it's just not there. "I don't know how to be any other way. How am I supposed to act when I'm faced with these situations? Or with something like these damn letters, which have now endangered your life as well? I can't just walk away from that."

"I know." He reaches over and takes my hand. "I just don't want to lose you because of it."

I'm not sure if he means he'd leave me one day because I have always put work first, or if he thinks going this hard is eventually going to get me killed. And honestly, it doesn't matter. The message itself is clear. I need to pull back, or else I might lose everything I hold dear.

"I hear you," I say. "But I don't know if I can change who I am."

"I don't want you to change who you are," he says. "I just want you to know you don't have to prove anything to anyone. Sometimes it's like you're fighting against this invisible force, that only you can see. That if maybe you fight just a little bit harder, *then* you'll finally get what you want.

"There will always be a case out there, or someone who likes to hurt other people. Or a killer on the loose. You can't solve them all, and you can't save the world, not on your own. I guess what I'm saying is, it's okay to let go every once in a while."

Let go. I've had those same thoughts myself from time to time. And while sometimes it feels like that's possible, most of the time it feels like letting go means I'll fall to my death.

"Hey," he says, rubbing the back of my hand with his thumb. "I'm here. You're not alone in this. You have me, and Zara. And probably Wes too if he can stop being a dumbass."

I smile. "How did this conversation become about me? We were talking about *you* working too much."

"I just needed you to see that you, of all people, don't need to be lecturing others on how hard they work," he says, grinning.

"Oh, is that so? Well, maybe the lesson here is that if *I*, the consummate workaholic am telling *you* to slow down, then you have already seriously overworked *yourself*."

He arches an eyebrow. "Am I crazy or are we telling each other the same thing here?"

"Maybe we should both learn to take our own advice," I offer.

"I will if you will," he says, holding out his fist for a bump.

"Deal," I reply, bumping him back.

Chapter Twenty-Six

SOMETIMES IT FEELS like this work is never going to end. We ended up going for Italian last night, which was so filling it put me in a food coma and I really did sleep almost ten hours before waking back up first thing this morning, ready to hit the case again.

But we've already been at it another hour and all I can see is the wall of information in front of me, blocking me from seeing who is behind it all. I still don't have anything other than circumstantial evidence on this guy, and I think he wants it that way. But I can worry about proving his guilt later. First, I need to find him.

Thankfully, Liam took my advice and has decided to stay out of the station today. He said he might try to go patch things up with his mother, or at least get her to patch things up with me. But I told him not to bother, there's nothing that woman can give me that I want. Honestly, I'd rather not have to deal with her again and I can't help but think the feeling is mutual.

After an hour of phone calls to even more gun stores, I can already feel the burnout looming. Maybe Liam is right; this case might not be solvable. At least, not with the information we currently have. Usually I have a handhold to grab, something that helps me figure out where the case is going. But this has been unique.

I think what irks me most of all is the fact he knows he can't be caught. Not without royally screwing up. If I were him, I don't think I'd be worried about the police at all. He probably doesn't even keep up with the news on these people. For some reason I get the feeling like when he makes a kill, that's what does it for him. He doesn't need to see the results of what he's done. He's gotten what he's needed. Unlike a normal serial killer who will often want to watch the gruesome aftermath, or at least see the terror and fear he's inspired. This guy cares for none of that. To him, it's no different than going out and hunting an animal.

He takes his time setting up. He gets himself into position. Then he waits for the perfect moment. And when he pulls the trigger—

My phone buzzes in my pocket, bringing me out of my thoughts.

"Slate," I say.

"Yeah, uh, hi. This is Rick Parker down at Mountain Arms and Weapons. We spoke on the phone yesterday."

"Right, how are you, Mr. Parker?" I ask, though I honestly don't remember. I spoke to so many gun shop owners I can't recall a one of them.

"Good, good," he says. "I was thinkin' about that Browning X-Bolt you were lookin' for. We haven't bought one of those, but I do have a buddy who got one a while back in a private sale."

I perk up. "Really? When?"

"Not sure. I just remember seein' it on his wall the last time I was over at his place. Me and him go out huntin' turkeys sometimes. But it's been the better part of a year since we last went."

Which means he's had the gun for more than a year, I think. "Mr. Parker, can you give me the name of your friend?"

"Sure, it's Nathanial Beltran. But everybody just calls 'em Nate."

"Do you know who sold him the weapon?" I ask.

"No clue. I jus' happened to remember it when I was sittin' on the couch last night watchin' Jeopardy. I got my rack above my TV and I remembered that Nate has his set up that way too and then I recalled seein' that gun and asking him about it. But like I said, it's been a while. He might not have it anymore."

"Do you happen to remember Mr. Beltran's address?" I ask.

"Yep," he replies and rattles it off. "He don't live too far. Just haven't seen him in a while."

"Thank you, Mr. Parker," I say, jotting down all the information. "Can I call you back if I have any additional questions?"

"Sure, sure," he replies. "But I dunno how much more help I can be."

I thank the man again and hang back up. So far everyone I've spoken to doesn't have a record of buying a Browning. Though it's a relatively rare gun. And if our killer wasn't willing to destroy the weapon as I assume he wasn't, then it would make a lot more sense to sell it in a private sale rather than to a public shop, to prevent someone like me from doing exactly what I've been doing.

Damn, this guy is not making this easy. But Mr. Parker's information has at least given me a potential lead. After all the sifting through cases we've done on this one so far, it feels like a big relief off my shoulders to have *something* to go off.

I look at the address. It's in a town called Bedford, Virginia. I've never been there, but it's not that far from my own hometown of Fairview. Still, I mostly stuck to the center of the state when I was young; I never ventured over this far west, not until I was in college. But it will be strange to head back in that direction again.

I grab my coat and head for the door.

∼

IT'S A TWO-AND-A-HALF-HOUR DRIVE TO BEDFORD, AND I reach the town just before lunch. It's a quaint little place, with a cute downtown, though a lot of the businesses look permanently closed. I pass a couple of signs pointing to local monuments and see the National D-Day Memorial is here, which I'm sure helps the town with tourism.

But I'm not here to sightsee, and I instead head for Mr. Beltran's address.

The house sits at the very end of a neighborhood where the road is barely large enough for one car, much less two. It's a dark brick house, one-story, though it looks relatively new. The lawn is manicured and there are some children's toys in the side yard, which is bound by a wooden fence. A gray Acura sits in the driveway. The road the house sits on continues along, but there's a sign not far past Mr. Beltran's home that designates the road as private property. I pull my car over to the side and park parallel to the home.

Considering it's still late afternoon on a Thursday, I don't really expect him to be home, but I have to start somewhere. I make my way up the short driveway and knock on the door, taking a few steps back with my badge at the ready.

A moment later the door opens to reveal a woman in her mid-forties. She's wearing what look like spandex pants and a halter top, and her blonde hair is pulled up and back. "Yes?" she asks.

"Good morning, is this the home of Nathaniel Beltran?" I hold up my badge.

"FBI? What do you want with Nate?" the woman asks. She has a pronounced accent; one I recognize from my youth.

"I need to ask him about a weapon he may have purchased about eighteen months ago," I say. "A Browning X-Bolt?"

"Oh, lawd," the woman says. "Come on in." She holds the door open for me and I enter the house. Wood paneling lines the hallway and the floor seems to be either laminate or linoleum, I can't tell. "I told Nate one day he was gonna get in trouble for all these damn guns he collects."

"How many does he have?" I ask, following the woman into the house.

"Hell if I know. But he acts like they're gonna stop makin' them or something." When we enter the living room I see what she means. No less than four gun racks hang on the walls, each of them full of six guns apiece. I know my weapons, but there are a lot here.

"Is this all of them?" I ask.

"Hell, no. There's another bedroom full in the back."

My mind goes to the children's toys I saw in the yard. "You have children?" I ask.

"Yes, but don't worry. They're all unloaded. I make sure of that, at least."

I shoot a glance back down the hallway. We passed a closed door on the way in. "Even in the back?"

She nods. "And I make him keep the ammunition out of reach. I ain't about to become one of those stories on the news where the kids got ahold of a gun and shot themselves or somebody else."

I nod, taking my time going around the room and looking at all the weapons in turn. "What does your husband do?" I ask.

"He works over at the milling plant. Has for years. He's usually gone by seven and not back until six at night."

"Kids at school?" I ask.

"Yes, thank God," she replies, sitting in one of the seats around a small table by the kitchen. "I don't know what I'm gonna do when summer rolls around. Those two take more than I can handle some days."

I spot the Browning up on the rack above the TV. Right where Mr. Parker said it would be. "Do you mind if I take that one down?" I ask, pointing to the weapon.

Mrs. Beltran screws up her face. "Well, maybe I should call Nate first. He doesn't like anyone messing with his guns," she says. I get the distinct feeling Nate isn't going to be very happy about an FBI agent in his house, looking at his "arsenal". And while this amount of weaponry is alarming, that's not what I'm here for. I just want this one gun. If I can prove this weapon is a match to some of our victims, then we'll finally have something solid.

"Let me just call him real quick," she says, pulling out her phone.

"Mrs. Beltran," I say before she can dial. "I'm not interested in your husband in any capacity. But we do believe he purchased that weapon from someone who may have used it illegally. It would be a big help to me if I could take the weapon for testing. I promise you will get it back."

She pinches her features and I can see there might even be a little fear in her eyes. She's not used to going against her husband's wishes. I can't help but start to wonder if there is something more sinister happening at the Beltran house. She flaps her empty hand at me, like I'm an errant fly. "Lemme just call real quick. It won't take but a second."

How bad would it be if I just took the weapon? It isn't like she could stop me. But I can't exactly go around illegally seizing someone's property, especially when it's a firearm. Talk about a shitstorm, given the climate around weapons nowadays. I can just imagine the headlines now. That's not a snake pit I want to get in the middle of.

"Hey, hon. Just callin' to let you know there's a lady here from the FBI. She wants one of your guns for—" Before she can even finish the sentence, a string of obscenities comes out the other end.

"I know, I know, I told her you didn't—well, I just let her in because—what do you mean? She's not doing anything, just —okay, okay, just be careful." She hangs up, giving me a sheepish look. "He'll be here in a few minutes. The plant isn't far."

It takes a lot of willpower not to roll my eyes. "I think it's probably best if I wait outside."

Chapter Twenty-Seven

I'M SITTING on the Beltran's porch when I see the truck come rumbling down the one-lane road. It's a black pickup, but I can't tell that it's a Dodge until it's a lot closer. Even from my vantage point on the porch I can see the man driving is red-faced and intense. I stand as he pulls in the driveway, and I make sure my hands are out and visible before he even gets out of the car.

"Mr. Beltran," I say.

"Jus' what in the hell do you think you're doin' on my property?" he yells back, storming out of his vehicle, leaving it running with the door open.

"A friend of yours, Rick Parker told me you might be able to help us out with a case," I say.

The mention of Mr. Parker and the word "help" seem to calm him for a moment. "What?"

I show him my badge. "My name is Agent Slate. Can we go inside and discuss this?"

"Discuss what, exactly?" he demands.

"I am investigating a case that might have involved a weapon you purchased eighteen months ago. I would like your permission to take the weapon for testing, to see if it matches the bullets we've recovered."

"And open myself up to the federal government coming down on my ass, no thank you," he says. "You can just remove yourself from the premises and we'll forget this ever happened."

I take a deep breath. Mr. Beltran smells of motor oil and dirt. He's got on what looks like a mechanic's uniform which covers his regular clothes and his name is stitched on a nametag that adorns his left chest. "If you want me to come back with a warrant, I will."

He pauses. "A warrant?"

"The weapon could be connected to a murder case," I tell him. "Multiple murder cases. We need to find out if it's a match. No amount of stonewalling by you will stop me. All you're doing is delaying things and potentially putting other people's lives in danger."

"I always knew this day was comin'," he says. "My pa warned me. Said one day they'd come for my guns. Well guess what? You're gonna have to pry them from my cold dead hands. Get your warrant."

I huff, placing my hands on my hips. It's the same spiel I've heard a dozen times before, rhetoric nailed into people's heads by cable news stations who are only looking to prop up their profits by scaring people into believing the government is "out to get them".

Maybe I can use that to my advantage.

"Mr. Beltran," I say calmly. "If I come back with a warrant, it isn't going to be for just one weapon. It will be for *all* of them. I will have the ATF seize every weapon you have in that house; do you understand me? And then *each* of them will be subjected to months of analysis. It could be the better part of a year before you see any of them again. Now unless you're willing to kill federal officers to keep that from happening, you are going to be defenseless in your own home for a least a few months." I can see the fear in his eyes as he plays through the scenarios in his head.

"*Or*, you can let me take the *one weapon* I care about, and it will be returned to you when I am done with it."

"And if it comes back a match how do I know you won't just haul me into jail?" he asks.

"Where were you on the night of Saturday the twenty-seventh?" I ask.

"Here, watching TV with my cousin. Dolly was hosting one of her Tupperware parties in the basement."

"Then people saw you here all night," I say.

"Yeah, I don't mind when Dolly has her parties. The view is always better." He says it with a creepy little smile.

Ugh, I think I just threw up a little. "Then you're not who I'm looking for," I say, though I do wish he would keep pushing me. I could find a reason to haul his ass in and I'm not too proud to say it would be *very* satisfying.

"I'm gonna need that in writing," he says.

"Mr. Beltran, I don't have time for this," I say. "Let me take the Browning or I come back with a van of agents. Your choice."

"Oh," he says, screwing up his face. "You want the Browning? The X-Bolt, right? I haven't used that thing since I bought it."

I'm not sure I want to ask what gun he *thought* I was talking about, but I'm willing to bet it's one he didn't exactly get legally. And now I *am* intrigued. "Then you'll let me take it?" I ask.

"Yeah, sure, what do I care?" he says, heading back over to his truck and turning it off.

*For the love of…*God, men can be so frustrating sometimes. I wait for him to head into the house. Mrs. Beltran gets up as soon as she sees him. "Hi, hon, did you—"

"Yeah, it's fine, Dol, we got it worked out." He heads for the weapon.

"Hang on," I tell him. "I'll remove it. You said you haven't used it since you purchased the weapon?"

"Nah, just hung it up and haven't touched it since." I pull on a pair of gloves before removing the weapon from the rack. He's right, there is a thin layer of dust on it. It's possible we might be able to pull an old print, but I'll have to get it back to forensics in Stillwater before I can be sure.

I head back outside and gingerly place the weapon in my backseat, after making sure it's unloaded. Beltran and his wife follow me out. Once I'm sure it's secure, I snap my gloves off and return to them.

"Who did you purchase the weapon from?"

"Old buddy of mine, lives down on Smith Mountain Lake. We used to go hunting together but he's been busy lately."

"Name?"

"Oh, Donald Kincaid. He's a little older than me."

"Do you have his address?" I ask.

"Something Bear Paw Road," he says. "I can't remember exactly." I find Mr. Beltran is being a lot more cooperative now that he doesn't think I'm taking whatever weapon he was talking about earlier. His entire demeanor has changed and his body posture has relaxed. He's definitely not our killer, otherwise he'd be a lot more worried about the Browning in my backseat.

"And when did you purchase it from him?" I ask.

"Well, it wasn't so much a purchase as a trade," he says. "He was lookin' to get rid of it, and I had this Bergara that I hadn't used in a while, so I thought it might be a good one for one."

My ears perk up. "A Bergara? What kind?"

"Uh, B-14, HMR I think."

All of a sudden my heart is thudding in my throat. "And when was this?"

"Around August or September of '19, I think. At the start

of hunting season. He was lookin' to get used to it so we'd take it out and I'd coax him through it."

"But you didn't want to try out the Browning?" I ask.

"Nah, I had this sweet new Stevens I'd just purchased. I used that most of the season. Snagged a ten-point buck with it too."

"Did you purchase the Bergara originally?" I ask.

"Yeah, about a year prior, why?" he asks.

"What kind of ammunition does it take?"

"Well, a few kinds, really. But I was using Hornady seven millimeters with it. I buy a lot of weapons," he almost smiles as he says it. I notice his wife isn't smiling along with him, though.

"All right, thank you Mr. Beltran," I say, putting my phone with the notes away. "Like I said, we'll return this weapon to you when we're done with it."

"Take as long as you want," he says. "Don't need it anytime soon." He's still smiling, but there's something else behind it, something I can't identify. I don't like how quickly he's made this heel turn. But at the same time, I don't want to look a gift horse in the mouth. If his information is accurate, I might have just found the name of our unsub.

As I'm leaving the Beltran's house, I pull out my phone and call Sybil. "I think I might have a hit on the weapon. Can you check the casings from Newsome and Crease to see if they could have come from a Bergara B-14 HMR?"

"Sure," she says on the other end. Her voice is slightly muffled like she's writing it down. "Shouldn't take long."

"Thanks," I tell her and hang up. I dial again, this time to Liam. I know he's supposed to have the day off, but he can do a little recon for me.

"Howdy," he says and I can see he's still in the hotel room in Stillwater. "How's it going?"

"I think I might know who the killer is," I say, my heart pounding as I drive. "I have one of the weapons in my possession. Can you do a background check for me on a Donald Kincaid, lives on Bear Paw Road, off Smith Mountain Lake?"

"Sure," he says. "Or, I can at least call it in. What's the deal?"

"I have the Browning I think we've been looking for in my backseat. I think there's an analysis office nearby in Roanoke. It will save me from coming all the way back up to Stillwater. And we might have a lead on the second weapon."

"Okay, I'll be in touch as soon as I have something on this guy."

"Thanks," I say, pulling out of the small neighborhood and heading back for the main road out of town. My emotions are running high right now coming off what could have been a very bad confrontation *and* the fact I might have just broken this thing wide open, but I can't let that distract me right now. I need to follow the evidence, keep our procedure in place.

But I hate that Liam can't be here with me. "Hey," I say before he hangs up. "I love you."

His entire face breaks out into a huge grin. "I love you too," he replies. "Be in touch soon."

I can't help but smile when I end the call. I don't care if I am all hopped up on adrenaline and endorphins right now, I'm going to ride it for all I've got. I don't get chances like this very often.

As I pull onto route four-sixty, all my thoughts are on getting this weapon processed as fast as possible.

And with any luck I'll get to begin a hunt of my own.

Chapter Twenty-Eight

I'M STANDING in the hallway of the Virginia Department of Forensic Science offices, which are located in a long brick building that's built next to a school in the city of Roanoke. The building shares resources with the Medical Examiners for the surrounding area, so it's an environment I'm familiar with.

After identifying myself and checking the weapon into evidence, I've been out in the hallway waiting for what seems like hours for someone to get back to me. In reality it's probably only been about forty-five minutes, but I can't keep myself from pacing the hallways, anxious to get the process moving.

"Agent Slate," a man dressed in a suit and a white lab coat says as he comes out of a nearby door close to the reception area. "I'm Richard Lynch, Assistant Director." He holds out his hand and I give it a quick shake.

"Pleasure," I say. "Have you had a chance to look at the weapon?"

"I'm afraid it's not that simple," he replies. "Unfortunately, we have a backlog and have been running behind."

"How far behind?" I ask.

"Right now for firearms we're in about a two week turn-around," he says.

"*Two weeks?* This guy is out there now. He just killed someone not more than a week ago. If I wait two weeks I could have more bodies on my hands."

"I understand," he says in that patronizing way that tells me he really doesn't. "But there's nothing I can do."

"The whole reason I came over here in the first place was so I didn't have to drive back up to Stillwater," I tell him. "Did you get the case file from Sybil Crowley?"

He nods. "We did, but—"

"Then you have the ballistics data, yes?" I ask.

"We do, but as—"

"So then all you have to do is compare the striations on the bullets to the ones in the weapon chamber. How difficult is that?"

"It's not that it's difficult," he replies. "But it's like I said, we have about a hundred other weapons—"

"Listen to me," I say, dropping the timbre of my voice. "This man has been out there killing without accountability for *years*. I am *this close* to finding him and you're going to stand here and tell me that an analysis that *I know* takes no more than an hour is going to take you two weeks?"

"Well, it's a bit more complicated—"

"Let me uncomplicate this for you," I tell him. "Unless any of your other cases deal with a killer who is randomly targeting his victims, I suggest you move this to the top of your queue. I have an informant who tells me he doesn't live too far from here. Do you remember how panicked everyone was when those two men started shooting people indiscriminately up in D.C. a few years back?"

He nods. "I was working at the Manassas branch then. I remember it very well."

"Then you'll remember just how unpredictable someone like this is. I need to get him in custody *now*. But in order to do that, I need something that connects him to the murders and right now all I have is that weapon in your possession. Understand?"

His eyebrows form a "V" like he's thinking hard about it, trying to weigh the moral implications of moving my case to the front of the line. "Let me see what I can do," he says. "If you wouldn't mind waiting here?"

"Thank you," I say, my voice genuine. He heads back through the door again and I find the best thing I can do is continue to pace. If I sit down, I'll just end up getting so restless I'll need to get up again.

When my phone buzzes in my pocket I'm so revved up I almost end up throwing it across the room I remove it so quickly.

"Slate."

"Agent Slate, it's Agent Sandel." The man's even-tempered voice is a surprise to my ears. I hadn't expected to hear him on the other end.

"Agent Sandel? Is everything okay?"

"Of course. I was calling to inform you of the information you requested. Agent Coll called and said you needed a favor."

"Background check?" I ask.

"On one Donald Kincaid. Eight-fifty-three Bear Paw Lane, Goodview, Virginia."

"You found him," I say.

"It wasn't difficult. You'll be interested to know he's clean. No criminal history, not even a parking violation or speeding ticket."

I wouldn't have expected anything less. "I'm treating him as our primary suspect. He sold our first weapon to another man and I suspect he purchased the weapon he's using right now from that same man. I need everything you've got on him."

"He's forty-four years old, married with two kids," he says.

"Graduated in two-thousand-two from Radford University with a degree in Economics, has lived at the same address for the past eighteen years. Wife is a nurse with Carilion Healthcare and he works for the Virginia Social Security Department. He's been an employee with them for…nine years."

"And before that?" I ask.

"He worked for a local bank, before they got bought out."

"How old are the kids?"

"Eleven and thirteen, though there isn't much in the records other than their birth certificates and where they go to school. He drives a two-thousand sixteen Ford Focus, light gray. You want the plate number?"

"Yeah," I say, copying the number down as he reads it. "Anything else?"

"Some retirement funds, a few insurance policies, nothing out of the ordinary. Mortgage on his lake house is only twenty-five percent paid off. He's not behind on any payments, but a cursory analysis reveals that he's probably living paycheck to paycheck."

"This is great, Elliott, thank you," I say, making the notes as fast as I can. "If he works for the Social Security Department he should have his fingerprints on file, correct?"

"He does," he replies. "You want them?"

I think back to the dust on that Browning from Beltran's house. What are the odds? "Yeah, go ahead and shoot them to me. They might be able to pull a print off the weapon down here."

"I'll send them immediately. Do you need anything else?" I really have to admire Agent Sandel. Despite butting heads with him on the Magus case, he's been nothing but helpful ever since I met him a few months ago. Both he and Agent Kane have really come through for me ever since the Bureau restructured. I need to make sure I show my gratitude somehow.

"I'll call if I need anything else. Where's Zara?"

"I don't know for sure," he says. "She left about an hour ago."

Huh. That's odd. Usually, you can't tear Zara away from work in the middle of the day. I'll have to make sure everything is okay with her later.

"Thanks, Elliott," I tell her. "I owe you one for this."

"No, you don't. It's part of our jobs. And I'm happy the bot worked," he replies. "When we first began testing there was a seventy percent chance of a system crash every time we ran a simulation. Fortunately, Zara figured it out."

The door opens again and Dr. Lynch sticks his head out. "No, it worked great. Thanks again, I've got to run."

"Anytime," he says.

I hang up and head back over to the door. "We're looking at it now," Lynch says. "Should only be another hour or so."

"I also need you to check it for prints," I tell him. "I'm going to forward your department a file. See if you can't pull any partials anywhere."

He huffs. "I hope you understand what we're doing here for you. This isn't a run-of-the-mill operation. There are usually forms to complete, a process to go through, it's not just—"

"Doctor," I say, holding up my hand. "I completely understand. And I appreciate your haste in this matter. How about you give me all the forms and I'll fill them out while you finish checking the weapon?"

He grumbles, then heads back inside.

I think I'm starting to grow on him.

～

TWO HOURS LATER, I'M LOOKING AT THE BROWNING X-BOLT sitting on a long, metal table in the back of the forensics department. A white-gloved technician came over and placed it right in front of me after Dr. Lynch invited me into the back to look at the weapon. Of course, that was after I spent a solid half-hour filling out requisition report after requisition report, making sure to initial that the FBI had *specifically requested* a rush and that we would be charged accordingly.

Wallace is going to love that one.

But right now, it doesn't matter. Instead, I turn my attention to Dr. Lynch who has set up a laptop on the metal table beside the weapon. "All right," he says, pulling up the file. "Here are the bullet examples we received from Stillwater," he says, opening the image files that have blown up pictures of the bullets that were recovered.

"And here are the images we recovered from firing the weapon. You're lucky we had the same type of ammunition in stock." He pulls up another set of pictures. "After careful examination, we can say with about a ninety percent certainty that this was the weapon used to fire the bullets you provided."

He points on the screen to a pair of diagonal striations that run down both sets of bullets. "The depth and character of these markings is near identical. Taking into account the age of the weapon and any natural degradation, I'm confident this weapon was used in your cases."

I relax and take a breath. I hadn't realized I'd been holding it in while he was speaking. "Any prints?"

"Two. But they're only partials. We compared them to the ones you provided. We also believe these are a match, but we can only say with a sixty percent certainty." He pulls up another pair of images, one set are the prints Elliott sent down, and another is a transparent film that's been backlit of what looks like a thumbprint. Small red circles on both images seem to correspond.

"Got 'em," I whisper. "Can you send me both of these reports?" I ask.

"Of course," he replies, turning to me and I can read the impatience in his body language. "I hope this has been to your satisfaction?"

I grin. "It's been a huge help."

"Good. Do you want the weapon transferred back up to Stillwater?" he asks.

I nod. "And I'll need you to forward all of this information to the Stillwater Police as well, care of Lee Salazar."

After thanking him again I head back out, pulling out my phone and calling Liam.

"Good news?"

"I think we got him," I say. "Prints match on the gun. He definitely killed Mrs. Havens and the others before he switched weapons."

"What about the Bergara? Are you going to try and seize it first?"

"Nope, I'm not waiting. This is at least four counts of murder. We're going after him," I say, pushing through the double doors. "I'm headed to the social security office right now."

"Em, you need backup," he says, his voice alarmed.

"Don't worry. As soon as I'm off the phone with you I'm getting in contact with the locals. They'll provide all the backup I need. Liam, I could have him in custody in the next hour if everything goes right."

"And if it doesn't?"

I huff. "I'll be careful, okay? I haven't forgotten our discussion."

"I should be there," he says.

Mrs. Coll's words echo through my brain. "You're exactly where you need to be. At that hotel recovering. I'll call you with an update as soon as I have it."

"I just wish you had another agent to watch your back," he says. "Not that I don't trust the locals, but they don't have the same training I do."

"I know. But hopefully we'll just be able to walk into his office and apprehend him. It's only three o'clock. He's probably typing away at his desk, oblivious." I unlock my car and slide in, programming the location of the nearest police station.

"I've got my fingers crossed for you," he says. "Good hunting."

We hang up and I head out, determined to see an end to this today. Kincaid has eluded capture for long enough; he's even eluded identification. Frankly it's only because of a lucky break that we've managed to track him down. It's time to turn the tables on the man. His victims have never seen him coming; it's time to see how he likes it.

Chapter Twenty-Nine

"Agent Slate, are we a go?" the voice crackles in my ear.

Unfortunately, finding Donald Kincaid hasn't been as simple as I'd hoped. When I arrived at the social security office with about half a dozen officers in tow, I was informed that Donald had taken a half day and left around noon. I was ready to curse my luck when I remembered I left Beltran's house a little after eleven-thirty. Odds are he called to warn Kincaid, which, if he's our killer, amounts to aiding and abetting. At the very least it's impeding an investigation.

While I would love to go back and tear Beltran a new one, I can't be in two places at once. Fortunately, I still have some help. I spoke with Jill back in Stillwater, who is mobilizing a small task force to head down to Beltran's home for his arrest. Because of the amount of weaponry on his property, I didn't want her going in by herself. He's already spooked enough as it is; when a half dozen cops show up on his lawn he might panic. But Jill is a capable officer, I have no doubt she can handle it.

Not only that, but Sybil has managed to confirm the Bergara Beltran sold to Kincaid is more than likely our weapon. We won't know for sure until we have it in our possession to test, but the markings on the rounds are consistent with those fired from a Bergara B-14 HMR. That has only strengthened my resolve that Kincaid is our man.

But there's no doubt armed and extremely dangerous. Against my better judgement I mobilized the local SWAT and headed to his home address. I don't have a great history with SWAT, local or not, but a case like this requires it. No Captain is going to let his guys go in without some additional protection, not when we can already attribute at least four kills to this guy.

We arrived at the Kincaid property about fifteen minutes ago and made sure to stay off any roads leading to or from the house so we wouldn't be spotted. And I just spent the better part of ten minutes trudging through the woods to get to Kincaid's house, which isn't on the lake itself, but is set back off one of the side streets. Local police have the roads secured in the event he tries to run.

For the past five minutes I've been staring at the house through a pair of binoculars, but there hasn't been any movement inside. A car sits in the driveway, but it's not Kincaid's Ford. Instead, it's his wife's Honda, which makes me just a bit nervous. The whole reason we've been holding is because if he's hiding out in there, she's probably in there with him and we don't want a hostage situation.

Knowing how callous Kincaid has been toward all his other victims, I'm not sure he wouldn't dispense the same cold threat on his wife as well. Thankfully, the children should be at school, but given the time, will be home soon. I've already sent another unit to intercept the bus.

"Agent Slate," the voice crackles again. "Are we clear to move in?"

It's either hold and wait for him to come out on his own or go in after him. If Beltran really did call and warn him, odds that he comes out of his house anytime soon are slim. And when he does, more than likely he'll be armed. I can't predict how he'll respond in a situation like this because I genuinely believe he never thought he'd be in this situation. He probably thought he'd be able to get away with it forever. That is, if my profile is correct.

"Move in," I finally say. "Keep it slow. Do not breach the house until everyone is in place."

I hate operations like this. First, I have to trust these people know what they're doing, but I haven't worked with any of these teams before. And then there's always the uncertainty element. What will Kincaid do if he's backed into a corner? What could he have already done? I have visions of us breaking through the doors and finding Mrs. Kincaid hanging from the ceiling fan, strung up like a chicken.

The first of the SWAT start moving in, their semi-automatic rifles out and close to the chest. I move forward as well, trying not to hurry myself along but instead take my time so I don't make too much noise. My weapon is out but pointed at the ground as I'm watching all the angles, trying to get a feel for the situation. The woods are deathly quiet, which unnerves me. All I can hear are a few distant cars driving by on nearby roads. While there's no snow this far south, the woods are blanketed in fallen leaves, making it slow going. Thankfully they're somewhat wet from a recent rain, which at least makes the approach easier.

There are three other officers near me, and we're all moving up on the south side of the house, as if we're coming from the lake. Another team is approaching from the north and we have the other team off to the east side. The house is one of those seventies models that isn't exactly square, so we're all approaching on something of a diagonal, meaning there is no west side. From our vantage point here, we can see the basement walk out and the back of the house, but I don't see any light on inside or movement in the windows.

If he's in there, he's staying low and quiet.

"Looks like we go——" A voice crackles in my ear before it's cut off by a huge explosion which comes from the front of the house.

I hit the ground, covering my head and can feel the residual rumble under the forest floor. Immediately my thoughts go back to New York, when Zara and I had that bomb strapped between us.

"Back! Get back! The house is rigged!" Another voice yells as other officers begin to try talking over each other.

"Pull back!" I tell the three guys I'm with. "Get to cover." I'm up and running back from the house as all four of us retreat to a safe distance. I expect gunfire any second to tear into my back.

"Echo One, what's your situation?" I ask into the comms as we're running.

"Hit some kind of trip wire. Donnelly is down, my God, he's missing his leg! I need emergency services! We've also got a massive fire over here."

"Copy, all units do not approach the house," I call into the radio. "Pull back to five hundred feet."

"Emergency services are close by," another voice says. Thankfully we had both the fire department and rescue squad on standby already.

I pull out my phone and call Captain Hoover back in Roanoke, explaining the situation. "We're going to need additional backup here. And the Bomb Squad. He could have the whole house rigged."

"I'll mobilize the force and get them to you as soon as possible. Can you hold?" the Captain says.

I glance back at the house, from my vantage point around the trunk of a wide tree. I don't see any change, other than the plume of black smoke rising from the other side of the roof. No weapons fire from any of the windows I can determine. I get back on the comms. "Anyone else hit? Anyone see him?"

"Delta clear."

"I don't see anything," the team leader of my group says. He's behind a log with his weapon pointed at the house, looking through the scope.

"He's bleeding out over here; someone get me a tourniquet!" Echo leader yells. I'm not sure he meant for that to go over comms.

I put the phone back to my ear. "We can hold. But you better hurry." In the distance I hear the familiar whine of the ambulance siren.

BY THE TIME THE BOMB SQUAD ARRIVES, ALL THE SWAT officers have pulled back to a safe distance and are holding. We're all keeping an eye on the house, but I've managed to make my way around the property to see the extent of the damage from the explosion. Thankfully, because of the recent rain, the fire from the explosion didn't spread very far and the fire department has it under control quickly. However, Echo One had to drag his man back away from the house like he was in goddamn Afghanistan to get him to safety. His leg is completely missing. I don't even know if he stepped on a mine or if there was something else out there. But it's changed my opinion of Kincaid.

Now I know he's definitely our man. Anyone who is willing to booby trap their own home is not a stable individual. Imagine if his kids had hit that, or someone else's kids that just happened to be playing around in the woods near his house. The odds of that are low, given how isolated the home is, but that he's done this in a populated area is certifiable.

The worst part is, we can't make any move on the house until we get the clear from the Bomb Squad. And that is taking hours. They get Donnelly strapped into the ambulance and are taking him to the closest hospital, but his life will never be the same again. It just means I get to add attempted murder of a police officer to Kincaid's list of offenses. I also now realize we can't wait for him to come out, even though it puts his wife's life in danger.

"Agent Slate," the sergeant who runs the Bomb Squad says, trotting up to me. I think his name is Callahan, but I'm not sure. When they arrived everything was in a state of flux.

"What's the situation?" I ask.

"Entire property is fenced," he says. "We've found six clay-mores so far. But there could be more. I'd suggest staying back until we can get some additional equipment out here. There's no telling how much he's buried out there in the woods."

"Dammit," I say, staring at the top of the house which is just barely visible over the small hill where we've set up our command center. We're far enough away that we shouldn't be in the line of sight of Kincaid's rifle. Not unless he can make bullets curve, that is. He knows we're coming after him; he could have a stronghold set up in there.

"I don't like any of this. What about the driveway? The hard surfaces?"

Callahan gives me a shrug. "Unless he's buried them under either one, I think they'd be okay. Especially if he's using them every day. But it's possible they are remote-acti-vated. He could have had them under there for years and has just now turned them on, which means the next person who walks up that sidewalk will end up like Donnelly. Or worse."

I slam my hand down on the folding table that's been set up before I turn to Captain Hoover, who has come in from Roanoke given how much this situation has developed. "Where are your snipers?"

He pulls out a map of the lake where he's circled Kincaid's house. "I've got one set up over here, across the lake," he says, making a small red dot on the other side of the lake. Because Kincaid's house isn't on the lake, he'll have a lot of woods to shoot through, assuming he can get a good shot. "And I have two more set up here, and here. They should just about be in position."

"Just make sure they don't mistake any of my guys for the target," Callahan says.

Hoover shoots him a look. "I think the large, silvery suits gives you away." He pauses, looking at the map. "My question is, why isn't he defending from inside the house? This would be the perfect time to start picking us off one at a time. Especially Callahan's men."

"That's what I'm trying to figure out," I say. "Maybe he has a panic room in there somewhere. And he's just betting we won't be able to get through it before his traps take us out."

"And the wife?"

"No doubt she's in there with him," I say.

Hoover's radio crackles and he picks it up, walking away. "Go ahead."

I turn back to Callahan. "Keep going, do what you can. I'll let you know if anything changes."

Callahan sighs, then picks up his helmet again. "Okay, but just keep in mind we're the ones with our asses hanging out over there. If he decides to start shooting—"

"Your suits, they're rated to take how much force upon impact?" I ask.

"These are level eight suits. Usually enough to protect us from most anything out there."

"That should be enough to stop a rifle round, right?"

He scoffs. "Feel free to grab a suit and test it out for yourself." He puts his metallic helmet back on and heads off, meeting with a couple of his guys near the base of the hill.

"Agent Slate," Captain Hoover says, approaching. "My guys are all in position. None of them see any activity inside the home. Lights may be off, but they can still see inside. There is *nothing* moving inside. Not even a dog."

"Can they see in every room?" I ask.

"Not every room. About seventy percent of the home."

I tap my foot against the wet leaves. Something about this doesn't seem right. If Kincaid wanted to go out in a blaze of glory, he should have taken his chance when the mine exploded. Except it's been quiet ever since. "Who was in charge of getting the kids off the school bus?" I ask.

"Mendelson, I think."

"Where's Mendelson?" I ask.

Hoover looks around, before pulling out the radio again. "Anyone seen Mendelson? What's the report on the bus?"

"Here, sir," Mendelson replies on the radio.

"What's your position?" Hoover asks.

"I'm over with traffic control on Poplar," he replies. "Keeping any vehicles away from the scene."

"Where are the kids?" Hoover asks as a pit forms in my stomach.

"They weren't on the bus, sir," Mendelson replies. "I meant to inform you, but with everything—"

"*Dammit,*" I say, breaking off in a run toward the house.

"Agent Slate, wait!" Hoover calls after me.

I crest the hill, staying on the hardtop of the driveway as I run toward the house. I can clearly see Callahan's people in their silver suits performing their perimeter search. And I can also see the blackened woods where the explosion happened, about ten feet out from the house.

"Agent?" Callahan calls out as I rush past him. "What are you doing?"

Dammit, dammit, dammit. He's smart. How could I forget he's smart?

Even though I know I probably don't need to, at twenty feet I take an extra jump and make sure I'm over where I think the perimeter runs around the house. A small walkway runs from the driveway to the front door.

"Agent Slate!" Callahan calls out.

Staring at the walkway I make a choice. Either I'm right, or this will be the last decision I ever make. But I don't think I'm wrong. In fact, I know I'm not. I take a few ginger steps forward, staying on the path, until I reach the front door.

If he booby-trapped the yard, he booby-trapped the house. I wave Callahan over. What little I can see of his face is twisted in confusion. But he follows my steps exactly until he's on the stone porch with me.

"That little stunt could have just gotten you killed. Are you insane?" he asks.

"Maybe. Can you check this door for any traps?"

He sighs and runs a small device over the entire frame of the door. "Looks like we might have something in the upper right corner." Glass windows frame both sides of the door. I take the butt of my gun and smash through the right window.

"What are you doing?" Callahan asks, ducking down.

I peer around the inside of the window, but see nothing out of the ordinary inside the house. No muzzle pointed at my face, which only strengthens my resolve. "You're clear."

Callahan gets up, then gingerly peers in. "Yep. Right there. Give me a second." He reaches in and messes with something for a moment while I hold my breath.

This may be the most reckless thing I've ever done, but time is of the essence. I need confirmation of my theory.

"There," Callahan says. "Pin is out and it's disarmed."

"Can I break it down?" I ask.

He takes a few steps back. "It's not going to explode, but if anything else happens I can't—"

"Good," I say and shove the heel of my boot into the door, cracking it on the first blow and breaking it open on the second. I have my weapon in my hand as I take a tender step inside.

"Donald Kincaid!" I yell out. "Marie Kincaid! FBI, show yourselves!"

The house is quiet. No noise, not even from a running

refrigerator or a heater. I turn back to Callahan. "Get Hoover. We need to go through this house, right now."

"But he could be——" Callahan begins.

I shake my head before he can finish. "No. I don't think so. I don't think he's been here at all."

Chapter Thirty

"Well, that's it," Hoover says, coming back into the hallway with his hands on his hips. "The entire house has been cleared. You were right."

I'm standing in Kincaid's living room, looking at the family pictures he has on the mantle above the fireplace. Happy pictures of him, his wife, and their two kids. He's smiling in all of them, looking like nothing more than a dad and husband. Just an average guy, living his life. Nothing out of the ordinary.

Hard to believe this is the face of a cold-blooded killer. The pictures alone are almost enough to make me question if we have the right guy or not. But then I look up to the rack above the pictures. A rack that's drilled right into the brick itself, and the gun that *isn't* there.

He keeps it out, on display for everyone to see. Almost like he's flaunting the fact he's doing this and no one knows it. He may even get off on it.

"Agent Slate?" Hoover asks. I turn to him. "Did you hear me?"

"He pulled the kids out of school this morning, didn't he?" I ask.

"We spoke with the district. He came in around noon, took them both on what was given as a *family emergency*."

Damn Beltran. I should have just stayed with him until I had eyes on Kincaid. Made sure he couldn't warn the man. But he'll go down for this too. Phone records will confirm what I already know, and I'll be more than happy to charge the man.

"You know, if it weren't for all the traps we found, I'd say we had the wrong guy," Hoover says. "But considering he just blew the leg off one of my men, I'm pretty sure we're on the right path."

"You mean we *were*," I say. Kincaid has had almost five hours now to put some distance between us and him. He could be headed anywhere. He could be as far as Knoxville, or Pittsburgh. "Did you put out the APB?"

Hoover nods. "We've got information about their car going to every adjacent state and we'll have a segment on local news channels as well. *Someone* will see them."

I wish I had his confidence. Someone will see them all right. But they'll see a happy, close-knit family. A family that doesn't look suspicious at all. It's the perfect cover. The only thing that really gives them away is the car. And I'd be willing to bet Kincaid has a spare set of license plates stashed away somewhere. He's too smart not to.

"Is Callahan done?" I ask.

Hoover nods. "There were trips on each of the entrances, but nothing else in the house. At least, nothing they could find. It looks like he just wanted to keep us away from the inside as long as possible."

"To give him more time to get away," I say.

"If you hadn't run up to the house, it very well could have been tomorrow before we got inside," Hoover says.

I let out a long breath. "Yeah, well, don't tell my SAC about it. Or anyone else I work with, otherwise I'll never hear the end of it." It was reckless and I know it, but at the same time, my gut told me this house would be empty, and I've started trusting it more. Better that than to second guess myself all the time. It's just that my gut likes to get me into sticky situations sometimes.

"We need a full accounting of this house. I want to know if he owns any other properties under other names, where the rest of the family lives, anything. Anything that might be able to point us to where he's gone."

"My men are already on it," Hoover says.

"Thanks, Captain," I say. "Your team has been great."

He nods, then heads back the way he came, presumably to supervise the search. I turn back to the pictures, studying them. Does Kincaid's family have any idea of who he really is? His kids obviously don't. Even though these pictures were no doubt cherry-picked, I don't see anything in the eyes of his kids that indicates anything but pure love for their father.

The wife too, for that matter. And if Kincaid is as smart as I think he is, he's never let it slip that he lives a double life. I was wrong about him originally. I'd pegged him as this cold, emotionless monster. But it turns out that while that may be true, he can also turn on another side of himself. And that's the side he presents to the world. I'm sure all of his coworkers think he's a great guy. And he's probably a very loving and supportive husband. Everything in these pictures suggests nothing else.

But I know. Beneath those smiles is something sinister. A dark mind who can kill without remorse, without pity. A mind that kills for fun.

I think we have a true Jekyll and Hyde situation here. I can't help but exhale as I pull out my phone and text Zara a picture of the mantle.

This look like a killer to you?

A few moments later the three little dots appear. *Don't tell me that's him.*

Yep.

Wow. Talk about the most boring guy alive.

I smile. *I think that was the point.*

Any luck finding him?

That's right, I haven't had time to let anyone know what's been going on here. Instead of texting back I just call her instead.

"Hey," she says. "You okay?"

"I don't know," I say honestly. I give her the basics of everything that's been happening, and this new dead end we've just slammed into. "Seriously though, he could be anywhere by now."

"You think he planned for this?" Zara asks.

"He must have. It was too clean. He gets a call from Beltran—who I'm about to have on a platter by the way—and then less than an hour later he's collected his kids, his wife, has the car packed and they're gone before anyone even knows he's not coming back from his lunch break. I was so wrong. I thought he was cocky enough to think he'd never get caught. But it seems like he planned for every contingency."

"I still don't get why he booby-trapped his house," Zara says.

"Delay tactic," I say. "Gives him more lead time. I just hope he isn't already on a plane out of the country. We've got his passport flagged if he tries. But if he's already gone—"

"Don't think about that," Zara says. "Plus, if he is, there are always ways of getting him back."

"Assuming we can find him," I say.

"You'll find him. Do you have his phone information? I could try and geotag him," she offers.

"I have a cell phone registered in his name, but I doubt he's using it. More than likely he's already gotten rid of his phone and is using a burner."

"What about his kids?" Zara asks.

"What?"

"Doesn't he have teens?"

I think back to the file. "Yeah, uh, eleven and thirteen I think."

"Do you think they still have *their* phones?"

I furrow my brow. "No way. Right? I mean, he'd make them turn them off or just throw them away, right?"

"Oh, sweet, innocent Em," Zara says. "You really don't know anything about kids, do you?"

"And you do?" I ask.

"I know they don't give those things up without a fight. Kids are *glued* to their phones. And who is to say that even if their dad did make them get rid of them, they don't have backups of their own?"

"You mean—" I say.

"Monkey see, monkey do," she replies. "If they're anywhere near as clever as he is, they'll have backups. Backups he knows nothing about."

"What are the odds of that?" I ask.

"For a normal family, I'd say about fifty-fifty," she replies. "But for *this* family, I think we have a good chance. You keep looking there, in case he's got a secret property stashed somewhere while I do some digging. What are the kids' names?"

"Uh, Claire and Adam," I say. "Do you really think you'll be able to find them?"

"Unless he's kept them sequestered their entire lives, they'll have a digital footprint," she says. "And they go to public school, right?"

"Right."

"Oh yeah, this is gonna be a breeze. Lemme call you back in thirty." She hangs up before I can say another word.

While I have no doubt in Zara's abilities, I'm not as confident Kincaid's kids are as devious as he is. Especially if they know nothing about their father. But then again, maybe some of that paranoia has just naturally rubbed off. If we could—

No. I can't think that way. I need to help out the officers here, see if we can find anything solid. A place where they might go until all this blows over. Though short of getting out of the country, I'm not sure where Kincaid thinks he can go where his face won't be plastered all over every post office from here to California.

I'm about to search again when my phone buzzes. Thinking it's Zara, I get ready to answer quickly, until I see it's a number with a northern Virginia area code. "Slate."

"Hey, it's Sergeant Hubbard," she says on the other end. "We've got Beltran in custody."

"Already?" I ask. "Did he put up a fight?"

"We thought he might," Jill says and I can tell from the ambient noise she's outside. "But as soon as he had six weapons pointed at his face he crumbled, even got on his knees, begging us. It was kind of pitiful."

A swell of satisfaction fills my chest. "Good. I need you to interrogate him." I give her a quick rundown of the situation that's unfolded here. "Make it seem like we're gonna pin the attempt on Donnelly's life on him. See if he knows where Kincaid might have gone."

"I would love nothing more," she says, and I can hear the pleasure in her voice. I'm sure she's had as "pleasant" of an exchange as I had with the man. "You sure you don't want to do it?"

"Can't," I say. "I need to stay here and coordinate. We need to get after this guy."

"Understood," she replies. "I'll be in touch as soon as I learn something."

I take a seat in one of the nearby chairs. At least that's one less thing to worry about. Part of me wasn't sure if Beltran was willing to back up all the bravado or not. But it seems like he was all bark and no bite. I need to remember to speak to the ATF. I'm sure they'll be interested in whatever he was so adamant about hiding from me.

As I'm sitting there, just trying to process the last couple of hours, my eyes wander. The living room is modest, like the rest of the house, and I can hear Hoover's men rustling around in the other rooms. But on one side of the fireplace is a stack of shelves, all full of books. I get up and start pulling them one by one, flipping through to see if I catch anything useful. Many of them are the classics, though they don't seem to have been used in a while. Though there are a few that catch my eye. I bend down and grab the stack of them. All books on fishing and boating. Including one which is something of a guide for buying a good boat.

"Captain?" I call out.

He sticks his head in the room as I hold up the book. "We are on a lake, after all."

"But the lake doesn't go anywhere. There's a dam at both ends. It's not traversable."

"Still, it's an avenue we need to explore. I want to know if he owns any boats that might be out on that lake right now."

"Got it," he says.

I set the book down and continue searching. But I'm not really focused on the search. I'm focused on my phone.

C'mon Z. We need a miracle.

Chapter Thirty-One

"You are going to love me," Zara says, after taking more than an hour to get back to me.

"Thirty minutes, huh?" I ask.

"Hey, I had to get Nadia to run interference on Wallace. I think he's getting suspicious because he hasn't heard from you."

"That's on purpose," I say. "I'm not reporting back to him until this is all over. Why do you think I haven't called in any backup yet?"

"Waitasecond," she says, in that mischievous voice of hers. "Are you *trying* to get him fired?"

"I never said that," I reply. "And you better watch what you say around there."

"You are so paranoid," she says. "My personal phone is clear of any bugs, trust me. And I always keep active dampers around my workspace."

"What are active dampers?" I ask.

"Something I just made up so you'd stop worrying so much!" she says.

"Ugh. Please just tell me you found something useful."

"Don't I always? It turns out I was right; Claire Kincaid is a *very* active socialite. At least online. And while it looks like her service *was* interrupted earlier today, as in, she wasn't online for about two hours, it has since been restored and she's still regularly chatting with her friends. But she's been careful enough not to make any posts."

"Damn," I say. "You were right."

"Of course I was right," she says confidently. "I usually am. Plus, if you really are going after Wallace, I want a piece of that. Can't let you take *all* the glory."

"I'm not going after Wallace or anyone else," I say. "I'm just covering my butt so when he tries to pull a fast one on me, I'm ready."

"Ooo, sneaky. I like it. So yeah, I've got a geo-location on Claire Kincaid. Her phone is pinging in central Virginia. Closest town is Blackstone."

I rack my brain. "Where the hell is Blackstone?"

"Tiny town. About thirty minutes southwest of Richmond."

"Is she moving?" I ask.

"As far as I can tell, yes. Heading in an easterly direction," Zara says.

"Where can he be taking them?"

"Richmond has an airport," Zara says. "Maybe he's looking to get them out of there."

I head for the front door, pushing my way past another officer who is still digging through Kincaid's stuff in his house. "Send me the information. I'll need to notify the local PD to be on the lookout for him. If we can keep the signal, we should be able to set up a roadblock."

"I've already sent it to your phone. May I take this opportunity to remind you that this is the *second* time I have saved your butt on this case?"

"I know!" I say. "Which is why you should be out here with me, instead of stuck in the office there."

"I would love to, but we've got something big going on here. I can't exactly get away."

"What is it?" I ask.

"I'll tell you when you get back," she says and for the first time I sense some hesitation in her voice.

"Z. What's going on?"

"It's nothing that can't wait," she replies. "Look, you just stop this guy. And for the love of all that is holy will you please be safe about it?"

I smirk. "I'll try. Thanks for the info."

I hang up and look through my emails, finding a new one from Zara. When I click the link, it takes me to a site very much like the one she and Agent Kane set up for me before. There's a map, and a dot. All I have to do is follow it. Though I wonder what exactly she's talking about could be going on back at the office. It's not like Zara to be cagy. Could it be related to the counterfeiting case she told me about earlier?

"Agent Slate." I turn to see Captain Hoover come jogging up. "We found out Kincaid owns a boat down at the slip. But I just got off the horn with the harbor master. He says the boat is in dry dock for the winter and no one has access but him. It's up on a shelf somewhere as far as anyone knows."

"That's okay, Captain," I say. "I think we have a new lead. But can you get me visual confirmation just to be sure?"

He nods. "Do we keep going here?"

"We think he may have been spotted in eastern Virginia. I'm gonna see if we can't pin him in. But we're still going to need as much evidence as we can find. Take whatever you need, we'll sort through it later."

"Got it, good luck," he says.

"You too."

～

It doesn't take but two calls with Richmond Police before they are already on the hunt for Kincaid. I gave them access to the information Zara shared, allowing them to track Claire Kincaid's phone in real time. I suppose Kincaid could have always stuffed it in the back of some trucker's trailer as another way to throw us off, but I'm hoping his kid is as devious as he is.

I decided to hand this off to Richmond PD instead of trying to track down Kincaid myself because he's got a three-hour lead on me and I'd never catch him in time. Though what's odd is he started out with a five-hour lead, and he still hasn't left the state of Virginia. I don't understand what he's waiting around for, or why he's lingering. I would have thought he would have picked a direction and just driven as fast as he could, but then again, I've underestimated him a few too many times.

He has a plan; I just need to figure out what it is. The variable here is I have to trust Richmond PD to apprehend him without incident. And more than likely he has three possible hostages in his vehicle.

I think back to what Zara said. Maybe I should inform Wallace, and get the go-ahead to pull federal agents from the Richmond office. I mean, they're *right there*. I've been holding off on informing Wallace because I was pissed at how dismissive he was about this case. About how he thought it didn't amount to anything, and that I was just "wasting my off time".

Grumbling as I get on Route 460 headed east, I pull out my phone and dial.

"Hey," Liam says. "How's it going? Jill said you guys are close to finding Kincaid. I would have called, but I didn't want to interrupt—"

"I need advice," I say.

"Is everything okay?" he asks in that soft way that was part of what made me fall in love with him in the first place.

"I need you to be honest with me. Do you think that by not telling Wallace about what's going on that I'm endangering the case?"

"I'm not sure I follow," he says. With one hand on the wheel, I lay it all out for him. The confrontation with Beltran, the raid on Kincaid's house, the explosion, the Bomb Squad. And then me taking a risk I shouldn't have before Zara coming through with his kid's phone.

"Wow, I am *never* leaving you to a case by yourself again," he says and I can hear the frustration in his voice. "You told me you were going to be more careful."

"I know," I say. "But it could have cost us hours, maybe even days. You know better than anyone you can't always be careful in this job. But I feel like I might be throwing it all away, especially if Richmond PD can't handle this guy."

"You think your decision is going to get them killed," he says.

"I'm just wondering if this little feud or whatever you want to call it with Wallace is compromising my judgement."

"Your emotions are running high, and you don't have the best track record with Wallace," he replies. "But also remember this was always a local case. Salazar asked you to come aboard. But I wouldn't let Richmond PD do anything other than hold him. Don't let them interrogate him without you there."

"Assuming his car isn't a bomb itself and he blows him and his entire family up as soon as someone gets close to them," I say.

"How far away are you?" he asks.

"Another two-and-a-half hours," I say. "*If* they manage to stop him before he reaches wherever he's going." He goes quiet on the other end. "What are you thinking?"

He sighs. "I think you need to call Wallace. If Janice was still your boss, wouldn't you inform her? To make sure every angle is covered? Because if this all goes sideways, who do you think he's going to blame?"

"*Dammit,*" I say.

"I know that's not the answer you wanted to hear."

"But it's the right call," I say. "Thank you for being honest. Sometimes I get so caught up in myself I have a hard time seeing the right thing to do."

"We all do," he says. "That's why we need other people. Especially you."

"Okay," I say, grinning. "You don't have to rub it in. I'll call him right now."

"Good," he says. "I think I'll head over to the station and wait on Jill. See if she needs any help with Beltran. Maybe we can still get something out of him."

"Only if you're feeling up to it," I say.

"Don't worry about me, I'll be fine."

"Okay. Thank you. And Liam?"

I can see his face as he says it. The way it lights up when I use this tone of voice. "Yeah?"

"I love you."

Chapter Thirty-Two

MY FINGER HOVERS over the green button for a second and I finally hit it, gritting my teeth as I grip the steering wheel tighter.

"Wallace." His voice is smooth, no-nonsense. I can just imagine him reading over expense reports or whatever it is he does in that office all day long.

"It's Slate," I say. "We have a situation down here."

He's quiet for a moment. "What kind of situation?"

I lay everything out for him, from tracking down all the victims to eventually finding Beltran and then Kincaid. I also inform him about the clusterfuck that occurred at Kincaid's house. By some miracle he doesn't interrupt until I'm done.

"Where is Kincaid now?" he asks.

"On Route forty, headed east, about twenty miles southwest of Richmond," I tell him. "We're tracking him using his daughter's phone, but I'm still a good two hours away. I'd like the authority to have federal agents intercept him."

"That's a negative," Wallace says. "Three hostages means we can't let him know we're on to him. I don't want this situation to spiral out of control. Where are you now?"

"Just outside the Roanoke Metro Area, headed east," I tell

him. "We need to stop him before he gets wherever he's going. He's got a plan; I know that much for sure. And he might find out about his daughter's phone at any second, which means we could lose him for good."

"I'm already in contact with the Richmond office," he says and I can hear him typing on the other end. "We'll get eyes on him, but I don't want him stopped until he reaches his destination."

"Sir, I don't think you understand. He could have a bomb in that car. What if he's headed for a heavily populated area?"

"I think he would have already done that, don't you?" Wallace asks.

Somehow, I grip the steering wheel tighter. "What, we're just supposed to sit back and wait?"

"We'll get a drone up there to keep a lock on the vehicle," Wallace says. "We're not going to lose him."

"You have to trust me here," I say. "This guy, he's not your ordinary killer. He's clever. Think about it, he's evaded anyone even identifying him for years. Killed without impunity, and he hides it all behind the veneer of a normal family man. We can't just let someone like that drive around doing whatever they want. We need to stop him."

"No, we need to get those three hostages out of the vehicle," Wallace says. "That's the top priority right now. I don't want to take any action that may endanger their lives. We let them get wherever they're going, wait until we can get control of the situation and then we'll apprehend Kincaid when it's safe."

"And if he manages to disappear before that happens?" I ask.

"He won't. Not with our surveillance on him."

I hit the steering wheel, pushing the accelerator even harder. "Sir, I think you're making a big mistake here. If Kincaid figures out we're—"

"Slate, I appreciate you've managed to get yourself in the

middle of yet another mess where you have no business," he says. "But let the Richmond office handle this one from here. You've done good work, identifying the killer. Now leave it up to the rest of the Bureau to bring him in."

"But—"

"No buts, Slate. That's an order. You were right, I should have looked at the case more closely. I'll coordinate with the Stillwater Police Chief on the rest of the facts of the case."

Now he wants to take it over. After all the hard work has been done. Why am I not surprised?

"That's it, then? I should just come back to the office?" I ask.

"You still have a few days of leave remaining, use them however you wish," he replies. "It doesn't seem like you've managed to take much time off after all. I would take it while you can get it. As soon as you get back you're going to have a full caseload." He hangs up without another word and I'm so mad I want to rip the steering wheel off my car and throw it out the window.

Instead, I pull off in a gravel lot on the side of the highway and get out, fuming. This is exactly why I didn't want to call Wallace in the first place. Somehow, I knew he would do something like this, but even I didn't realize he'd take me off the case and tell me to *go back on vacation*. The man obviously doesn't know me at all.

And he's not taking Kincaid seriously. He's treating him like any other unsub, and he's not. He's cunning, clever and devious. And he's got a plan to get him and his family out of here.

Wait a second. *He's taking his family with him.* Someone like him—a cold-blooded killer with no empathy or remorse at all should have no problem leaving their family behind, even if they spent years working on their "outside" persona. But he's taking a big risk keeping them with him, unless he truly intends to use them as hostages. It would have been so much easier for him to leave and disappear alone. He could have traveled easier, left the country easier, and yet he decided to pull his kids out of school, go home and gather his wife, and then leave.

I think back to the pictures in the living room. Maybe it all wasn't so much a persona after all. Could he really care for them? It's not unheard of, but generally, especially with sociopaths, they have no attachments whatsoever. Everything about their connections are fake, because they don't know how to make real, emotional connections to other people. All they can do is imitate them. And some of them can imitate them very, very well.

But what if Kincaid isn't one of those people? What if he really cares for his family? Could it be possible that he's both a cold-blooded killer *and* a loving father and husband? What if I've been looking at this wrong the whole time? What if his killing isn't out of some thrill or desire to hurt people, but instead something he's *compelled* to do. That might explain why there's no regularity to the kills. He only does it when he feels like he needs to get it out of his system.

That sounds horrible, and it is, but it changes the game. *If* I'm right. It's always possible the only reason he collected his family was to use them as bargaining chips in the event he was caught. But I'm not so sure.

I get back in the car and peel away, headed east with the app pointing me in the right direction. I need to know. There might be a way to salvage this whole situation before it spirals out of control.

~

Two hours later I'm still heading east with no updates from the Richmond office or anyone else. The blip on Zara's map still shows Kincaid's daughter is active online, though the dot seems to have stopped somewhere around the Norfolk area. I can't tell exactly where until I get a little closer, and I'm still a good hour out from there.

I've been pushing the speed limit the entire way, and thankfully there's little to no traffic in this part of the state, but as I close in on the metro area, it starts to become more difficult to navigate. Unable to help myself I call into the Richmond FBI office to inquire about the status of the operation. Not being able to be in the middle of things is driving me insane.

As I'm on hold with Richmond my phone beeps, indicating another call coming in. I switch over, putting Richmond on hold. "Hello?"

"Em, where are you?" Liam asks.

"I'm about an hour outside Norfolk, why?"

"Jill and I just finished interrogating Beltran. It seems the man has a lot to say when he's not in a house surrounded by a hundred firearms."

"That's good news," I say. "I wish I had similarly good news, but Wallace took the case away from me when I called."

"You're kidding," he says.

"Nope. He agreed the FBI should get involved, but then decided the person who has been working the case this entire time shouldn't be the one in charge," I tell him. "I can't figure that man out. Sometimes it's like he *needs* me to work a case and other times he doesn't want me anywhere near them. It's so damn frustrating."

"I'm sorry, Em. So what are you still doing down there, then?"

"Because I'm not about to let some pencil pusher tell me what case I'm working," I reply. "I don't care if he is my boss or not."

"Any word on Kincaid?" he asks.

"I'm on hold with the Richmond office now. Though I doubt they'll give me anything."

"Then I'm glad I called. After we worked Beltran over for about fifteen minutes, he let it slip that Kincaid owns a boat."

"Yeah, the one on the lake, I know," I say. "I already confirmed it's being stored for the winter."

"No, a *big* boat," Liam says. "Like a sailboat. It's moored at Lynnhaven Marina, though I don't know the slip number. But Beltran says the name on the back of the boat is *Deep Blue C.* As in the letter."

"That's where he's going," I say, finally understanding his plan. "He's not looking to leave through the airport. He's going to put his family on the boat and sail somewhere. It's a lot easier to get through customs on a boat than it is at an airport."

"I thought you said they were going to roadblock him before he could get anywhere."

"That was the original plan, before Wallace changed it," I explain. "He thinks Kincaid is going to use his family as hostages."

"But you don't?"

"It feels wrong to me," I say. "I think he genuinely cares for them. He's trying to get all of them to safety together. Can you give me the address of that marina?"

"Sure," Liam says before rattling it off. "Are you going to inform the Richmond office?" he asks.

"If they ever pick back up," I tell him. "But they don't seem very interested in talking to me."

"Keep at it," he says. "We'll try to get anything else we can out of Beltran."

"Thanks," I tell him and hang up. When I switch back over to the other line, I'm still on hold. "Son of a—" I'd bet anything this is Wallace's doing. He's black bagged me, making sure I don't continue to interfere with the investigation. But *why?* Why is it so important that I don't work this case? Similarly, why was it so important that I *did* work the Bellefleur case?

I just don't get it.

As I'm sitting in traffic, I switch back to the app that showed the location of Claire Kincaid, but it seems to have stopped. When I pull up the location on Google Maps, I find myself staring at a parking garage in the middle of Virginia Beach.

Finally, the line clicks through. "This is Agent Forsythe, how can I help you?"

"Agent Slate, D.C. office," I tell him. "I'm the one who tracked down Kincaid. Have you apprehended him?"

"Agent Slate, I'm not sure I'm able to give out that information," Forsythe says. Her voice has a hard edge to it.

"Are you the SAC?" I ask.

"I am."

"And did you get a directive from SAC Wallace not to give me operational information on this case?"

There's silence on the other end of the line. "I'll take that as a yes. Well, you may want to know that Donald Kincaid owns an off-the-books sailboat docked at Lynnhaven Marina. And if you don't already have him in custody, there's a good chance that's where he is right now. Preparing to sail off, never to be seen again."

There's rustling on the other side of the phone. "How do you know that?"

"Do you have him in custody?" I ask again.

She sighs. "No. We found his car abandoned in a parking garage, with the girl's phone still inside. At some point he switched vehicles. We don't know where he is."

"Now you do," I tell her. "He's going for that marina. He's looking for a way out of the country that won't require him to look at a security camera. Get a team down there, now. Block the waterway and stop all traffic."

"I'll send my men in that direction," she says. "But it's rush hour. It's going to take them some time."

"I'm headed there now as well," I say. "Do whatever it

takes. Local PD, hell, if there's a mall security guard nearby, I don't care. Get someone to stop that boat."

Her voice takes on a new resolve. "Right. Thank you, Agent Slate. We'll be in touch."

No, you won't, I think after she hangs up. But at least now she'll think twice the next time she talks to Fletcher Wallace.

I just hope one of us can get to the marina in time.

Chapter Thirty-Three

It's an agonizing forty-five minutes before I reach the marina due to all the additional traffic. All the honking in the world doesn't do any good unless you have actual lights and sirens on your car, which I do not. But I was able to take advantage of a couple shoulders and closed lanes, which got me here a lot faster than I thought it would.

When I pull in, the sun is already beginning to set and the nearby lights are already reflecting off the water. The Lynnhaven Marina is nestled among residential homes on all sides, making this a perfect place to keep a boat if you're not looking for any prying eyes. From the outside it looks like an unassuming little beach community, where each house has access to their own waterway. The marina itself is on the other side of all the homes, where there are only about fifty ships moored. The only commercial buildings are on the marina itself, a couple of restaurants, and even a wedding venue. I head in, looking at the backs of all the boats to see if I see *Deep Blue C*, but I can't find it. There also doesn't seem to be anyone else here. I guess Forsythe's people haven't made it here yet.

Damn. I'm sure we've already missed him. The man had a

good two-and-half-hour head start on me. Of course he's already gone. Why did I call Wallace? I should have just gone with my gut. If I had, Richmond PD would have intercepted him before he ever got this far and he'd be in custody right now. The whole reason I second-guessed myself was because of Kincaid's wife and kids, who now I don't believe were ever in any real danger.

At least Wallace won't be able to blame me for this one. It's on the record that *he* decided not to intercept when we had the chance. I just hate that we've lost Kincaid, possibly for good. He could sail down to Cuba or the Cayman Islands if he wanted. In fact, I wouldn't be surprised if he already has something set up down there for all of them. Maybe a trust of some kind they can live off until they get back on their feet.

But if I'm right, and he *is* compelled to kill, he'll only be able to go so long before he does it again.

And that's when I see it. *Deep Blue C* scrawled across the back of a boat as I pass. The lights on the lower deck are on, but I don't see any movement. Why haven't they left yet? What's the delay?

I keep driving past slowly, like I'm looking for something else, or headed down to the restaurant at the end of the concrete pier. There's a small parking area where I turn in and park the car. I pull my phone back out and dial Forsythe again. But before they can even transfer me, I give them my badge number and inform them of the situation. I also notify them I'm going in and not waiting, because he could pull that boat out at any second.

I check my weapon, make sure the safety is off, then place it back in its holster before I get out of the car. The evening is breezy, but still chilly. I bet this place is a hotbed of activity in the summer. But right now, there's no one around.

Casually making my way down the marina again, I spot the same ship. A figure is sitting on the edge of the boat, but from their size it has to be one of the kids. There's still no sign of Kincaid anywhere. As I get closer I realize it's the daughter, Claire. She's looking out on the water with longing in her eyes, like she knows she'll probably never see this place again. No doubt her father has informed her they're never coming back here.

I check my surroundings again and see there is no one around. "Claire?" I ask, causing the girl to look up. She's so close I can almost touch her.

Her face morphs into confusion when she sees me. "Yeah?"

"I'm Emily," I say, holding out my hand. She reaches over, though she frowns like she doesn't know why a stranger wants to shake her hand. When she takes it, and I snatch the opportunity to pull her closer to me, which throws her off balance enough that I'm able to grab her off the boat so she's on the marina with me.

"Hey, what the—" she says as I catch a hint of panic in her eyes.

"Put her down!" A man's voice says and I look up to see Donald Kincaid, not more than eight feet away from me, a gun in one hand and a socket wrench in the other.

I've managed to get Claire behind me, but she's trying to get back on the boat and I have to hold her back. "Mr. Kincaid," I say. "My name is Special Agent Emily Slate. I'm with the FBI."

His face tightens, but he doesn't move an inch otherwise.

"I'm here to arrest you," I say so he understands the full gravity of the situation.

"Let me go!" Claire yells from behind me, but I manage to hold her back.

"You're not arresting anyone," Kincaid says. "You're going to let my daughter go and then we're going to leave."

"I can't do that," I tell him. "You're wanted in connection with at least four murders. And probably a lot more. Put the gun down and surrender yourself."

"Not going to happen," he says with a stern voice. "I haven't come this far to be stopped by you."

"Daddy, what's she talking about?" Claire asks. Even though she's a teen, she's still in that daddy phase.

"Nothing honey, just let me talk to the lady real quick, okay?" His voice is gruff, but it wavers at the same time. He's afraid.

"Don? Is everything okay?" a female voice from down below asks.

"Fine," he calls back. "Don't come up."

I shake my head at him. "It's over Mr. Kincaid. Additional agents are on the way. We already have the waterway blocked. Give yourself up now."

"*I can't,*" he says through clenched teeth. "Don't you understand?" The man almost seems on the edge of tears.

"You're a smart man, you know this is already over," I tell him.

"Not if I shoot you," he says. "You know I'm capable of doing it."

I nod. "I know you are. But I don't think you *want* to, do you? You didn't *want* to shoot Josh Newsome. He just happened to be there, didn't he? Wrong place, wrong time."

Kincaid gives me a slow shake of his head. "I did want to. Because if it was him, it wouldn't be anyone else."

"Why him?" I ask.

He pulls his lips between his teeth for a moment, his eyes flashing behind me at his daughter. "Because he was an easy target."

"You passed him on the trail that evening, didn't you?" I ask. "You saw an opportunity. Knew they'd probably be staying at that little lean-to. So you set yourself up in the woods to take the shot."

"I couldn't go back home without doing it," he admits. "I didn't want—" He stops abruptly as I see a boy of about eleven appear at his side. "Adam."

"Dad, what's going on?" he asks. "Mom is ready to leave." The boy sees me and his eyes go wide.

"You didn't want to unleash your compulsion on your family," I finish for Kincaid and his eyes drop.

"I've been this way a long time, Agent," he says. "But all I've ever wanted was a normal family."

"The only problem with that is other people have to pay the price for what you wanted," I say. "You couldn't unleash your desires on those you loved the most, so you went out and chose random people. People who didn't mean anything to you. People who would just let you *get it out of your system.*"

"Dad?" Claire asks from behind me. "What's going on?"

Kincaid's eyes are swimming with tears, but they haven't fallen down his cheeks yet. He already knows he can't escape. "I thought...I thought if I was careful enough, no one would ever know."

"Mr. Kincaid," I say. "No one wants to put the people they love in danger. I've made that mistake in the past myself. And I've recognized that in order to do what is best for them, I have to make sacrifices. We can't have it all. And I can tell you right now, that by standing there, threatening me, you are putting your family's life in danger. You are doing exactly what you swore you'd never do. And you know it."

He winces, then winces again as the sensation washes over him. He lowers the weapon and I hold out my hand. Claire has stopped fighting behind me. Kincaid looks at me one more time, maybe in a vain hope that I might be willing just to let him go. But I know he sees the resolve in my eyes. The determination. I take the weapon from him and remove the clip, then unload the chamber. I step back as Kincaid falls to his knees, sobbing. The socket wrench clatters to the deck. His son only looks at me while Claire stands off to the side, holding herself.

"What's going on up—" a woman says, coming up the stairs from the lower deck.

"Mrs. Kincaid," I say. "I'm Agent Slate with the FBI. Your husband has just surrendered to our custody."

She furrows her brow, staring at her husband as I hear the first sirens in the distant background. They're only a few minutes away. I step back and give the family the last moments they'll have together. Kincaid is openly sobbing now. I don't know if it's all the death he's caused, finally washing over him, or—more likely—that he's been caught, and he knows he'll never see his family outside of a prison wall again.

All of us stand there, watching and waiting as the man melts down before us. But I know what he is, what he's become in order to maintain this farce of a life. And even though part of me wants to feel sorry for him, I don't let myself feel it. Instead, I think about all those people who never get to see their families again.

As Forsythe's people arrive and secure the scene, I keep their faces in my mind. *Not* Kincaid's.

Chapter Thirty-Four

I TAKE A SEAT, my feet killing me from being on them for three days straight. Liam takes a seat beside me, smiling and giving my hand a squeeze as we wait for Chief Salazar to join us.

"Morning," Jill says as she steps into the room and leans up against one of the walls behind us. "Everyone sleep well?"

"I slept *hard*," I admit. After Kincaid was arrested, I had to stay with him and the family as he was processed in Virginia Beach before he could be transported back to Richmond to await charges. To say his family felt some animosity toward me would be an understatement, but it was nothing compared to how they felt about him once they'd learned who he was and what he'd done. From what Agent Forsythe has told me, the wife has already filed for a divorce and possession of all his assets. Not that he had many to begin with. Apparently, most of Kincaid's money had been spent on setting up contingency plans.

"Sorry, sorry," Salazar says, coming in and rounding the desk before taking a seat. "Thanks for coming in. I know you two are anxious to get back to D.C."

"Some more than others," I say.

Salazar doesn't seem to notice my sarcasm.

"Good news first, after a thorough search they managed to find your missing Bergara hidden in his boat and it's a perfect match to all the casings that have been recovered so far. We're working with a host of other agencies to try and determine if there are any more victims we can add to the list. So far we're up to sixteen."

Liam whistles. "Over how long of a period?"

"Nine years," Salazar says. "We're still using the tool the FBI developed to help us narrow the search." He gives me an appreciative nod. "Sergeant Hubbard already knows this, but we've formally charged Beltran and he's being held in our lockup until we can get a court date. Either his wife doesn't want to or can't post bail."

Probably both, I think.

"More than likely we'll get a plea deal out of him. But I suspect he's got a long time before he'll see the light of day again."

"And Kincaid? Any updates?" I ask.

"Until we have a final victim count, he's being charged with the cases we *know* he's connected to, along with the attempted murder of that SWAT officer down in Roanoke. We've also added child endangerment, conspiracy and a few other charges to the list. You don't have to worry about Kincaid. Best he can hope for is life in prison."

"I just wonder what will happen when his compulsion rears its head in there," I say.

"He's also undergoing psychiatric care from what Richmond tells me. Anything they can do to help them find more victims. Apparently after his wife filed for divorce, he's gone silent."

"He doesn't have anything to fight for anymore," I say. "Nothing to look forward to."

Salazar picks up a couple of papers and stacks them on his desk. "That very well could be. But, I don't want to hold you up too long. The real reason I wanted to see you was because I wanted to thank the three of you for being so diligent on this case. What looked like a cold case in the making has turned out to be one of the biggest wins for this department, even though it's not technically our case anymore."

"It will still look good on your record," I tell him. "You're doing a good job turning Stillwater around."

"I appreciate that, Agent Slate, thank you," he says. "Liam, I don't suppose I can convince you to come back to work for us here. We need good people and Jill tells me you're about as good as it gets."

He smiles and I know the flattery is probably embarrassing the hell out of him. But he doesn't let it show. "Thank you, Chief. But I've been down this road before. I'm happy where I am."

Salazar leans in. "I can't say I blame you. I also wanted you to know that the department has taken up a collection for your father. We'll do anything we can to help with his medical care."

"You don't have to do that," Liam says.

"I know. But we want to. It's the least we can do for his years of service to this community. I wish we could have kept you both." He turns his attention behind us. "Sergeant Hubbard, I want you to know you're in consideration for promotion to Lieutenant. Make sure you've studied up for the test, I'm going to need you by my side over the next few months."

I turn to Jill who lifts her eyebrows at the news. She uncrosses her arms and stands at attention. "Yes, sir. Thank you, sir."

"No need," Salazar says. "You've proven you can handle a lot more than you've been given. I want to make sure you're an integral part of rebuilding this department." He then turns to me. "And I know offering you a job is an exercise in futility, so I'll just say thank you again. Thanks to you, the department is getting more recognition, which will help when it comes to election time. The mayor has already indicated we should see a bigger budget next year, which will help with hiring and making sure what happened here under Burke never happens again."

I take his hand and shake it. "I'm glad I was some help. Thanks for trusting me with the case."

"I spoke with your boss, SAC Wallace?" he says. "He tells me this kind of thing is routine for you."

I shoot a look at Liam. "I wouldn't say *routine*. Just…I have a lot of experience."

"Well, we can't thank you enough." He smiles, looking around the room. "All of you."

"ARE YOU SURE I CAN'T MAKE YOU SOMETHING TO TAKE WITH you?" Mrs. Coll says as Liam leans in for a hug. We've already packed up my car with all our stuff and are preparing to head back to D.C. But we had one final stop we had to make before we made the trek back.

"I'm fine, Mom, thanks," he says. Normally I'd think he was just being nice to placate her, but in the past three days I haven't seen him use his inhaler nearly as often. I think keeping him off duty and away from the action really has helped him to heal.

"Okay," she says. "If you're sure." Her face is pinched with worry and is almost the same face I saw when she first came into Liam's hospital room in Millridge.

"Dad," Liam says, wrapping his arms around his father.

"Be good, son. Stay out of trouble."

"No deal," he says. "They kind of keep us in it all the time."

Mr. Coll chuckles as he slaps his son's shoulder. "I guess they do. Make us proud." He then turns to me. "Emily."

"Mr. Coll," I say, cautious.

"You keep an eye on 'im. I know you won't let anythin' happen to him." He reaches in for a hug, surprising me.

"I'll do my best," I say, wrapping my arms around the bear of a man. He's strong, but also gentle at the same time. I haven't felt a hug like that since my own father died. He lets go and smiles at me, holding me by the shoulders for a moment before letting go.

I give Mrs. Coll a respectful nod as I'm sure that's all she wants from me and we head back to the car.

"Emily," Mrs. Coll calls out and I stop, cursing inside my head. *Almost made it.*

I turn to her, putting on my best fake smile.

She stares into my eyes for what seems like a long time, then reaches out with a quickness I didn't know she had before pulling me close, pressing her head against my chest. "Thank you for watching out for him."

She lets go almost as quickly as she'd grabbed me, stepping back and wiping her eyes. "Of course," I say gently, astonished by her reaction. Maybe she's acting this way because I didn't take Liam with me down to southern Virginia, and I didn't put him through the chase with Kincaid. I admit it was more difficult without him but giving him the time he needed to heal was the best thing for him. And I think, at least I hope, that she knows I realize that now.

Now if I could just take that advice myself. But if Zara is right, we're headed back into a shitstorm when we return to D.C.

We say our goodbyes again before getting back into the car. "Wow, didn't see that coming," I say.

"I told you, my mom is a really loving person. In her own way," he replies. "Anyway, thanks for coming back here with me. I think it would have been a lot harder without you."

"Oh, you mean if I hadn't been here to interrupt on all that partying with your brother," I say, smiling.

"No way, he may like that kind of stuff, but that part of

my life is over. I never want to step into another place with a fog machine again."

"Well, I'm glad I had the chance to meet your family," I say. "Though I kind of feel like I should have asked your parents for permission to move in with you. They're so protective."

He laughs. "Nah. They just don't know the meaning of the word boundary. Why do you think I was so anxious to get out of this place to begin with?"

We share a laugh as I pull out of the driveway and head back in the direction of D.C., leaving the town of Stillwater behind us.

Epilogue

THERE'S NOTHING LEFT.

Well, not *nothing*. But as far as a usable house goes, it's no longer functional. From where I'm parked, I can still see the yellow police tape around the property. It surrounds the charred remains like a fence, keeping everyone out. People climb over the rubble, sifting through with their tools hoping to find something useful. I'm sure Detective Michaels is down there with his arson specialist, going over every square inch. Looking for the evidence.

Looking for me.

Maybe they'll find my stash. It wasn't like I'd planned on burning the building down. But when that *interloper* came looking around the house, I realized I had no choice. Why did he have to come and ruin everything? If I'd wanted a man around, I would have gone out and found one. I'd seen him before, on the TV with Emily. But I don't know who he is, not yet anyway. He's obviously someone very important to her, otherwise he wouldn't have been there.

But why hadn't Emily come herself? I thought the letters had been very clear. As clear as I could make them, anyway. It was supposed to be *her*, not him, not anyone else.

Just her. And her alone.

We were going to talk. Maybe even have tea. I was going to explain it all, and then she would have agreed to stay here with me.

But when I saw him in the house, snooping around, I panicked. Grabbed the kerosene from the old barn. I thought maybe someone had found out about me. I thought they'd come for me. It wasn't until I saw him lying outside on the grass, barely breathing that I recognized him as belonging to *her*.

I guess it's a good thing I didn't kill him, but it wouldn't have made much difference in the end. And she *had* eventually come, but only to be with him. I watched from the parking lot as she ran inside the hospital, her long, dark hair bouncing behind her. Seeing her in the flesh was enough to send shivers up my arms.

I never thought I'd see that face again. But there she was, less than a hundred yards from me.

I should have gone in then, confronted her, convinced her to come with me. As soon as she saw me, she wouldn't have had a choice. She needs to tend to *me*, not him.

And now she's gone again. Disappeared, back to the city and her job and everything else. And I'm left here, alone again.

I round my vehicle, opening the passenger side door and reach in, grabbing two more letters. The last ones I have. They were my backups; in case she didn't show up with the first letters. Now, it seems I have no choice but to send them. She won't come back if I don't.

But…the letters aren't working. She isn't *listening.* I need something else. I need…I need to go to her. To show her the truth. To make her understand.

I tear the letters to shreds, throwing them on the ground and stomping on them because it feels good. *Stomp. Stomp.* Into the cold dirt you go.

If Emily Slate won't come to Millridge, I'll have to go get her. To bring her back and show her myself. She'll never understand otherwise.

I open the trunk of the car, and it creaks as the old metal scrapes against itself. Inside the trunk are two bags. One holds everything I have left. I unzip it and sort through the things inside, making sure I don't need any other supplies before I leave. I may be gone for a while.

The other bag…that's for Emily. I notice though that it's shifted as I drove up here to get a better look at the house from a distance. A stark white femur sticks out of the bag, as if it's pointing at me. I gingerly push it back inside the burlap sack, along with all the others. *Whole again. You'll be safe in there until I can show you to her.*

Until I can show her everything she's missing. Everything she doesn't understand. Her mother would have never told her the truth.

But I will.

I'm not afraid.

I'm coming, my beautiful, charming girl.

Just hang on.

I'm coming.

The End?

To be continued…

Want to read more about Emily?

WHO DO YOU TRUST WHEN EVERYONE IS A SUSPECT?

· · ·

IN THE SEEDY UNDERBELLY OF THE NATION'S CAPITAL, A DRUG deal gone wrong ignites a firestorm which threatens to pull the entire city into a turf war.

Special Agent Emily Slate, still investigating the possibility she may have a living family member is brought in to help determine who is killing criminals and why. Someone is looking to position themselves as the new leader of the criminal underworld. The only question is who would be so brazen? And can they stop the backlash before innocent people are caught in the crossfire?

Teaming up with a new department, Emily, Zara, Liam are given the impossible assignment of finding the culprit. But tracking down this killer is easier said than done. The only evidence left behind is the professional way in which the victims were dispatched.

As she teeters on the precipice between law and lawlessness, between the questions of her lineage and the clear call of justice, one thing remains certain: Emily Slate will stop at nothing to reveal the truth, no matter how perilous the path may be.

Find out more in *Ties that Bind, Emily Slate Mystery Thriller Book 13*.

To get your copy of TIES THAT BIND, CLICK HERE or scan the code below with your phone.

FREE book offer!

Where did it all go wrong for Emily?

I HOPE YOU ENJOYED *EDGE OF THE WOODS*. IF YOU'D LIKE TO learn more about Emily's backstory and what happened in the days following her husband's unfortunate death, including what almost got her kicked out of the FBI, then you're in luck! *Her Last Shot* introduces Emily and tells the story of the case that almost ended her career. Interested? CLICK HERE to get your free copy now!

Not Available Anywhere Else!

You'll also be the first to know when each book in the Emily Slate series is available!

CLICK HERE or scan the code below to download for FREE!

The Emily Slate FBI Mystery Series

Coming Soon!

A Note from Alex

Hi there!

Thanks so much for reading *Edge of the Woods*! If you're anything like me you've been chomping at the bit to see Emily and Liam's relationship develop a little more. Things may have started out bumpy between them and they've both been through the wringer, but I can think of nothing better than to always know someone out there has your back, which is something Emily desperately needs in her life. Whether you started at the beginning or come into this series in the middle, I can't thank you enough for continuing to stick with me and Emily as we go on these adventures together. Don't worry, there are plenty more to come!

If you haven't already, please take a moment to leave a review or recommend this series to a fellow book lover. It really helps me as a writer and is the best way to make sure there are plenty more *Emily Slate* books in the future.

As always, thank you for being a loyal reader,

Alex